"Do you want the job or not?" Isaac asked.

"I don't think the owner likes me much. Who says he won't fire me as soon as I show up for a shift?"

"Me. I say so."

"And who are you?" Clare asked.

That was a question Isaac would never answer—not honestly, at least. He'd never tell her about his time with the San Antonio PD SWAT or why he left. He definitely wouldn't share that he was working with Jason Jones, the Supervisory Special Agent out of the FBI's San Antonio office, to catch a hit man who'd been on the lam for a year.

"I'm just a guy who's trying to make a living. You look like you need a break. You want the job or not?"

Clare scraped her bottom lip with her teeth. It was a gesture he'd already seen once. He decided it was the face she made when weighing her options and something he found sexy as hell.

"Why are you being so nice to me?"

"You want an honest answer?"

"Absolutely," she said.

"I have no idea." He paused. "The job. Yes or no?"

"Yes," she said, breathless. "Of course, yes."

Dear Reader,

I can't begin to tell you how excited I am to introduce a brand-new miniseries. Set in southern Texas, I was able to bring together several things that fascinate and frighten me. The complex mind of a serial killer is set loose in the wild and untamed Southwest. Then I added in a hero with a dark past of his own and a heroine on the run.

Now, if you've read my Dear Reader letters before, you know that I always love my hero. Isaac Patton is no exception. He's smart, brave and, because of his past, has shut himself off from the rest of the world. Then he meets the heroine and all that changes.

The character I don't usually mention in these letters is the heroine. But this time, I have to tell you about Clare Chamberlain. More than a woman with secrets of her own, she is every bit as smart and brave as Isaac. So, when the two meet, they struggle to maintain the protective walls they've built around their hearts. Even worse for the main characters (but better for us!) is that all of this happens during the winter holidays.

Finally, there's a new villain and he's as dangerous as they come. So, now you see why I'm so excited!

Thank you always for spending your time with me!

Regards,

Jennifer D. Bokal

TEXAS LAW: UNDERCOVER JUSTICE

Jennifer D. Bokal

HARLEQUIN
ROMANTIC
SUSPENSE

Recycling programs
for this product may
not exist in your area.

ISBN-13: 978-1-335-73817-2

Texas Law: Undercover Justice

Copyright © 2022 by Jennifer D. Bokal

For questions and comments about the quality of this book, please contact us at CustomerService@Harlequin.com.

Harlequin Enterprises ULC
22 Adelaide St. West, 41st Floor
Toronto, Ontario M5H 4E3, Canada
www.Harlequin.com

Printed in U.S.A.

Jennifer D. Bokal penned her first book at age eight. An early lover of the written word, she decided to follow her passion and become a full-time writer. From then on, she didn't look back. She earned a Master of Arts in creative writing from Wilkes University and became a member of Romance Writers of America and International Thriller Writers.

Winner of the Sexy Scribbler in 2015, Jennifer is the author of several books, including the Harlequin Romantic Suspense series Rocky Mountain Justice, the connected series Wyoming Nights, and several books that are part of the Colton continuity.

Happily married to her own alpha male for more than twenty-five years, she enjoys writing stories that explore the wonders of love. Jen and her manly husband live in upstate New York. They have three beautiful grown daughters, two very spoiled dogs and a cat who runs the house.

Books by Jennifer D. Bokal

Harlequin Romantic Suspense

Texas Law

Texas Law: Undercover Justice

The Coltons of Colorado

Colton's Rogue Investigation

Wyoming Nights

Under the Agent's Protection
Agent's Mountain Rescue
Agent's Wyoming Mission
The Agent's Deadly Liaison

The Coltons of Grave Gulch

A Colton Internal Affair

Visit the Author Profile page at Harlequin.com for more titles.

To John, Always.

Prologue

Decker Newcombe was very good at one thing. Delivering death.

Sitting in the passenger's seat, he stared through the dusty windshield at the front doors of the Pleasant Pines County office building. A month earlier, he'd registered at the Pleasant Pines Inn. Using an alias, he'd spent a week in Wyoming conducting reconnaissance. Playing the part of a developer interested in a tract of land, he'd gained access to the offices and had even managed to wander about the place freely while "researching" the deed.

From his time in town earlier, he knew that the building was closed for the evening, leaving only an elderly guard on duty.

Decker held a photograph of his latest target—Chloe

Ryder, the local district attorney. Months ago, she'd indicted all the members of the Transgressors, a local motorcycle club, on charges of trafficking—both drugs and humans. Everyone ended up in jail and the DA had been targeted by the national motorcycle club for termination. Decker had been given the kill contract.

To date, Decker had killed over seventeen people and never been charged with a single murder. As a rule, he never took contracts on public officials—the risk was always higher than the reward. Yet, this hit was worth so much cash—a cool 500K—he was on board. After his contact took his commission and the getaway driver was paid, Decker would still make $415,000—the biggest haul of his career.

His plan was a simple drive-by shooting, catching Chloe on the street as she left work. Afterward, the driver would take them to another car that was stashed a few miles outside of town. Before the district attorney was even pronounced dead, Decker would be gone.

The driver, a guy named Paolo, lifted a cigarette to his lips and inhaled. The tip of the cigarette burned to ash. With an exhale, he filled the car with smog.

"What time is it?" Paolo asked for what seemed like the hundredth time.

Decker glanced at the other man from the corner of his eye. "What do you care? You got some place better to be?"

"No, man. It's just, well, you said she left work every day at six thirty. It's almost seven now."

During his scouting trip, Chloe had followed a strict schedule. He didn't like that she hadn't come out of her office—forcing him to wait close to thirty minutes. "Maybe she's working late."

Paolo took another drag from the cigarette. "What are we supposed to do now?"

Decker was loaded with pent-up energy—a spring, ready to explode. It was always like this before he carried out a kill. The adrenaline enabled him to act on his violent impulses, without thought or care. It made him feel powerful, invincible—and it made him incredibly dangerous.

Decker never took his eyes from the door. "It's her time to die."

Paolo shook his head. "How're we supposed to do the job if she doesn't come out of the building?"

"Well, I guess we'll go and get her." Decker decided on the next move in an instant. From his earlier visit, he knew that the DA's offices were on the first floor in the back of the building. He knew that the sheriff had her offices on the second floor, but at this time of the evening all three deputies were either on patrol or at home. He knew that the door was left unlocked until 10:00 p.m. and that a single guard stood watch. He also knew that none of the zoned alarms were set until the guard went home. "The way I figure it, we have five minutes to get the job done. More than that and we'll be trapped by the local law."

"Five minutes," Paolo echoed. "Got it."

"You ready?"

Paolo held a handgun in his lap. Pulling back on the slide, he chambered a round. "Yeah, man. I'm ready."

Decker's gun was tucked into the small of his back, the hard metal biting his flesh. He reveled in the pain.

It kept him focused. Vaulting from the car, he sprinted up the steps. Paolo left the car's ignition running and was right behind him.

Pulling open the unlocked doors, he rushed into the dim lobby.

The guard, a man with a white mustache and a brown uniform, sat behind a desk. He stood as Decker and Paolo entered. "Hey, it's after hours. You can't be here."

Decker lifted the gun and fired once, its blast echoing in the cavernous space. The bullet struck the man in the chest. The guard slammed into the wall at his back, then pitched forward, falling face-first onto the desk.

Decker raced down the hall.

The DA's workspace took up a quarter of the ground level, with Chloe's personal office in the back corner. Sweat dampened Decker's back, and his shirt stuck to his skin. Standing in the reception area, he pressed himself against the wall. Paolo stood beside a door.

Holding up his hand, Decker lifted his fingers, signaling to his partner.

One. Two. Three.

Decker kicked the door open. Gun already aimed, he crossed the threshold.

A man with a comb-over and round glasses sat behind the desk, holding a phone to his ear.

His skin, already pale, turned the color of spoiled milk.

Decker asked, "Who are you?"

"I'm Jake Loeb, the district attorney."

Paolo snorted. "That's a lie. Chloe Ryder, she's the DA."

"Chloe works for the Attorney General's office now,"

said Jake, a tremor in his voice. "She left Pleasant Pines last week."

"Last week?" Decker echoed. His face flushed with anger.

It was the first time that his intel had ever failed him—and just maybe, the worst mistake he'd ever made, too. All the recon he'd done. All the days he'd gotten coffee at that crappy Main Street diner, hoping he'd remain unrecognized—and gloating a little when his disguises kept the locals from seeing him for the killer he was.

But not hearing the gossip about Chloe Ryder's promotion had cost him, huge. It would be a blow to his reputation for sure—and now, thanks to the screwup, he had a mess on his hands. The objective, always, was to get in and out without detection. Now, he'd be forced to leave a trail of bodies.

But there was no other way. Not if he wanted to survive.

Jake swallowed. "What do you want?"

The words brought him back into focus—and amplified his rage even more. "Not you," said Decker, he lifted the gun.

"Please. No. What do you want?" the attorney begged. "I can help you with anything…"

What he wanted was to kill Chloe Ryder. What he couldn't have were witnesses. He pulled the trigger. The bullet ripped a hole in the guy's neck and painted the back wall with red. The report boomed, rattling the window. Moving to the door, Decker said, "The clock's ticking, man."

They raced down the hallway and their footfalls rang

out in the empty corridor. Paolo was at his side. The car idled at the curb, a cloud of exhaust billowing around it.

They hadn't killed Chloe Ryder, but they'd assassinated the district attorney. The job—sort of—was done. Now, the Transgressors had to pay up.

Decker pushed the door open as a clap of thunder ricocheted off the walls. He glanced over his shoulder. Stumbling, Paolo held his middle. A red stain bloomed on his abdomen.

Paolo had been shot. But by who?

Turning his head, Derek saw the security guard was once again on his feet. His white mustache was wet with spit and stained red by blood. A tendril of smoke rose from the barrel of his gun. His hand shaking with pain, he raised it again to shoot, but Decker turned—fired once—and blew off the top of the old man's skull. The guard's weapon clattered to the floor.

"C'mon, man." Decker slipped his shoulder under Paolo's arm. "The guard definitely called the cops. We have to get the hell out of here."

Dragging the other man to the car, Decker shoved Paolo into the back seat. After stripping off the flannel shirt he wore, he tossed it to the injured man. "Put this on the wound. Press down hard."

Slipping behind the steering wheel, he slammed the car door shut and pulled away. His mind raced as he drove. Paolo's injury looked bad. There was a lot of blood and no exit wound. He needed to find someone who'd treat a gunshot wound and not call the cops.

Fat snowflakes fell as he sped into the gathering darkness. What they needed was to get out of Wyoming and disappear. With the money they'd just earned, they could go just about any place. Maybe Mexico. South America.

Anywhere was better than here.

"Hey, Paolo?" Decker called over his shoulder. "First, you get patched up and then we'll go south of the border while you recuperate. How's that sound? Tequila's the best medicine in the world."

There was no response.

According to the information he'd been given, the extra car was hidden behind an old barn. He followed the digital map along a narrow lane off the main highway until he spotted the structure, looming in the night. He parked, pulling in close and glanced at the bac seat. Paolo's hand rested on his middle, his eyes stared at nothing. The upholstery was soaked with blood. Reaching for Paolo's wrist, Decker felt for a pulse.

He found nothing.

This job was different from all the ones before. Most of his other victims were criminals already. The police investigation into those deaths were perfunctory, at best. This time, he had killed a DA. The cops wouldn't stop until someone was charged with the murder.

What now?

Decker knew that, once again, he had to act.

He found a couple of gallon jugs filled with gasoline stashed in the trunk of the getaway car. He pulled away from the barn, threw it into Park and left the ignition running before returning to Paolo. Decker dumped gas on the front seat and then fished Paolo's lighter from his pocket. Fumes leaked from the car, burning his nose and eyes. Standing at a distance, he flicked the lighter and a flame sprung to life. He tossed it into the car. The driver's seat erupted with a whoosh of heat and fire.

He didn't wait around to watch the car burn.

After sliding behind the wheel of the second car and pulling onto the road, a tendril of sweat snaked down the side of his neck. Burning the car to destroy all the evidence would damn well stall the authorities for a while—but he knew it wasn't a foolproof solution. Because of that, he had to disappear—and not just for a few days or even a couple of weeks. Decker had to lay low for months, a year. Maybe longer. Only when the case was considered cold, could he resurface.

He quit thinking about tomorrow, or next week, or even next year and let his mind go blank.

As he drove south through the night, Decker knew it was no use fighting it. Destruction was his nature.

Chapter 1

One Year Later

Clare Chamberlain looked at the dashboard and sighed. The gas gauge was almost flat. Her worldly wealth—a crumpled $100 bill—was shoved into her pocket. It was enough for half a tank of the premium gas her car needed, with change left over for a soda and a sandwich.

And then?

Then, she'd be flat-ass broke.

The dusty plains of south Texas stretched out in all directions, disappearing over the horizon. She hadn't seen a car for miles. In the distance, the sun winked—glinting off glass and metal.

She leaned forward, her chest pressing into the steering wheel.

What was it? A town? A mirage?

Clare continued to drive. A sign on a metal post stood at the roadside. "Welcome to Mercy, Texas."

Mercy, Texas, was little more than a wide spot in the road. At an intersection, a single light flashed red in all directions. There was a gas station/convenience store. A post office inhabited a trailer that was the same dust-brown as the landscape. Across the street from the post office was the Mercy Motel—something her father would have called a motor inn. A wide parking lot separated the motel from a long cinderblock building with a bar named House of Steele. There was also a tattoo parlor called Gettin' Ink'd. More than a dozen motorcycles filled the parking lot.

Clare turned into the gas station. Parking the car next to the pump, she tried not to stare at the topless neon woman flashing atop the bar/tattoo parlor. As she got out of the car, her knees ached. Her head throbbed. Her hands had gone numb from hours of driving. It felt good to stand, but this was no place for a respite.

She fished the money from her pocket, the bill damp with perspiration.

Damn. It was only $50.

Had she really spent all her money?

Fine, then. It was half a tank and a coffee.

After that... Well, Clare didn't know what came after now.

She stopped her fill-up at $40, jiggling the handle to get the last drops of gasoline into the tank.

In the convenience store, a tinsel garland was taped to the front of the counter. "Silver Bells" played softly, although she could see neither radio nor speaker.

Was it really almost Christmas? A wooden-block calendar sat next to the cash register.

December 20.

There was no way she could go home. Which meant that Clare was about to spend her first Christmas alone.

An old man with a stained baseball cap looked up from a gun magazine. "Afternoon," he said. "You lost?"

Truer words had never been spoken. "Just passing through."

She poured herself a coffee, took a long drink and topped off the cup. There went a dollar. She grabbed a bag of chips for $1 as well. Setting the money on the counter, Clare slid the bill toward the man.

He made change.

"Thanks." She scooped up the money and shoved it into her pocket.

"Uh-huh." His eyes were already back on the magazine.

On the way to the car, she ripped open the bag of chips and shoved several in her mouth. It had been more than a day since she'd last eaten. And now the change she got from the gas station had to pay for her next meal—and the one after that.

Clare had left her home because staying meant she'd be risking her life. She knew that to be a fact.

But starving wouldn't be better.

She looked back at the bar. On the door, she could make out a red-and-white help-wanted sign. From her side of the road, she couldn't tell what position they had open. But she wasn't sure it mattered.

It brought up another question, though.

What kind of people lived and worked in a town like

Mercy? From the looks of the place, Clare could only imagine they were people who had fallen so far from grace they had no other options. People who were alone in the world.

Then again, what was Clare?

Driving across the street, she parked at the back of the lot. The building with House of Steele and Gettin' Ink'd was a squat rectangle. There were no windows, only two doors. One word was scrawled on the help-wanted sign. *Bartender.*

That was the first bit of good luck she'd had since leaving home.

In grad school, she'd tended bar for a semester. Of course, that had been more than fifteen years ago. And yeah, it was at a trendy nightspot in a university town, not a seedy biker bar. But wasn't pouring beer the same all over the world?

For a moment, she realized that she could be walking into anything—exposing herself to anyone. She wiped her damp palms over the thighs of her jeans. At this point, she had no other options.

She opened the car door and slipped her tote bag over her shoulder.

Clare Chamberlain was certain of one thing and one thing only. If she wanted to live, she needed to disappear.

And she knew deep in her soul that Mercy, Texas, was the last place that anyone would ever come looking.

Isaac Patton stood beside a row of taps and wiped down the wooden bar. At the beginning of the op, it had all been so simple. Set out a trap for Decker New-combe and wait.

Yet, waiting was all he'd done for nearly a year.

The life of a bartender in a backwater Texas town had swallowed him whole, and now felt more real than his old existence. Some days, the memory of his job as a member of San Antonio's SWAT team or a private security operative felt more like a dream than real life. What had given him the audacity to think he could start his own firm?

He glanced around the bar. A handful of round tables were filled with members of the Transgressors, the local motorcycle club who used the bar as their clubhouse. Most played cards. A few stared at their illuminated phone screens. Ryan Steele, his business partner—in a manner of speaking—was texting furiously at a table in the corner.

A black-and-white Christmas movie played on one big-screen TV with the sound muted, while another displayed a replay of the previous night's college foot-ball game. A set of red and green lights outlined a large mirror that hung behind the bar.

Isaac caught his reflection in the glass. He almost didn't recognize himself. The eyes that looked back at him had a hollow, defeated quality. He'd let his blond hair grow out of his usual crewcut. His cheeks and chin were covered in stubble. Though he'd kept up a fitness routine while undercover—pushups, sit-ups, and running—even that had gotten old.

The outside door opened, and a wedge of sunlight cut across the cement floor. Silhouetted in the light was a female form. Long legs, long golden hair, curvy hips. The woman's face was hidden in the shadow, but he imagined that she was pretty. His shoulders tensed and the immediate reaction left him unsettled.

Isaac straightened his spine. He had to ignore the rising emotions—no matter what. Because if there was one thing he'd learned during his life, it was that feelings of any kind were best avoided.

Tossing the rag into a bin of soapy water, he asked, "Can I help you?"

The woman stepped inside, her eyes darting to the tables and the dozen or so rough men. He'd seen wary glances cast at the gang members more than once. This bar was the first stop on a quick descent into hell. Yet, this woman seemed different from the others. She wore a pair of jeans and a silk tank top. Both were rumpled, but Isaac guessed they were good quality. The large tan and brown tote bag she had slung over her shoulder was expensive, too. He looked for jewelry—specifically a wedding ring. She wore none.

"Can I help you?" he asked again.

"I was wondering," the woman said, chewing on her bottom lip. "I saw your help-wanted sign. I'm here for the job." She cast a glance at the bikers, who all stared back. She returned her gaze to Isaac. "I can tend bar."

He asked, "Do you really want to work in a place like this?"

She shrugged one shoulder. "At the moment, I don't have a whole lot of other choices. I do have experience."

"What's your name?" Isaac asked.

"Clare," she said.

"Clare what?"

"Just Clare."

"I'll take it from here," Ryan cut in. Setting his phone aside, he rose to his feet.

If Isaac was forced to describe his relationship with Ryan in a word, he'd pick *complicated*. The biker was an integral part of the plan to catch Decker. As the hitman's former business manager, Steele was brought in by Isaac and his federal partners. As part of the bargain made with Ryan, he was set up as the owner of the bar, tattoo parlor and motel. Even though Decker had gone to ground months ago, after the disastrous hit gone wrong in Pleasant Pines, once the hitman needed his money, he'd come looking for Ryan.

And when that happened, Isaac would be ready.

His attention on the new arrival, Ryan continued, "Let's see what you can do, Just Clare. Can you draw a beer from the tap?"

Clare met Isaac's gaze. "Can I?"

Keeping up the cover story, he said, "That guy owns this place. I just work here." Stepping away from the taps, he continued, "It's all yours."

Ryan lifted his chin. "Go on."

After setting her bag on the bar, she made her way to Isaac's side. Taking a glass from a stack, she pulled back on the tap. She kept the glass tilted to prevent a foam head from forming. Once the glass was filled with golden liquid, she set the beer on the bar.

"Not bad." Ryan lifted the beer and took a sip. Setting it back down, he smirked. "Do you know what's in a Long Island Iced Tea?"

She lifted her chin. "Do you?"

The members of the MC chuckled. Narrowing his eyes, Ryan glared at Clare.

"She got you on that one," a man from the crowd called out.

"Besides," Clare continued, "at a place like this, it's mostly beer and shots. I can obviously pull a beer, and anyone can pour a shot." She met his gaze and held it steadily. "What about it? Am I hired?"

At six-two, Ryan Steele was every bit as tall as Isaac. He wore his dark hair long, but his temper was short. He was the kind of guy people avoided. Yet, Clare had stood up to him. Isaac admired her for that courage.

Maybe she did have the spine to work in this place.

"You?" Ryan scratched at the stubble on his chin and shook his head. "Naw, Isaac is right. You're all wrong for our place. If you want to stay, order a drink. If not, get the hell out."

He shouldn't care about what happened to Clare but for some reason, he did. A filmy mirror hung behind the bottles of liquor. His reflection—light brown hair, gray eyes—filled a corner of the glass. He watched Clare as she bit her bottom lip hard.

She let out a long breath. "Look, I need this job. Just give me another chance."

Watching in the mirror, Isaac held his breath.

Ryan returned to his seat. Stretching his legs in front of him, he folded his arms over his chest. "I don't think if I gave you twenty chances, you'd be any better."

"Really, I can do it," she insisted.

Picking up his phone, Ryan turned his attention to the screen. Clare and her troubles were already forgotten as far as he was concerned.

Isaac exhaled as Clare rounded the bar. She went to grab her tote bag, but accidentally knocked it from the counter. The contents spilled all over the floor. A small black flash drive. A wallet. Lipstick. Sunglasses. Cell phone. With a curse, she shoved her belongings back into the bag. Eyes straight ahead, she strode toward the door.

Then, Clare was gone.

"Look," said one of the bikers. He picked up a car's fob from the floor. Hooking a finger through a metal ring, he let it dangle from his finger. "She forgot her keys. How long do you think it'll take for her to work up the nerve to come back and get them?"

The crowd roared with laughter.

His hand instinctively made a fist. The need to take care of Clare, inexplicable as it was, clouded his vision. He rounded the bar. Standing before the gang member, he held out his hand. "I'll take them out to her."

"You're ruining the fun," said Ryan. "We could take bets. I'll ante up a Benjamin that it takes her more than twenty minutes."

Isaac didn't move. "Hand them over."

"Whatever, man." The guy slapped the keys into Isaac's outstretched hand.

From his last days on the San Antonio SWAT team, Isaac had made it a point to never build relationships at work. As he walked to the door, he reminded himself that doing the decent thing wasn't the same as making a personal connection. He'd return the keys and head back into the bar. It'd take him two minutes—no more.

Pushing the door open, he stepped into the afternoon sun. The light left him momentarily dazed. Yet, Clare was impossible to miss. Standing next to a black luxury sedan, she dug through her tote bag with a look of panic on her face.

"You dropped these." Holding up the fob, he approached her.

"Oh," said Clare, with an exhale. "You found them." She hesitated. "Thank you for bringing them out. I hated the idea of going back inside."

Clare held out her hand and Isaac pressed the keys into her palm. Her skin was soft and warm. Up close, he could see that her eyes were a deep shade of blue.

"I don't think that you're the type to turn your back on a challenge." Isaac withdrew his hand.

She gripped the keys. "Thanks again."

"If you don't mind me saying, you aren't like most of the women who work at the bar."

"What's that supposed to mean?" she asked.

"You have a nice car. Nice clothes. Nice bag. Seems like someone's been taking care of you."

"I can take care of myself," she said, unlocking the car door with the push of a button.

"Why go into a place like that?" Isaac hooked his thumb toward the bar. "And ask for a job."

"Because, like I said, I'm taking care of myself." Clare worked her jaw back and forth. "I'd better go."

"Where are you headed?"

She pulled the car door open. From where he stood, he could see a pillow and blanket. Fast-food wrappers. A small suitcase. She was on the run. Who was she running from and why?

"Why do you care?" she asked.

He lifted a shoulder. "Just making conversation."

"Well, don't," said Clare.

Isaac knew everyone had a past. But it was obvious that he'd pushed Clare for more information than she wanted to give. It was time to let her get back on the road. He should just walk away. Instead, he remained in his spot.

Fishing a wad of cash from his pocket, he pulled off two Benjamins. "You seem down on your luck. I hope this helps you get to someplace better."

"I don't want your charity," she said stiffly, ignoring his outstretched hand.

He reached over and set the bills on the hood of her car. "Suit yourself."

A hint of anger flashed in her eyes. "Keep your money. I don't need it."

Isaac knew that was a lie. He also knew that Clare would keep the cash if he refused to take it back. He turned toward the bar.

"Hey," she called out. "What's your name?"

He stopped walking and turned to face the woman. She held the bills in her hand, the afternoon sun turning her hair golden. "Isaac Patton."

"Thank you, Isaac."

"For what?"

"For bringing out the keys. For giving me—" she looked at the bills flapping in the wind and her eyes widened "—two-hundred dollars. For being the first truly nice person I've spoken to in weeks."

He nodded. "Take care, Just Clare."

She didn't move.

Neither did he.

Maybe it was the heat from the Texas sun that turned him a little crazy. Maybe it was that Clare had called him nice—something he hadn't heard in quite a while. Maybe it was the fact that Christmas was just a few days away and he felt like doing the right thing. Whatever the reason, Isaac asked, "You really want a job at the bar?"

"Define *want*," she said, with a short laugh. "I *need* to make some money."

Sure, Ryan told her to pound sand, but Isaac definitely had his thumb on all the owner's pressure points. What's more, Isaac knew how to squeeze. If he said that Clare was hired, Ryan had no choice but to agree. "I only need help through the New Year. All the jobs are off the books, so don't expect a paycheck or anything. Whatever tips you earn are yours to keep. There're a few rooms at the motel that are rented long-term. I know one with a free bed. You'd have a roommate, but it's better than sleeping in your car."

Clare's eyes flashed again—with anger, pride and something else. What had it been? Hurt? Shame? She slammed the car door shut. "Who says I'm sleeping in my car?"

"If you aren't, why you got a bed set up in your back seat? Why all the food wrappers?"

"Maybe I like to keep my pillow and blanket with me."

Isaac had to admit that he liked Clare's moxie. Maybe that was his problem.

She was a mystery that needed solving. After months of waiting for Decker Newcombe to surface with no luck, finding someone with a story to unravel, someone who, just maybe, could use his help, left him feeling like, well, he'd washed the grit of the world off his hands. "Look around you. Everyone here is down on their luck. Or worse, they got no luck at all. Do you want the job or not?"

"I don't think the owner likes me much. Who says he won't fire me as soon as I show up for a shift?"

"Me. I say so."

"And who are you?"

That was a question Isaac would never answer—not honestly, at least. He'd never tell her about his time with the San Antonio PD SWAT or why he'd left. He definitely wouldn't share that he was working undercover with the FBI's San Antonio office to catch a hitman who'd been on the lam for a year.

After a beat, he said, "I'm just a guy who's trying to make a living. You look like you need a break. You want the job or not?"

Clare scraped her bottom lip with her teeth. It was a gesture he'd already seen once. It was clearly a sign of nerves and something he found sexy as hell.

"Can I ask you a question?" She didn't wait for his answer. "Why are you being so nice to me?"

"Honestly?"

"Absolutely," she said.

"I have no idea." He paused. "The job. Yes, or no?"

"Yes," she said, breathless. "Of course, yes."

"Park in front of room seven. You'll have to move your car later, but for now you can unload your stuff."

He watched as she slid into her sedan and started the engine. She pulled into a space as he walked across the parking lot. Clare turned off the engine as he stepped on the sidewalk. She got out of the car, and he wrapped his knuckles on the door. "Trinity. It's me, Isaac."

The door opened a moment later. Trinity, a tall redhead, was wearing a threadbare T-shirt and baggy shorts. Tattoos covered much of her exposed flesh. A tiger lounged on one bicep. A pink python with eyes like emeralds was coiled around her calf and thigh. Eye makeup was smeared across her cheeks. "Hey, handsome. What can I do for you?"

"You got a new roommate." He stepped aside. "This is Just Clare. She's the new bartender."

"Don't worry, honey," said Trinity, reading the discomfort in Clare's expression. "Most of us don't use last names neither." She looked Clare over from the top of her head to the tips of her shoes. "What're you doing here? You look a little too well-off for a town like this."

Isaac answered the question. "She's tending bar with me. Starts tonight."

"I'm one of the tattoo artists," said Trinity, opening the door farther. "Come in, honey."

Clutching the tote bag to her chest, Clare said, "Thanks."

"Trinity, I'm putting you in charge. Make sure Clare looks right."

Trinity placed her palm on Patton's chest. "I'd do anything for you, you know that. Right?"

Stepping back, he let Trinity's touch slip away. "I'm counting on you," he said, stilling her with a look.

Walking away, Isaac could feel the women standing at the door, watching his back. In all his time undercover, Isaac had vowed never to get involved with anyone associated with any case he was working on. After a few short minutes with Clare, he'd already violated that rule by offering her assistance. And the thing was, he felt there were other rules which wouldn't matter too much to Isaac as far as Clare was concerned.

Maybe Ryan was right, and she had to go.

No. He'd never send Clare away. Not when she clearly needed protection from something. Or some*one*.

Which meant that she'd stay. And become a distraction that he couldn't afford.

Chapter 2

At 7:45 p.m., Clare sat in a wooden chair covered with a worn blue velour. The motel room was like many of the nondescript ones she'd seen before. Two full-size beds were separated by a small nightstand with a lamp. There was also a chest of drawers against the wall, along with a desk and a mirror.

There were differences, though. The room was obviously lived in—Trinity's clothes and makeup covered most every surface. She had also taken the time to decorate the drab space for the holiday, which gave it a bit of cheer. She'd set up a small Christmas tree in the corner near the single window. The artificial tree was four feet tall and covered in white lights and decorations in every shade of blue.

Clare couldn't explain it—the cluttered room and the

Christmas tree felt homey. After she'd gotten settled, she returned to the gas station and purchased a raspberry cereal bar. For tonight, it was her dinner. It left her almost no money, but she hoped that it was temporary. For the first time in months, she actually felt like she could relax. Then again, it'd be a mistake to let her guard down.

Her new roommate had offered to do her makeup for the first shift. It was an offer that Clare accepted. The other woman swiped a makeup brush through a palette of bright blue eyeshadow. She tapped off the excess.

"Close your eyes." Trinity wore a light pink robe. Her red wavy hair was pulled into a ponytail. A silver locket hung around her neck.

Clare hesitated a moment before letting her lids shut.

"I know this color seems like a bit much," Trinity said, applying the shadow. "But you'd be surprised how it looks when the lights are low."

Eyes still shut, Clare said, "I'm just pouring beers. Nobody will care how I look."

"That's what you think." She applied shadow to the other lid. "If you're behind the bar looking fine, you'll make more in tips." Trinity grabbed another brush, filling it with bright white shadow. "This is the highlighter. Keep your eyes closed."

Clare squeezed her lids shut again.

"Can I ask you a question?" Trinity asked.

"Sure."

"You ever work at a place like this?"

"I tended bar when I was in grad school near campus." She paused, trying to find a way to show that she belonged. "It was a popular hangout. On the weekends, there'd be a line at the bar that was five or six deep."

"Open your eyes." Clare did as she was told as Trinity examined her handiwork. "Filling pitchers of beer for frat guys is a lot different than working at this bar."

A jolt ran through her body, and she sat up straighter. "Why's that?"

"All those bikers hang out here. It can get pretty wild some nights. Violent. They do some business and it's not exactly legal."

She probably shouldn't be shocked. What's more, she was on the run because she'd learned that nothing—and nobody—were ever what they seemed.

Then again, here nobody wanted her dead. Memories swirled around Clare, threatening to pull her under and drown her with regrets.

She cleared her throat and tried to think of a way to change the subject. She asked about the first thing that came to her thoughts. "Tell me about Isaac." Huh. Apparently, the muscular bartender was still on her mind. "He seems nice."

"Isaac is probably the only decent guy around here, but he keeps to himself. Far as I can tell, he's never dated anyone. Never takes anyone back to his room. Never even flirts." She shrugged as if that was everything to know about Isaac Patton.

Honestly, Clare shouldn't be giving the guy a second thought, and yet, she was curious. "You said he doesn't date anyone here. Why not?"

Trinity smeared glue on a set of false eyelashes. "It's not an issue of liking or disliking—he just keeps his distance, that's all. I don't know really why. We like him, that's for sure. Isaac's handsome. He's tall. Built. Has the most amazing gray eyes that look like cracked glass. What's not to like?" She reached for Clare's lids. "Look up. Don't move."

Clare stared at the ceiling as Trinity applied the false lashes. As she waited, Clare knew she'd never stay in Mercy, Texas, long enough to find out more about Isaac. She just needed to make enough money to get to Mexico. From there, who knew? Maybe she'd try Costa Rica or Argentina. Someplace she could never be found.

Trinity applied red lipstick to Clare's mouth. "The bar opens at eight o'clock and closes at two in the morning. The first and last hours can be dead, but in between you'll be busy."

"This town is so small, though. Where do all the people come from?" From what Clare could tell, there wasn't another town for miles and miles.

"There are several ranches in the area and all the hands and sometimes the foremen show up after work. San Antonio is only a couple of hours away. Encantador is about twenty miles from here. But people come from Austin and Dallas, too. South of the border. Even as far away as Houston."

Clare felt as if she'd stepped through the proverbial looking glass, and everything she thought to be real was just an illusion. "People come from hours away for what? How crazy is the party?"

"This is a biker bar. It can get really crazy." Trinity drew her brows together. "Oh, honey, you really don't know what you've wandered into, do you?"

Clare didn't answer, but her expression clearly gave her away.

The other woman continued, "Isaac asked me to take care of you, so I'm going to give you some advice. Get back into that fancy car of yours and go. Whatever you left behind is better than where you are now."

Her throat began to close, making it nearly impossible to breathe "I'm never going back."

Shrugging, Trinity said, "Suit yourself." While applying blush to Clare's cheeks, the other woman ran her tongue over her teeth. "I'm done. What do you think?"

She glanced in a wall-mounted mirror. The woman who looked back was almost unrecognizable. She certainly had on more makeup than Clare would have ever worn, even to go out to a formal event, but Trinity was right—despite the wild colors, the overall effect made her eyes stand out more. The shirt—on loan from Trinity—was low and tight. It was all so very unlike her, and yet, Clare noticed something in her reflection that she hadn't seen in a long time. There was a spark in her eyes. What was it? Defiance? Confidence? Resolve?

In the end, she decided that it didn't matter. Whatever it was, it had given her the ability to strike out on her own. Certainly, her rediscovered self-assurance would help her to survive.

And if not? Her shoulders slumped. Well, then she'd fake it as long as she could.

Isaac stood behind the bar and kept his eye on the front door. Sure, he was always vigilant about who entered the House of Steele but tonight was different. Tonight, he was watching for Clare.

He'd told himself that it was stupid to shave and control his hair with a little gel. But he'd done it anyway. When he glanced in the mirror behind the bar, his own reflection was at least familiar. He turned back to the room.

A rock 'n' roll version of "Santa Claus is Comin' to Town" blared from the speakers. Spotlights swept erratically around the darkened room. A disco ball hung from the ceiling, scattering multicolored reflections across the floor. A few patrons sat at the bar and sipped drinks.

"Another one?" A ranch hand from the nearby Double S lifted his beer. The cattle ranch was one of the few in the area that actually turned a profit. The agricultural market had taken a hit in recent years with the rise of the corporate run–farms and unpredictable weather. Many of the small family ranches had sold their land, or simply folded.

Not the Double S. Run by the Sauter family for generations it was managed by Sage Sauter currently. The ranch started producing grass-fed beef before it was in demand and that toehold in the organic beef market kept them in business.

"Sure thing." Isaac grabbed a cold can from the fridge and popped the top. "How's Sage?" he asked, mentioning the only female ranch owner for miles.

"Same as always."

"Tough and fair?" Isaac asked.

"'Bout sums it up." The ranch hand gulped his beer. "You got plans for the holidays?"

"Does pouring beers count?" When he'd first started working the case, he'd been certain that Decker would quickly resurface for his money. All Isaac had to do was wait. Nearly a year later, he'd grown tired despite his dedication to nailing the bastard. He couldn't stop thinking about the life that was going on without him.

Was he about to miss visiting with family in San Antonio? The thought of spending Christmas alone burned a hole inside his chest. Yet, he wondered about Clare. He'd told her that she could stay through the New Year. But would she?

He pointed to beer. "You want that on your tab?"

Wiping his mouth with the back of his hand, the ranch hand said, "If you don't mind."

As Isaac marked the drink on the bill, the door opened. He looked up as Clare stepped into the room. He swallowed and dropped his gaze. Yet, he couldn't help but look at her again. Her shirt hugged her breasts like a second skin. The neckline dipped low, revealing likely more of her cleavage than she realized. He averted his gaze, reminding himself of his rule not to get involved with anyone—and to focus on his singular goal.

Approaching the bar, she gave a tight smile. "Trinity told me that the shift started at eight o'clock. I'm ready to get started. What do you want me to do?" She paused. "And did you talk to your boss? You're sure I won't get kicked out?"

Isaac had yet to speak to Ryan. Then again, tonight it didn't matter. He'd left Mercy and wouldn't be back before last call. He said simply, "The owner's not here tonight. I'll talk to him when he gets back."

"Okay, then," she said.

Isaac cleared his throat. "When was the last time you tended bar?"

"Grad school. About fifteen years ago."

"You still remember how to work a tap, so that's a

start," said Isaac. "Come back here and I'll show you where we keep everything."

She rounded the bar and stood at Isaac's side. The scent of her perfume—both floral and musky—washed over him. He held his breath for a moment, distracted by her scent. Shaking his head, he tried to focus. There would be a full house tonight. If she couldn't handle the crowd, things could get ugly.

Pointing to a small refrigerator, he began, "We keep the bottled beer in there. Beer glasses are under the taps. Shot glasses are under the liquor." He paused, distracted again by the brush of her arm on his as she leaned over to look at the layout of glasses beneath the counter.

Isaac forced himself to return to his instructions. "There are several cocktail waitresses and guys like to buy them drinks. If one of them orders a shot for herself, give her this." He held up a whiskey bottle. "It's filled with weak iced tea. They'll know what they're getting, so don't be worried about that."

She took the bottle from him. Her fingertips grazed the back of his hand, and again, that electric charge surged up his arm. She examined the amber liquid. "Smart idea, to make sure that the servers can stay sober."

It was exactly why they drank tea, yet he was surprised by her reaction. Had he expected her to be disapproving? Maybe because of the expensive bag and the luxurious car, he'd thought she wouldn't understand. But she did. For a moment, he was disappointed, and Isaac knew why. At least if she'd been judgmental, he'd have a reason to dislike her.

Isaac made it a point to never ask anyone about their

personal life. Having to answer questions put people on guard—and suspicions were the last thing he wanted. Yet, he couldn't keep himself from asking, "So, what'd you study?"

"In grad school?" she asked, before answering his question, but not saying too much. "Environmental engineering."

"Not many engineers around here." Still, he knew that education meant little. People's lives could take almost any kind of turn, up or down. He really should go back to minding his own business. But Clare had piqued his interest. "You ever work as an engineer?"

Clare lifted one shoulder and let it drop. "For a while at the EPA."

"I've never met anyone from the Environmental Protection Agency. What did you do when you worked there?"

She picked up a cocktail napkin and wiped down the bar. "Nothing interesting. Regulations and stuff."

It wasn't much of an answer. But his first impression of Clare was right. She was well educated and came from a financially comfortable background. Now he was certain there was more to her story.

Sure, he shouldn't care where Clare came from or where she was going. But he did.

He said, "Looks like you got settled and that Trinity's treating you right."

Clare gave a quick nod. "Thanks for setting me up in her room. She's been really helpful."

"She's been at Gettin' Ink'd since before I started working in Mercy. She's good people."

"So." Clare drew out the single word. "How'd *you* end up in Mercy?"

"I was in a Wyoming jail because a bar fight got out of hand," he began his well-practiced cover story. In fact, he'd told the lie so many times, it almost felt like the truth. "Ryan was my cellmate for a few weeks. He told me to look him up when I got out. I had no intention of ever contacting him." He shrugged. "But with my record, it was tough to find work. I remembered him mentioning this bar, so I made the call and Ryan offered me a job." He shrugged. "And here I am."

She nodded, seemingly buying his story without hesitation.

"Do you live in the motel, too?"

He nodded. "Room three."

"Anyone with you?" She discreetly placed a bottle of water for herself underneath the bar, then glanced back at him. "Wife? Kids?"

"This is hardly a place for a child to grow up," he said. "But no, I'm not married. Divorced once. No kids, and I haven't spoken to my ex in years."

She watched him for a minute. "Aren't you going to ask me if I'm married or have kids?"

"Don't need to. You aren't wearing a wedding band, so you aren't married. If you had kids, then you'd home with them—not tending bar in the desert a few days before Christmas."

"You can be married and not wear a wedding ring," she said, challenging him.

"People do it all the time—but not someone like you." He paused. "Tell me I'm wrong."

Clare hesitated, then shook her head. "You aren't wrong. What you are is perceptive."

"It's a blessing and a curse," he joked. Christ, when had he become so comfortable with Clare?

One of the patrons tapped his empty glass on the wooden top. Clare set the whisky bottle back in its place and moved down the bar. "What are you drinking?" she asked.

The electric charge still surged through his veins as he watched her go. It didn't matter if her scent teased his senses, or if her touch made his body go rock-hard. If he wanted sex, that was something he could find. Easily. But he was in this hellhole to serve a higher purpose. He'd sacrificed almost a year of his life working undercover and now wasn't the time to get sidetracked.

As Isaac watched Clare begin to serve customers, he reminded himself that she was on the run, from someone or something. Whatever she was tangled up in meant danger to his case. And he couldn't—hell, wouldn't—risk temptation when there was so much more at stake.

By 2:15 a.m., the bar was empty save for Clare and Isaac. She couldn't remember a time when her back or her feet hurt worse. For almost six hours straight, she'd served beers and shots to a growing crowd of rowdy—and increasingly drunk—patrons. But she welcomed the pain. It meant she had worked hard and earned some money—money that put her closer to the escape she desperately needed.

Or so she hoped, anyway.

"You did good." Isaac placed a stack of cash on the

bar. "It's half of the tips," he continued, then lowered his voice. "But don't count it here. Wait until you're alone."

Stuffing the wad into the front pocket of her jeans, Clare nodded. "Understood."

"You earned it." He took a bottle of beer from the small fridge. "You want something a little stronger than that water you were sipping all night?"

What she wanted was to sleep for hours. Since leaving her home in Columbus, Clare hadn't dozed for more than a few hours at a time. Afterward, she woke in the clutches of the same nightmare, and somehow more tired than when she closed her eyes. Maybe a beer—along with the fatigue from working—was the right mix for her to get some decent sleep. She reached for the bottle. "That'd be nice."

While opening his own beer, Isaac said, "Must've been hard standing on your feet, after being behind the wheel for so long."

She guessed that he was digging for information about her, but it would be a mistake to share too much with a guy as observant and discerning as Isaac. "I'm okay," she said, not giving away anything about her past. Yet, that didn't mean she wasn't curious about the House of Steele. "It seemed busy tonight."

He took a long swallow from the bottle. Setting it on the bar, he said, "It's always busy."

She nodded and took a drink. The beer landed in her stomach like an explosion. She really should've eaten something more than the gas station chips and the cereal bar. Honestly, she'd been nervous about her shift. The roll of bills was heavy in her pocket. How much had she made? Or maybe she should be asking a different question. How much did it cost to start a new life?

"There were a lot more people here than I expected to see. I mean, this place definitely is in the middle of nowhere…" She let her final word unravel into an unspoken question.

Isaac said nothing, just sipped his beer.

Clare tried again. "Why is this place so popular?"

"Let me give you some advice. Don't ask questions. You won't like the answers."

Like a boulder had been dropped on her shoulders, Clare felt a weight pressing her down. "Got it."

He eyed her carefully. "Are you going to be able to work here for the next few weeks? I really need the help through New Year's Eve. It's a good time to make a lot of tips. Bad time to be short staffed."

"How much are you talking about?" she asked.

He shrugged. "Over a thousand bucks, easy."

"I'll be here," she promised. Hell, she thought, for that much cash, she could stand it. At least, she thought she could.

"We're closed on Christmas Day if you want to visit family or whatever."

Christmas in Mercy. Now that was a joyless thought. She had no place else to go. Nobody else to see. "I'll be here then, too."

His gaze skimmed her expression. "You look exhausted."

She tried to make a joke. "I must look better than I feel."

He gave a quick laugh. "Let's call it a night." Isaac moved from behind the bar. "Come on. I gotta lock up."

Isaac punched a code into a keypad near the door. The alarm beeped three times. He opened the door for Clare.

After tossing the bottle into the trash, she walked to the front door and stepped outside. Isaac pulled the door closed. Using a key that he carried in his pants pocket, he locked the dead bolt. Only then did he give the handle a hard pull. Satisfied that the bar was secure, he shoved the key back into his pocket and gave a sigh that Clare could only describe as weary.

Night stretched over the open landscape, replacing the blinding sun and furnace-like midday heat with a sky of velvety black, along with a cold that bit into Clare's flesh and chilled her to her bones.

The motel was on the far side of the parking lot, an ocean of darkness between two islands of light. It wasn't that far away. Still, her pulse raced at the thought of walking alone. Clare wondered if she'd always been this afraid of the dark. Some days, it was all but impossible to remember who she'd been before her final night in Ohio.

Folding her arms across her chest, she stood on the cracked sidewalk and shivered.

"Damn," Isaac cursed. "It's cold."

"I didn't expect it to be this chilly." She rubbed her hands over her shoulders.

"I'll walk you back to the motel," he said, before quickly adding, "Just to make sure you get back to the room. It may look quiet here, but you never know who might show up around closing time."

As they walked through the night, she realized it was the first time in months that she'd actually felt...safe. It was more than finding a temporary place to live. It was Isaac and the fact that he'd seen her need and offered help. Cash. Shelter. A job.

There was more to his story—more to his life—than just a guy who threw beers at a roadside bar in Mercy, Texas. She was sure of that.

Who was Isaac Patton, really?

They stood in front of room seven. A single bulb hung over the door, buzzing loudly. Trinity had given Clare a spare key, which was in the same pocket as her money. She pulled it out, careful to leave the tips in place.

"Well," she began, key in hand. "I better—"

"Yeah, I should probably—" He spoke at the same time, then hooked his thumb over his shoulder. "You know, get going."

"Thanks, again." She turned for the door and tried to slide the key home. Metal scraped against metal, and it stopped. Clare jiggled the key and tried to tug it free. It was no good—the key was stuck. "Dammit," she cursed.

"Here," said Isaac, reaching around her. "Let me."

His hand covered her own and Clare's pulse spiked. His breath warmed her shoulder. She knew that she should move away, but she was rooted to the spot.

"Sometimes, you just have to ease it in," Isaac said, his voice dark and seductive.

He pushed her hand and the key slid home. For a moment, they stood with his palm on the back of her hand. Her pulse raced and her skin tingled. Clare let herself take in the moment. This was the first time in a long while that she'd felt a physical connection to another person.

To a man.

Then again, whatever she felt didn't matter. Mercy was only a temporary pit stop. As soon as she had enough money to disappear, she'd leave—and never look back.

Chapter 3

There was a rattling noise an instant before the door opened. Clare stumbled forward as the key slid from her grip.

Trinity stood on the threshold. Her face was clean, and her auburn hair was wound into a messy bun at the top of her head. "There you are," she said. "I heard something and thought maybe you couldn't work the lock." She paused. "It sticks sometimes."

"I warned her," said Isaac. He'd stepped away from the door and was already part of the shadows. "I have to go." He lifted a hand. "Good night."

"Good night," she called after him. Her voice cracked. It didn't matter. Isaac was already gone and blending with the darkness.

"Jeeze, it's freezing out here." Trinity stepped away from the door. "Come on in. This is your place, after all."

Following Trinity into the room, she closed the door. The lights on the tree twinkled and a *Friends* rerun played on a boxy TV. After standing outside, the room was hot—almost stifling. Or maybe it was having Isaac's hand on hers that left Clare flushed.

"How was your night?" Trinity asked. "From the tattoo parlor, it looked like you were busy."

"We were." Clare slumped onto the bed. The mattress sagged in the middle, yet she didn't care. After weeks of fitful naps in the back seat of her car, any bed was a luxury.

"I was just about to change," said Trinity. "But I'll go to the bathroom and give us both some privacy."

Clare took the moment of solitude to count her haul. The wad of bills was thick. Isaac had taken the time to organize the money. There were more $1 and $5 bills than $10s or $20s. Even so, she was surprised to discover she'd made $482. Along with the $200 he'd given her, she had almost $700. After almost two weeks of working at the House of Steele, she might save thousands of dollars.

For the first time since leaving her old life, she thanked her lucky stars. After slipping out of her sneakers, Clare rolled the bills into two separate piles and shoved each into the toe of a shoe. That was followed by a sweaty sock. She stashed her shoes in her suitcase and engaged the combination lock. Her roommate seemed nice, but she wasn't about to trust anyone.

Trinity exited the bathroom.

"You hungry? I know how I get after working a long shift."

The last thing she'd eaten was that cereal bar, hours ago. "Starved."

Trinity opened the top drawer of the dresser. "I always stock up on snacks whenever I can get a ride to the grocery store in Encantador. Help yourself." She removed an oatmeal cream pie and took a bite. "Really, I don't mind sharing."

Rising from the bed, Clare moved to the dresser. The drawer was filled with individually wrapped cookies, chips, pretzels and crackers. At the sight of the food, her stomach grumbled loudly. She took a pack of crackers with peanut butter and sat back on the bed. "Thanks."

After opening the crackers, she shoved one into her mouth. Chewing, she closed her eyes. Sure, it was silly to think that a stale peanut butter cracker was good, much less delicious. But to her, it was the best thing she'd eaten in a while. She swallowed and sighed. "That's tasty."

"Don't be shy. I can tell you weren't lying when you said that you were starving." Trinity tossed pretzels and chocolate chip cookies—both in bags—at Clare. The snacks hit the mattress. "Out here, we gotta take care of each other. Nobody else gives a crap about what happens in Mercy."

Scooping the bags closer, she gave a mirthless laugh. "This is more than I've eaten all week."

"Help yourself to the food whenever you want. You hear me?"

She nodded and ate another cracker. "I do."

Trinity remained on her feet and finished her oatmeal cream pie. She threw the wrapper in the garbage and held out her hand for Clare's trash. "The only problem with food in the room is you can't leave anything out. It attracts bugs. Big bugs." She circled her fingers, presumably showing the size of insect invaders.

Clare shivered. "I guess everything is bigger in Texas." She opened the pretzels and shoved several into her mouth.

"In the mood for a glass of vino?" her roommate asked, filling a paper cup with red wine. "A little holiday cheer in a cup."

Clare wasn't, especially after the beer, but she said, "Sure."

Trinity filled a second cup. Holding out the drink, she said, "Here you go."

"Thanks." Clare sipped the wine. The alcohol slid through her veins, relaxing her further. Although she had to wonder if chasing a beer with wine was really the best idea in her exhausted condition.

"Not often that I get a GWN."

"GWN?" Clare repeated.

"Girls' Wine Night," said Trinity. "You probably go to cocktail parties and have fun all of the time."

"I used to." When Clare married into a family filled with old Ohio money, she'd understood that there would be lots of expected socializing. But... "And I hated every minute."

Trinity barked with a laugh. "Damn, you're funny."

"Maybe Isaac would let me do a comedy night. What do you think?" Clare teased, finishing the last of her pretzels.

"Maybe..." Trinity sipped her wine, grinning.

At one time in her life, making small talk had been

easy. Now, she couldn't think of anything else to say. "What about your night? Did you have any customers?"

Sitting on her own bed, Trinity took a swallow of wine. "Oh, sure. Someone always wants a new tat. Mostly, I'm paid to keep my mouth shut about how the Transgressors use the bar as a place to do business."

"Oh." Clare's face was hot. She'd been warned more than once not to ask questions. And she'd been working so hard to keep up with the pace as the night went on that she hadn't had time to really pay attention to the goings-on among the customers. "I didn't mean to pry... I'm sorry..."

"Don't be sorry." Trinity held up a necklace that was around her neck. It was the locket Clare had noticed earlier. Slowly, she opened the front. Instead of a picture, fine strands of hair were tied with a tiny pink ribbon.

"I have a daughter," said Trinity. "Right now, she's with her father. One day soon, I'll save enough money to hire a fancy lawyer and get my visitation rights back."

"What..." she began, before deciding better than to snoop. Trinity was her first ally since leaving Columbus. She didn't want to alienate the woman who had taken her in and been so nice to her. She gave a quick smile. "I'm sure you will."

Trinity eyed her shrewdly. "Go ahead and ask."

She shook her head, wanting to do nothing more than sleep. "Doesn't matter."

Letting the necklace dangle between her fingers, Trinity took a sip of wine. "You want to know what happened? Right? As in why don't I have custody of my child?"

It's exactly what Clare wanted to know. "Like I said, it doesn't matter to me. Everyone has a story." Hadn't

Isaac said something like that earlier? Maybe there was a good bit of wisdom in his words. Just thinking about him brought a smile to her lips. Must be the wine. She took another sip.

"I don't mind you asking. It helps to talk it out. My ex-husband is an alright guy. And he is a good dad. When we got together, we both partied a little. That stopped when I got pregnant. But after I had the baby…" She paused. "You got kids?"

Clare shook her head. "No kids."

"Well, being a mom is the hardest thing ever. You actually work twenty-four/seven. If the kid's awake, you gotta take care of them. Even when they're asleep, there's stuff to do. And I was trying so hard to quit drinking. I really was. But sometimes, when I couldn't handle anything, I guess…" She sighed. "I guess sometimes I just gave in to that need. It caused a lot of problems.

"One day in our apartment complex's laundry room, I complained to a neighbor about being tired. He seemed so understanding and we started off as friends. Things progressed, and you know." Trinity shrugged. "The affair led to a divorce. The bastard I'd fallen for didn't want kids. Because I was young, dumb and in love, I didn't sue for custody. I was struggling with my own addictions. I missed several visits, and my ex-husband took me to court to terminate my parental rights. I didn't fight him. Not long after, the guy I was with left me. I took up with another guy—worse than the first. Seems like I dated every lousy man in Texas before I figured out what was important. Now I'm trying to get my life straightened out." Trinity placed her palm over the locket, pressing both into her chest. "Until then, this is all I have of my baby girl."

Clare sipped her wine and thought of her family. Her father died of cancer years before. Her mom was still alive and had relocated to Hawaii. She hadn't called her mom in all these months, too afraid that someone might be tracing those calls. By now, she could only imagine how worried her mother would be. Her throat tightened with guilt. "Must be hard to be away from your daughter during the holidays."

"It's hard every day, but yeah—Christmas is the worst. I mailed presents already. Her dad will let her call in the morning, and we'll talk. It's nice, but it's not enough." She sipped her wine. "What about you? What's your life story?"

"Just one lousy guy. And yeah, I married him." Clare chewed on the inside of her lip. She shouldn't have shared so much about her past. Maybe the beer and wine were making her a chatty...and reckless.

Trinity lifted her paper cup. "To lousy men. May we learn to avoid them."

Touching her cup to Trinity's, Clare said, "Cheers."

Exhaustion began to set into her limbs. Stretching out on the mattress, Clare pulled the comforter over her legs and chest.

Trinity settled onto her own bed. "No kids. No husband. What about siblings? Parents?"

Clare knew enough to not give away too many details. Still, she couldn't ignore Trinity's question. "No siblings. Lost my dad to cancer, but my mom is still around," she said, giving a true but vague answer.

"You close to your mom?"

After everything that had happened, she thought every day of calling her mother. Then again, what could her mom do from the other side of an ocean?

"We talk now and again." Clare folded the pillow and relaxed into the mattress.

"Well, speaking for all moms everywhere, we always want to hear from our kids." She paused a beat. "How'd you end up here, then?"

"This is where life led me," said Clare with a shrug.

"You drive a fancy car. You have expensive clothes and bags. That means you came from a life of privilege. It also means you have choices beyond pouring beers at some bar in the back-ass of beyond." Trinity's gaze hardened a little. "No one just chooses to be here. But you did, Clare."

Trinity wasn't wrong. But she wasn't completely right, either.

She sighed, not sure how much she could—or should—reveal. "Something bad happened. It was…where I used to work. If I stayed, there would've been trouble. For a lot of people," said Clare, skirting the truth as closely as she dared. "I had to get out. And I had to leave everything behind. Just get up and…go." Clare took a big sip of her wine, hoping she'd be able to choke it down along with the emotion clogging her throat.

"I thought my job was hard." Taking the last swallow of her wine, Trinity nodded. "You know, Clare, you're okay." She held up a hand. "No, I mean it. When Isaac showed up with you, I wasn't sure what to think. But you're alright. Not many I'd call a friend around here, so I'm glad you're my roommate." Trinity picked up the empty glasses and threw them both in the trash can.

Clare gave a quiet laugh. She couldn't help but recall her monied acquaintances in Columbus. In all those years, she'd never felt at ease with any of them. But Trinity was different in a good way. "I'm glad that I'm your roommate, too."

Trinity picked up a phone from the nightstand. "What's your number? Then we can text each other if things get boring at work."

Clare hesitated. "Oh, I really don't use my phone for much."

"I get it—a phone bill can be expensive. I'll just get your number for emergencies."

In all honesty, Clare hadn't bothered to memorize the number to the new cell phone. She took it from her bag and turned on the power. After creating a new contact, she handed the phone to Trinity. "You put in your information."

She typed on the screen. "I'll send myself a message from your phone."

She handed the phone back to Clare. The message read Hey sis.

"So, what happened to your lousy husband?" Trinity stretched out on the bed.

Had Clare said too much? She'd stopped in Mercy to disappear, not to bring up her past. "Divorced. I haven't spoken to him since I signed the papers."

Maybe she was starving for more than food but actual human contact. Besides, Clare had only agreed to stay until New Year's. She'd be long gone before she was asked any questions that she didn't want to answer.

"That's the best way to do it. No loose ends."

She gave a sleepy nod. Yet, for her ex-husband, Clare

was someone who knew too much. That made her more of a live wire than merely a loose end. Her eyes drifted closed.

"Hey, aren't you going to change?"

"No," Clare mumbled, knowing that sleep was close to claiming her. In her dreams, there were strobing lights and pulsing music. A shadow moved at the edge of the lights. The figure had no face, yet she knew it was her ex-husband.

Kyle.

Even embroiled in the dream, Clare was haunted by fear. Where was he? And what would he do if he ever tracked her down?

Decker needed two things. Information and his money. The search for both led him to Encantador, Texas. It was a town of just 2,800 souls that sat thirty miles north of the Mexican border.

Turning off the headlights, he drove down Main Street. All the storefronts were dark. Then again, at this hour nothing would be open. A flashing yellow light hung above an intersection, and he slowed his approach. The last thing he wanted was to get stopped by a local cop. After a year in hiding, Decker followed all the traffic laws like they were his religion. On the corner, a brown sign was affixed to a post. *Library, two blocks.*

With a smile, he followed the sign. Set at the end of a dead-end street, the library was in the perfect location. It was made of golden brick and a red sign was staked to the lawn. *Protected by South Texas Alarm System, San Antonio.* After a slow drive around the block, he was confident that his initial guess was right.

There were no cameras. Certain that the security was basic—and no match for him—he parked his car next to the building. After slipping on a pair of old gloved, he picked the lock. Next, he found the alarm's keypad and quickly circumvented the system. It would take several minutes for the security company in San Antonio to realize that the library was off-line. Then several more minutes would pass as they ran diagnostics. A few minutes more before they called the police. Then, how long until the police came to check?

His best guess was that he had ten to fifteen minutes. By then, he would have to be gone without a trace.

Standing on the threshold, he took a moment to get the layout. There was a single large room. Shelves with books ringed the perimeter and stood in rows. The back of the space was filled with round tables and partitioned desks. To his left was a smaller room. Through the door, he could see a mural of a beach and smaller tables. Decker assumed that was the children's area.

In the back corner, he found what he needed. A dozen computer monitors sat at individual workstations. Moving to a computer, he hit the power button. The screen blinked to life. A helpful card was taped to the monitor with the computer's password and internet login. After entering the keystrokes, he was on the internet.

He found the site for the Wyoming State Police. It took two minutes to hack into the database and another forty-five seconds to find his file.

Pinned to the top of the e-file was an old mug shot of Decker holding a placard with his ID. His blond hair was long, and his beard was shaggy.

There was a report about the murder of Jacob Loeb,

District Attorney of Pleasant Pines. Decker's DNA and fingerprints had been found in the getaway car, along with Paolo's body. Apparently, the fire hadn't been as total as Decker had hoped. Video footage from a doorbell camera showed Decker's car as he drove from Pleasant Pines.

The state had all the evidence they needed to throw him in jail for the rest of his life. Or worse, give him the death penalty. Then again, they had to find him first.

He continued to read the report. The case was assigned to a detective with the state police. The last entry was more than six months ago, when someone who resembled Decker had been seen at a local grocery store. Since then, there was nothing.

It meant his evasion tactics seemed to be working. Still…he couldn't afford unnecessary risks.

He entered the name of another person with Wyoming's DOC. Ryan Steele. Ryan's file was thinner than his own, but he had to find out if his old buddy had been caught up in the murder investigation of the DA. If Ryan was in jail, it'd be hard for Decker to get his cash. But if he was a free man…

It looked like Ryan had been remanded to custody for questioning following the death of Loeb and then released. Decker smiled. He couldn't wait to hear how his pal had gotten out of that mess. Knowing Ryan, it was quite a story. He closed the report.

His file still filled the screen. Moving the cursor to the *X* at the top of the page, he stopped. At the bottom of the file was a link. *DNA analysis, Newcombe, Decker.*

He paused. He still had a lot to do. First, he had to change his appearance—maybe he should create a more conservative, boring look. To do that, he'd need a haircut and presentable clothes. The library had to have scissors somewhere. Plus, if he were lucky, there'd be something that fit him in the Lost and Found. Once he was done, he still had to clean away every trace that he'd been in the library at all.

Did he have time to read another report?

He knew the answer was a definite *no.*

Then again, had the cops linked him to other crimes through his DNA? Decker needed to find out. He clicked the link.

The report gave genetic makeup as being mostly from the United Kingdom. There was a list of names that went back for generations and meant nothing. Decker had heard that the police used DNA taken from genealogy tests to link people to unsolved crimes, but this was different. They'd analyzed his family history. But why?

One name, Jeremiah Newcombe, was highlighted. A notation had been added: *genetic link to sociopathy?*

He closed the file but remained in his seat. His pulse pounded, resonating in his ears. He should just leave it alone and walk away, but he couldn't. Decker opened a new search and entered the name *Jeremiah Newcombe.*

In seconds, over one-hundred thousand hits appeared on the screen.

Leaning closer to the computer, he whispered, "What in the actual hell."

A headline from an article posted seven years ago was at the top of the search. "Identity of Jack the Ripper discovered through DNA."

The article read:

During the fall of 1888, London's eastside neighborhood of Whitechapel was gripped in terror. One of England's first documented serial killers, Jack the Ripper, was thought to be responsible for the murder and mutilation of five female prostitutes. Despite Scotland Yard's theories about the killer's identity, the actual name of Jack the Ripper has been a mystery for more than a century.

That is, until now.

In late 2007, it was discovered that the clothing of Jack the Ripper's second victim—Annie Chapman—had been saved in storage. Through analysis, two samples of DNA were taken from the dress. The first sample belonged to Chapman herself. The second sample belonged to an unknown male.

Recent discoveries have linked the second DNA sample to a Whitechapel baker, Jeremiah Newcombe. At the time of the killings, Newcombe was questioned by detectives but there was never enough evidence to bring charges. In the late 1890s, Newcombe emigrated to America and his name faded into obscurity.

Decker stared at the computer. His heart hammered against his chest. It couldn't be true.

"Jack the Ripper?" His voice was loud in the silent library. "I'm related to Jack the Ripper?"

He closed the file and conducted one final search. A shoebox lid, filled with stubby pencils and scraps of paper, sat next to the computer. Using a pencil and slip of paper, he wrote down a title and catalog number.

Decker cleared the history from the computer. Sure, any investigator would be able to pull up the search history from this particular hard drive. But if he left no trace that he'd been in the library, nobody would ever care to look.

A container of antibacterial wipes sat on the table's edge. A handwritten note was taped to the tube. *Kill the germs. Wipe down the keyboard and mouse after each use.* For once, Decker found a rule that he was happy to follow. With the computer and table free of prints, he pocketed the wipe—no sense in leaving behind evidence.

Taking the slip of paper with him, he walked through the history section and scanned the titles. He stopped and pulled a book from the shelf. *The Complete Guide to Jack the Ripper.*

Was he really related to the world's most notorious serial killer? It was a stunning—if kind of ridiculous— idea to wrap his brain around. Then again, Decker had always been drawn to death. He knew the desire to kill was a part of him.

Maybe those DNA results were right. Murder was literally in his blood.

Chapter 4

Arms tucked behind his head, Isaac lay on the bed and stared at the ceiling. He had yet to strip out of his clothes, but it didn't matter. He was too keyed up to sleep, and after pacing the room, he'd finally forced himself to stop, knowing he'd have to find another way to calm his restless mind. Certainly, staring at his four walls wasn't going to help.

Not tonight, anyway.

For the past year, he'd lived in the single room at the hotel. In all that time, he'd tried to make the place, if not homey, at least livable.

The small space was divided into three parts. A recliner, a footlocker that doubled as a coffee table, and lamp and four-tiered bookshelf sat near the door. The middle of the room held a bed, along with a dresser and TV. On the side farthest from the door was a dorm-sized fridge, small microwave and another set of shelves with dishes, food and a single-serve coffee maker on top.

He'd turned the TV to a twenty-four-hour sports channel. Nothing the overnight commentators said about a severe storm warning in Texas canceling upcoming games caught or kept his attention. What's worse, the constant drone wasn't enough to bore him to sleep, either.

He didn't have to wonder why he was lying in bed and awake. It was Clare.

What would've happened if they hadn't been interrupted by Trinity? He would have kissed her. But, then what? Would he have asked her to come to his room?

Would she have said yes?

The thought of Clare's naked body beneath him came to Isaac with a painful clarity. The image left him hard. He gritted his teeth and exhaled slowly. Was now the time to take matters in hand? Although he suspected the fantasy would be nothing compared to the reality of having Clare in his arms, in his bed.

His thoughts were suddenly interrupted by his phone, which sat on the bedside table and pinged with an incoming message. Sure, getting a text in the middle of the night was rarely because of good news. Still, Isaac was happy for the distraction. Sitting up, he scrubbed his face with hands and reached for the phone.

The message was from Jason Jones.

"Dammit," he muttered. The Supervisory Special Agent was the last person Isaac wanted to hear from—especially at this hour.

I need something to report back to DC by the end of the year.

"Bureaucracy," he grunted, while reaching for the TV remote. He turned off the sports channel. "The boring side of police work."

Another text followed.

I can't justify spending all this money if there are no results. Otherwise, it looks like I'm paying you for a yearlong vacation.

A vacation? Really? Clearly, Jason had never been to Mercy.

This is what he was going to hit him with at 3:00 a.m? Threats of closing the op? Isaac sent his own text: Trust me This is no vacation.

Then again, he understood that the SSA's problem was professional—and personal.

Decker had killed Jacob Loeb, but his actual target had been Chloe Ryder. She was now the AG, but she was also married to Jason's older brother, Marcus, and the mother to Jason's only niece. At the time of the hit, Isaac was working for Rocky Mountain Justice in Denver. Marcus was a colleague from the Wyoming branch. It was Isaac who came up with the idea to lay a trap for Decker. Ryan was on board—and the money owed to the hitman was bait. It was an audacious play—something the FBI loathed.

For Jason, getting Decker was personal. Until the hitman was in custody, the Jones family wouldn't be safe.

That's why the SSA agreed to the plan. He placed

Isaac as a single undercover operative in Texas. And what did Isaac get out of the bargain? Once Decker was in custody, Isaac would be his own boss.

For a split second, his mind returned to that old op. It had been four years ago already when he entered that dank hallway. And yet, as he sat in his room, he could still smell the stink of gunpowder. He could still hear the gurgling sound—like a clogged pipe. His hands were still hot with blood that sprayed like a fountain. Sure, the debacle hadn't been Isaac's fault. Since that fateful night, everything changed, and his old life was like an ill-fitting suit. He'd left the San Antonio PD within a month.

He'd gotten a job with Rocky Mountain Justice. But the job in private security was a bad match, too. The owner promoted teamwork too much. After San Antonio, the last thing Isaac wanted was to be part of a team. While he knew that he needed Jason to continue his one-man operation, Isaac resented the interruption to his solitude. He sent another text. What do you need?

Jason's reply was immediate. Something to take to my supervisors. Anything at all.

That was going to be a trick, because right now what Isaac had was absolutely freaking *nothing*.

Jason's next text read, Proof of life. Better yet, get me a location for Newcombe.

Isaac replied: Here I thought you were going to ask me for something hard. Sure, he knew better than to be sarcastic with Jason. But what the hell did he care?

He sent another text immediately.

If I knew that Newcombe was alive and his whereabouts, this case would be closed.

Jason sent another text.

Actionable intel by the end of the year. Or your op will be closed.

Isaac cursed. He knew what would happen if the Newcombe operation failed. It'd be more than a waste of money for the government—Isaac's reputation would be ruined.

Decker spent less than ten minutes changing his appearance. Using the scissors he found at the checkout desk, he gave himself a quick haircut and shave. He changed into a blazer and T-shirt he found in the Lost and Found. He quickly cleaned everything he touched as best he could on his way out of the building.

He left Encantador, putting a few miles between himself and the small town before pulling a burner phone from his pocket. Powering it up, he waited as the screen blinked to life, then entered a number that he'd memorized years earlier and listened as it rang.

The call was answered. "This better be good. Calling me from an unlisted number in the middle of the freaking night."

The gruff voice was almost as familiar to Decker as his own. "Ryan, man. Good to hear you."

Across the miles, he could hear the hiss as Ryan sucked in a breath. "Decker, what the… It's been a year, man. I thought you were in South America—or dead."

"I had a safe house about eight miles south of the border. Just a shack on a bluff. A well for water. Generator for power. An extra set of everything I'd ever need. An old lady who lived nearby delivered food twice a month."

"A safe house?" Ryan sounded equal parts impressed and perturbed. "I never heard anything about you having a safe house."

"If everyone knows, then it's not safe. Is it? I set it up years ago in case I needed to disappear for a few weeks."

"A few weeks? You've been gone for a whole damned year." Ryan's tone had risen. When he spoke again, he lowered his voice. "What do you want?"

"I need some information, man. Where are you?"

"Ever heard of a place called Mercy, Texas?"

Now that was an interesting twist. Based on the dust road signs he'd seen, Mercy was less than thirty miles from Encantador. Did he want Ryan to know he was that close? No, not yet. "Never been. Is it nice?"

"It's the exact opposite of nice."

Decker guffawed. "What are you doing there?"

"Got my own place." Pride was evident in Ryan's tone. "Bar. Tattoo parlor. Motel."

How'd Ryan come up with all the cash he'd need to start three businesses? Lip curling in anger, he realized Ryan must have used all the money from Decker's hit in Wyoming to set himself up.

The one person he thought he could trust was a self-serving piece of garbage.

Anger roared through him like a locomotive. Gripping the steering wheel tighter, he stared into the night as he drove.

Now wasn't the time to lose his cool. He still needed Ryan for whatever cash was left and information. The crazy notation about Jack the Ripper came to mind. "Did you ever hear anything about the cops doing DNA testing?"

"DNA? What kind of whacked-out question is that?"

"Nothing," he said quickly. "Never mind." Then, he was all business. "You know why I'm calling you, right?"

"You called 'cause you missed me, Decker."

He laughed again. "No, numb nuts. I need my money."

Silence stretched out as he drove.

After a full minute, Ryan spoke. "That might be a problem, Decker."

Ice crept into his voice. "You better find a solution, man. I need to get my butt into a country with no extradition to the US. And fast. I can't live in hiding anymore."

"Like I said, that's going to be a problem…"

Before Ryan could say more, he interrupted, "I don't want to hear excuses. I want my damn money. You got businesses, that means you got cash."

"I've got employees. Overhead. Hell, being legit means I gotta pay taxes and insurance and crap like that."

One word stuck with Decker. *Employees.* His vision went red. He could feel blood, silky and hot, wash over his hands. A bead of sweat dotted his upper lip. He licked it away, tasting the salt of his own skin. "It'd be a shame for something to happen to one of them people you gotta pay."

"You wouldn't do that, man. These are my people. My responsibility…"

Before Ryan could say anything else, he hung up. His friend had always been the smart one. It was no wonder that he owned a place of his own—even if it was in the middle of nowhere. He threw the phone out the window and glanced in the sideview mirror as it bounced across the pavement. Then again, if Ryan really was smart, he wouldn't have stolen from Decker.

After the text exchange with Jason, there was no way Isaac would get any shut-eye now. After shoving the phone into his pocket and grabbing the key to his room, Isaac stepped into the night. The motel consisted of twelve rooms, all on a single level. Three lights had been installed in the roof's overhang, and they lit up the walkway. He leaned against the brick wall, cooled by the night air.

Isaac refused to fail.

But he couldn't think of a way to succeed.

He stared into the night. Near the bar, a shadow moved, and Isaac froze. It was a person, but who?

Silently, he shifted to the end of the motel, and let his eyes adjust to the darkness. The figure was male; he could tell that by the height and broad shoulders. A second later, the flame of a lighter came to life as a cigarette was lit. Even at a distance, he could see a face. It was Ryan Steele.

He needed to pass on Jones's warning about the op being closed. Now was the perfect time.

Quickly and quietly, he crossed the parking lot. While still shrouded in shadows, he spoke. "What're you doing out here?"

Ryan pressed a hand to his chest. "Christ Almighty.

You scared the crap outta me. What the hell are you doing?"

Isaac stepped closer. Even in the dark, he could see the other man clearly. The pulse on his neck raced. His skin was pale. Ryan had been more than startled—as he'd said—but he was scared. Sure, Isaac had caught him unawares. But it wasn't enough of a surprise to cause the extreme reaction. The man also held his phone. Maybe he was expecting a call. Or maybe he'd just received one.

Isaac bet on the latter. "Who was on the phone?"

"You know, in a lot of ways, the real world is worse than jail. At least in lockup, I didn't have a personal guard. Here, I got you for a shadow."

"Cry me a freakin' river. You're out of jail. You have a chance to expunge your record. This is a sweetheart of a deal for you—especially since you've delivered two things. Jack and shit."

Ryan took a final inhale from his cigarette before flicking the butt into the night. "I heard that you let the blonde stay. What's her name? Clare?"

He could see Ryan's tactics from a mile away. He wanted to change the subject, challenge his authority and get Isaac rattled. The thing was, Clare did leave Isaac shook. He refused to bring her into the conversation.

Ryan continued, "She work for you at… What's your agency called? Texas Law? Is she a fed, or something?"

Shaking his head, he said, "I always work alone."

"Then, she's got to go. She made me look like an ass with her Long Island Iced Tea comment. Besides, this is my business, and you got no right—" Ryan began.

Isaac's temper flared. Poking his finger into the other man's chest, he growled, "I've got every right. The federal government owns this property. Unless you want to go back to jail, you'd best remember one thing. I own you." He paused a beat, glancing over his shoulder at the darkened hotel windows behind them, then lowered his voice. "We gotta talk about something else."

"Like what? You want my Christmas list?"

If Ryan Steele weren't such a jerk, Isaac might think he was funny. "We have to talk about Decker Newcombe."

Ryan smirked, "Too bad. I was hoping for a new gaming system."

"Cut the crap. Where's your pal?"

"Dunno." He fished a pack of smokes from his pocket and tapped out a filtered end. He caught it between his lips and shoved the pack back in his pocket. With the unlit cigarette in his mouth, he continued, "But if I knew, I'd tell you. I understand why I'm here."

"You turn over Decker and you get your criminal record expunged." Isaac didn't need to repeat the deal. They both understood the roles they played. Then again, he needed Ryan to be more than mere bait. If Decker was out there, he'd have to be lured into the trap. "I need you to call around. Ask questions. See if there are rumors, at least."

"Rumors, at least?" Ryan repeated. "What's going on? You sound pretty freakin' desperate, pal."

Isaac was, but he'd never admit as much to the likes of Ryan. Still, in giving the new order, he'd shown too much of his hand. Too bad it couldn't be helped. "I need something to give to the feds. And I'm not your pal."

Ryan took a lighter from his pocket. One handed, he flicked the flame to life and touched the fire to the tip of his cigarette. "What if there's nothing new to give?"

"By the end of the year all this—" he opened his arms, taking in the motel, bar and tattoo parlor "—will go away. You, too."

Ryan inhaled deeply. "I hate this, you know." He spoke words that were filled with smoke. It was akin to talking to a dragon. "This life isn't fun anymore. Drinking makes me sick. I've never gone for drugs— seen them mess up too many people. I like the women, but only if they like me first." He tapped ash from the end of his cigarette. "I want that second chance."

Isaac studied his face. "You really want to start over? Then you gotta earn it. Get me something." Isaac clamped his jaw shut. He was walking a pretty thin line between leaning on Ryan and begging the guy for his help. He'd be damned before he let the ex-con know just how bad the investigation was going.

Exhaustion flattened him in an instant, like being hit by a runaway eighteen-wheeler. His legs ached. His head pounded. His eyes were gritty. Isaac pinched the bridge of his nose. "We'll talk tomorrow."

"Isaac." Ryan's voice was harsh. "I want the blonde gone by morning."

Damn. Isaac wasn't in the mood for a fight. Then again, he wasn't going to make Clare leave—not now, at least. "No."

"You saw what happened in the bar today. I told her to get lost, but she's still here. How am I supposed to look like the boss with you undermining me?"

It was a reasonable question. He sighed. "Anyone asks, tell 'em it's a Christmas present for me."

"You think you deserve a Christmas present?" Ryan scratched his cheek with his middle finger. "Let me think."

Isaac wasn't sure if he should laugh or punch the guy in the mouth. "Say what you want, but Clare stays."

He turned for his room.

"Hey. Isaac." The words rang out like a shot.

Now what? He was too damn tired to think. He faced Ryan. "Yeah?"

"Just remember, I want a gaming system for Christmas—and a nice one, too."

The word *game* hit Isaac like a punch. "Let me see your phone."

"No way, man. I'm not giving you my phone."

He took a step toward Ryan. "Give me your phone or I'm taking it from you."

Placing his hand over his pocket, he asked, "Why do you need my phone? You have one of your own."

"I want to see what game you were playing, that's why." Even in the dark, he could see Ryan go pale. He'd found a nerve—now all he had to do was squeeze. "If you're lying to me, I'll have you back in jail tonight. You'll be charged with a dozen crimes. Accessory to murder. Money laundering. The feds will bring you up on RICO charges." He held out his hand.

With a curse, Ryan fished the phone from his pocket. He pressed it into Isaac's hand. "Fine. He called just now. I was going to tell you, I swear. I just had to get my head on straight… Besides, the number's blocked. It won't help you at all."

Isaac was too astonished to be furious. "Tonight? Now? What'd he say?"

"He said he's been hiding out in Mexico for a year at a safe house."

"Where in Mexico?" he asked, his pulse racing with excitement. There'd be time to answer questions later. But not here in the middle of the parking lot where they might be overheard. "Come with me."

This was the moment he'd been waiting for—and he wasn't about to waste another second.

Chapter 5

As they walked back to Isaac's room, each step was filled with a certainty that he hadn't felt in a long, long time. He worked the key into the lock and opened the door. After turning on the light, he gestured to the single chair. "Have a seat," he said to Ryan.

Isaac stayed on his feet and took out his phone. He placed a call to SSA Jones. The phone began to ring, and he turned on the speaker function.

Jason answered. "This better be good."

"Decker Newcombe called." Isaac tried to keep the excitement from his voice, but it was damn near impossible. He was a kid at Christmas, getting the best present ever. "Just now, Ryan Steele heard from him." He paused a beat and added, "He's here now and you're on speaker."

"This better not be some prank. Because if it is, I'm not amused."

He ignored the comment, though it did dampen his enthusiasm. "Decker's been hiding in a Mexican safe house. I didn't waste time with a debrief before contacting you."

"I'm listening."

Ryan took several minutes to share what had happened. He started with receiving a call from a blocked number—it was Decker, who was looking for his money. He had more information about the safe house. There was a well. A generator. It was located eight miles from the border. He ended his debriefing by saying, "He asked a real crazy question about DNA testing. Either of you know anything about that?"

Isaac shook his head. "I don't. What about you, Jason?"

"Nothing on my end. But local law enforcement agencies have been more aggressive in testing unknown DNA found at crime scenes against what the FBI has collected in CODIS." He turned the conversation from the Combined DNA Index System, and back to Decker's whereabouts. "What else can you tell me about the safe house?"

"Nothing, man," said Ryan, before repeating, "Just that it was eight miles south of the border."

Jason sighed. "The US–Mexican border is nearly two-thousand miles. That's a lot of ground to cover. Decker could be anywhere."

Isaac's temper flared. "You wanted intel, you got intel."

"Actionable intel," Jason corrected, then sighed. "At least we know he's close to the US and not planning on leaving without his money. Looks like the trap is finally working. I'll see what we can do with satellite images. Have you gotten the number?"

"Not yet." Isaac still had Ryan's phone. If he was lucky—and good—he'd be able to access the phone's memory and access the call log. The phone was locked. He held it up to Ryan's face. The biker stared back at him before realization hit his expression.

"Hey, man. You can't do that."

Isaac glared before looking back at the unlocked phone. It took him only minutes to find the most recent call and entered a code to circumvent the block. He repeated the number for Jason while writing on a scrap of paper. Then, he tossed the phone to Ryan. "There you go."

Ryan stared at the phone. "You got a number for Decker? How, man? The call was blocked."

Jason was the one who answered. "Everything received by a phone is stored in the memory somewhere. All you need to do is know where to look."

"So, how does a number help us?" Ryan asked.

"If Decker's phone is still on, we should be able to find him." He knelt in front of the footlocker and entered the combination into the padlock. Opening the lid, he removed a computer. He closed the lid once again and used the metal crate as a seat. With the laptop balanced on his knees, he powered up the device. "I subscribed to a service that will let me access information from cell towers."

It was Ryan again who spoke. "Can anyone get that information?"

Isaac tilted his head from side to side as he typed. "It's

not for the public, but law enforcement agencies can get access. Me, too. Jason would have no problem getting the information, but I imagine he'd have to go to the office to access the server."

"Confirmed," said Jason. "But I'm headed to the office now, anyway."

Once inside the server, Isaac entered the number and hit the return key. It took only minutes for a map to appear on the screen, along with a red flashing dot. "We got a hit," he said for the sake of Jason, who was still waiting on the other line.

"Is that really Decker?" Ryan asked, leaning toward the computer.

"It's the phone that called your number," said Jason, clarifying. "But if the cell is attached to the man, then yeah, we got Decker." He asked, "You got a location for me?"

Isaac read off a set of GPS coordinates. Then, he worked the map's aspect. The picture went fuzzy as the program was recalibrated.

"Holy crap," Ryan whispered as the picture became clear. "That's just down the road—right outside of Encantador."

Isaac was already on his feet. "I've got to go and check that out."

"Be careful," said Jason. "And report back with anything you find."

With a beep, the call was ended by the agent.

"I'm going with you." Ryan stood as well.

Isaac slipped on his coat but didn't argue. He could use the extra set of hands. Besides, Ryan had just as much at stake in finding Decker.

Ryan opened the door and impatiently swept his arm toward the night. The gesture was an unmistakable invitation for Isaac to exit his own room. "C'mon, man. We know where Decker was, but we don't know where he's going."

"Give me a second." From the footlocker, Isaac removed three more items. A translucent evidence bag, a box of surgical gloves and a Glock 19 with ammo.

Without another word, they left his room. As they walked away from the motel, his pulse was still racing. Decker Newcombe was close, and Isaac was going to bring him to justice.

Clare wasn't sure what woke her, but she lay on the sagging mattress and stared into the dark. The outline of the Christmas tree was visible from the light filtering in through the seam of the curtains.

There it was again. Male voices. Was it Kyle? Had he finally found her? She froze, not daring to breathe. There was something about the timbre of the voice that was familiar. Definitely not Kyle, though. She rose from the bed and crossed the room, careful not to bump into Trinity's bed. She stood at the side of the window and looked out into the night.

Just as she had heard, two men were outside and talking.

The lights were on under the roof's overhang, making it easy to see Isaac and Ryan.

"You think we'll find him?" Ryan asked.

"We can only hope," said Isaac. "I've got my Glock in the glove box in case we do meet your old buddy."

Ryan said, "I need something from the bar. It'll only take a second."

"Hurry up," Isaac called, his tone sharp.

They walked away from the motel, their shadows blending with the night.

What the hell?

"Hey." The single word was whispered, and Clare started. She spun around. Trinity was sitting up in bed, her form darker in the shadowy room. "You okay?"

Clare gulped down a breath. "Yeah. You startled me, that's all."

"Everything okay out there?"

"Sorry for waking you. I thought I heard voices."

"Is someone outside?"

"No." Clare wasn't sure why she lied. She maneuvered through the dark back to her own bed. She peeled back the covers and slipped between the sheets. "It must've been a bad dream or something."

"Try to get some rest. You've had a long day."

Even in the dark, Clare smiled. Finding a friend in Trinity really had been the first good thing to happen in months. "Thanks. I appreciate it."

Trinity's breathing became slow and rhythmic within minutes. Yet, Clare was still awake. She stared at the window, the sliver of light and the outline of the tree— all the while, hoping that sleep would reclaim her. Isaac and Ryan were obviously looking for someone. But who were they looking for? And why did they need guns?

Isaac unlocked the truck and Ryan slipped into the passenger seat. As Isaac settled in behind the steering wheel, Ryan laid a Heckler and Koch across his lap.

So, that's what he had to grab. He shook his head.

If Ryan noticed the gesture, he said nothing. "All this time, man. And here we are."

Isaac turned the key in the ignition and let the engine run. "What are you talking about?"

Ryan gazed at the bar. "How long have we been working this cover together now? Almost a year? And finally, Decker's back. I'll be honest with you, I thought your plan was out there from the beginning, but it worked."

Isaac pulled out of the parking lot and for the first time, he wondered if tonight was a setup. Was the phone call a ploy to get Isaac into the desert so he could be murdered by Ryan and Decker? A chill ran down his spine.

If that were the case, why now?

No, he had to trust Ryan—even if he didn't really trust anyone at all.

Ryan kept talking, "I still can't figure out how you worked that deal. Hell, I can't understand why you'd convince the feds to clear my record. I'm not the kind of guy people should help out."

Isaac stared into the night as he drove "Is that a Freudian slip?" He glanced at the gun on Ryan's lap. "You're suddenly making me regret that I okayed letting you carry a weapon—even if it's for a good cause."

Ryan stilled. "Why would you say that?"

He shrugged. "I'm just saying that you've been a very good boy, Ryan—as far as I know. Don't go giving me a reason to think otherwise. Especially if we're riding off into the desert alone together." He tightened his grip on the steering wheel. "Besides, I'm a better—and faster—shot than you."

Ryan snorted. "A cop? Never."

Isaac smiled, but his gaze was cold. "You'd be surprised what we ex-cops can do, partner."

The headlights cut through the darkness. As they approached the phone's location, he knew that they weren't going to find Decker. The stretch of road was empty for miles.

Isaac parked on the road's shoulder, his thoughts racing.

Ryan looked out the window. "What the hell was he doing out here? Think he's still around?"

From the beginning, Isaac knew they might not find the hitman. "We've only got an approximate location on his phone—not him." He turned off the engine, the night suddenly filled with silence. "But the phone's around here somewhere. If we find it, there's a lot we might learn about Decker."

Ryan unfastened his seat belt and opened the door. "Sure, let's look for a phone on the side of the road in the middle of the night. Sounds like fun. Easy, too."

Sometimes the dumb jokes were slightly amusing, but not tonight. Could the guy not keep his mouth shut? Isaac thought not. From the glove box he removed a flashlight. He held it out to Ryan. "You need this?"

"I'll use the light on my phone."

The ease with which Ryan handled the situation reminded him of his last partner at San Antonio SWAT. Miguel had been the kind of guy who rolled with the punches as well. He also told corny dad jokes. A feeling of affinity for Miguel squeezed his chest. For a moment, Ryan wasn't as annoying.

"Take these." He held out a pair of latex gloves. "Put these on before you pick up anything important."

"Yeah, I know. I've been arrested a few times. I've seen how you cops do things."

Isaac ignored the comment. Jumping from the truck, Isaac swept the flashlight's beam across the ground. He walked to the road's edge and looked into the night. In the distance, a coyote howled.

"What's the range of your tracker?" Ryan asked.

"One-hundred yards." Isaac stepped off the shoulder and onto the plains that stretched out for miles. "And please don't complain that one-hundred yards in any direction is a lot of space to cover. You offered to come along."

He grumbled, "Yeah, I remember."

For a few minutes, they searched in silence. Isaac turned back to the road and that's when he saw it. Hidden under a clump of tumbleweed was the reflective face of a phone. "I got it."

Isaac donned a pair of gloves to keep from transferring fingerprints before picking up the phone. He pulled the evidence bag from his pocket and placed the phone inside.

Without comment, they walked to his truck. As his tires hit the pavement, a line of pink showed on the eastern horizon.

He placed a call to Jason. "I have the phone," said Isaac as the SSA answered. "He must have tossed it from the car after he made the call." San Antonio was only a few hours away. "I'll bring it to you now." And after that, he could drop Ryan off at a restaurant or something for a few hours. Then he'd have time to stop by his parents' house for a preholiday visit.

"Negative on you coming to the office. Decker is

close and I don't want anything to appear out of the ordinary—like a long-time employee disappearing. Or my undercover operative not being on the property if the subject shows up." Jason sighed and Isaac imagined that he was weighing his options.

Ryan offered a solution. "There's a delivery place in Encantador. They can get packages to San Antonio within a few hours."

"Done. Deliver the phone but get back to Mercy as soon as possible. From there, it's business as usual."

Isaac asked, "What about the satellites? Have you gotten anything that can scan the area?"

"The request is moving up the chain of command at DOJ. With it being so close to Christmas, not everyone's in the office. They're being tracked down. We'll have to use satellites from Defense and that's going to be a whole different approval process. I have no doubt it'll get done. But it's taking some time. What makes it all worse is that there's a storm coming up from the Gulf of Mexico." Jason continued, "Get me the phone. Business as usual." He ended the call.

"Wow," said Ryan. "Your buddy is a real prince of a guy."

Isaac laughed. "Let's invite him to the bar. Have a beer. Watch a game."

"Did you just make a joke? After a whole year of knowing you, I thought you lacked the sense of humor gene." He paused a beat. "There was something else that Decker said last night. When I told him that I was in business for myself, he made a comment like, 'It'd be a shame for something to happen to one of them people you gotta pay.' You think we should call back Jason and tell him?"

A threat from a man like Decker should be taken seriously. But it left Isaac with a single question. "I'm not sure how much the feds care. Don't get me wrong, they don't want anyone to die. But would Jason intervene?" Actually, he knew the answer. The fed wouldn't change his plans. "We'll mention it to him next time with speak."

"Alright then." Leaning back in the seat, Ryan stretched his legs out and closed his eyes. Eyes still closed, he said, "Wake me when we get to Mercy."

Isaac shook his head and watched the sky. The horizon was filled with pink, rose and amber. *Red in the morning, sailor's warning.*

The new day promised to be long. Isaac still had to stay undercover and work the bar.

He would be beyond tired. This time, he didn't mind.

For the first time in a long while, his investigation seemed to be moving in the right direction. And the sooner he wrapped it up, the sooner he could get the hell out of Mercy.

Trinity wasn't used to having another person in her room. It wasn't that Clare was obnoxious or even that she snored. But the soft breathing of another human being in the opposite bed kept her from her usual deep sleep.

By 6:00 a.m., her head throbbed. She couldn't stand to toss and turn for another minute. She needed a cup of strong coffee. True, she had a coffee maker in her room, but it hissed and shook with every single-serve cup.

That'd wake Clare and honestly—Trinity was happy to be a considerate roommate. She took a moment to think and came up with a plan. She could grab them both drinks at the gas station.

Rising quietly, she stripped out of her T-shirt and shorts before donning a pair of jeans and sweatshirt.

True, Trinity wasn't used to thinking of other people. Yet, she liked Clare and figured she could use a treat. Picking up her phone, she sent a message.

Went to get us coffee. I can make a latte at the gas station. It's good. BRB.

Slipping out the door, Trinity pulled it closed behind her. The parking lot that stretched between the bar and motel was empty, save for a single car that sat near the road. Sunlight glinted off the windshield. Tucking her hands into her pockets, she strode across the pavement.

Nearing the road, she shaded her eyes and looked at the horizon for any traffic. There was nothing.

"Excuse me." The car's door opened, and a blond man stepped out.

Trinity staggered back, her heartbeat racing. "Holy crap." She pressed a palm to her chest. "You startled me."

To Trinity, the guy—with his short messy hair and thick-rimmed glasses—looked like an accountant after an all-night party. He smiled. "Sorry, I didn't mean to scare you. I'm a little turned around and was hoping you could help me figure out how to get back on the road."

Of course, the guy was lost. Nobody came to Mercy on purpose.

"Sure." She stepped closer. "You got a map on your phone, or something?"

"Yeah. It fell onto the floor but it's in here, somewhere." The guy ducked into the car. He called out, "Give me a second."

Trinity moved closer still. As she stood behind him, she noticed a rattlesnake tattoo on his neck that seemed out of character. And his hair was more than messy. The haircut was choppy, a total crap job.

Something wasn't right. She scanned the parking lot. It was still empty. A tinge of fear crept up the back of her neck. "You know, I can just give you directions."

The guy riffled through the junk on his seat. "What?"

Leaning down, she raised her voice to be heard. "Where are you headed? I can just give you—"

Then, he struck. The belt was around Trinity's neck before she even knew what was happening. The leather bit into her flesh. She clawed the strap, trying to pull it free. Her necklace broke. The chain slid from her throat. She saw the locket hit the pavement and she wanted to cry out. But every part of her body burned with the need for air. Her pulse echoed in her skull, like waves crashing on the shore.

The guy was close, his breath hot on her shoulder. Reaching behind her, Trinity punched, scratched, clawed. Her fingernails grazed flesh.

With a curse, the guy pulled the belt tighter. "Do that again and I'll kill you slow."

"What?" she said, gasping for air. "Why?"

Trinity's arms were too heavy to lift, and she could no longer fight. Her vision blurred and darkness crept in from the sides. For a single instant, as the pain melted away, she wondered what came next.

Then there was nothing.

For the first time in almost two months, Clare woke up feeling truly refreshed. Her mind was clear. Her muscles were relaxed, instead of aching and cramped from sleeping curled up in the back seat of the car. Stretching in the bed, she took in the hotel room. Trinity's bed was empty. Clothes were tossed into piles on the floor. Makeup and jewelry were scattered across the top of the nightstand and the chest of drawers. The little Christmas tree still stood next to the wall, its glossy ornaments glowing in the sunlight creeping around the window shades.

On the floor was Clare's tote. She rolled to her side and leaned over the edge of the bed. Peering into the bag, she exhaled. The flash drive and the phone, along with pictures of the documents, were both in the bag.

Clare knew that the time had come. She couldn't keep running forever, which meant that she had to do something.

She could contact the media.

Or maybe the local police.

What she really wanted was to call her mom—if for no other reason than to speak to a person who knew and loved her.

Trinity's wisdom from the night before rang loudly in her mind. *Speaking for moms everywhere, we always want to hear from our kids.*

In all this time on the run from Kyle, all those lonely nights on the road, she hadn't reached out, even though she knew her mom would be worried. Sharing what she'd found, or any hint of her location, would put her only parent at risk. But if she made a call, she didn't have to tell her mother anything important—just enough to let her mom know she was safe.

A digital clock sat on the nightstand, the numbers a darker gray on a smoky background. It was 7:12 a.m. In Kauai, it'd be the middle of the night. But if Clare didn't call now, she knew she'd lose her nerve.

The cell was a pay-by-the-month smartphone that had been purchased in Indiana. At the time, Clare paid cash for the device and six months of service. She'd entered no contact information but knew her mother's number by heart. She placed the call and waited as the phone began to ring. For an instant, Clare hoped to get voice mail.

"Hello?" The voice on the other end of the line was thick with sleep.

"Hi, Mom. It's me."

"Oh, Clare, honey. It is you! Where are you? How are you? I heard from Kyle and have been so worried…"

Clare tensed. She should've known that her ex would reach out to her mother.

Her mom was still talking. "I know what it's like to have a breakdown and need to get away. Really, I do. Are you back in Columbus? I'll book a flight. It might be a day or two. You know how hard it is to get to the mainland."

A breakdown? So that's what Kyle had been telling people. "No, Mom, I'm not in Ohio. And I want you to stay away from Kyle. He's a dangerous man, Mom."

"He said that was part of your breakdown, honey. That you'd been making up stories about him."

How had Clare ever loved such a manipulative son

of a bitch? "Mom, listen to me. I didn't have a break-down. I'm not paranoid," she said, although the last part wasn't exactly true. "Kyle and his father, well, they've done some things. Trust me." Her voice had risen. She paused and breathed. "I just called to let you know that I'm okay."

"I love hearing your voice, but I want to see you. Where you are? I'll come to you."

Clare closed her eyes and let her mind fill with happy dreams of seeing her mother again. But those dreams would never become a reality—not with Kyle and his family still out there. "I can't see you right now." Her chest was tight, but she drew in a breath. "It might be a while, but I'll call when I can."

"Why won't you let me help, Clare?"

"Because it's better for us all if I take care of things myself."

Her mother made a small sound. Clare couldn't tell if it was a laugh or a cry. "You've always been so indepen-dent. Even as a little girl. *Me do.* That was your favor-ite phrase. *Can I get you cereal?* Same answer always. *No, me do.*"

Emotion clogged her throat, and she swallowed hard. Once she could speak, she made sure her tone was con-trolled. "I'm sorry, Mom. I really am. I called to let you know that I'm okay. I didn't have a breakdown. And Kyle isn't the guy we thought he was."

"Can you tell me anything?"

"I don't want to drag you into this." She rubbed her eyes and sighed. "Promise me one thing. Do not call Kyle or his dad. If they reach out to you, say nothing about talking to me, or where I am."

"I don't know where you are. Really you haven't told me anything…"

Love gripped her heart and squeezed hard. "One more thing. Merry Christmas."

"Merry Christmas, Clare. I love you."

"Love you, too."

Clare ended the call and stared at the phone. A hard kernel of regret was stuck in her throat. No. She wouldn't feel bad for calling her own mother. But she knew that reaching out hadn't been the best plan, either.

The phone pinged as a message notification appeared on the screen. The appearance of a text left her confused. Nobody had her contact information. She pressed her thumb onto the bubble.

It was from Trinity.

Went to get us coffee. I can make a latte at the gas station. It's good. BRB.

There was also a time stamp: 5:57 a.m.

She glanced at the clock again. It was 7:16 a.m. Trinity had been gone for over an hour. Or maybe, she'd been gone, come back and left again. Maybe to do her laundry or something…

Pulling her knees to her chest, Clare scanned the room once more. This time she looked for a take-out cup, filled with coffee that would be cool by now.

Nothing.

Sure, Clare didn't know Trinity well—or even at all, really. Just because her roommate had offered to grab an extra cup of joe, it didn't obligate her to bring one back.

For a moment, she was sucked back into memory,

to her darkened office at Chamberlain Plastics Manufacturing.

A cup of tepid coffee sat at her elbow. The computer's illuminated screen was the only light. She'd opened the file several minutes before and had read the contents twice, still unable to believe the words in front of her. Her pulse raced. Her chest was tight, and her lungs burned with each breath.

"Hey." *Kyle's voice seemed to come from nowhere. He crossed the threshold, and the motion sensor clicked. Lights flooded the room.* "What are you doing here, sitting all alone in the dark?"

Swallowing, Clare realized that she didn't know where—or how to begin. "Umm..."

"You look tense." *Kyle wore a dark suit, white shirt and no tie. His blond hair was freshly cut, and just starting to show a touch of gray at the temples. Standing behind her, Kyle began to knead her shoulders. He continued,* "Maybe all this volunteer nonsense is too much for you. You're working late and all the tension is settling in your shoulders."

Nonsense. The one word helped her find her voice. "I found a problem," *she said. For the past several years, she'd worked with a non-profit that turned unused land into parks. She was researching a possible site owned by Chamberlain Enterprises.* "With the tract of land."

"Problem?" *he echoed.* "What kind?"

She shifted to the side, so he could see the screen. "Look." *She pointed to the internal memo written by her father-in-law, chairman of the company Kyle's family had owned for decades.*

"So, it's a memorandum from my dad." *He leaned*

closer. His breath was hot on her neck. "Written, what, twenty-one years ago. So, what about it?"

"Kyle. Do you see what it says?" She pointed to the screen again.

His palms still rested on her shoulder and his grip tightened.

"Ow, Kyle. You're hurting me..."

He let his hands slip from her shoulder. "Sorry. It's just..." He paused. "Dammit. I just don't know what you expect me to do. He is my father, after all."

She turned in her seat to look up at her husband. "I don't expect you to do anything. It's us. We're in this together and we'll figure out what to do."

He looked down at her and smiled. "I'm glad I have you with me. I'd hate to face all this alone." He flicked his fingers at the computer and the document on the screen.

She stood. Kyle pulled her to him, wrapping her in a hug. His arms were stiff, trapping Clare next to his chest. Of course, her husband was shocked that the company his family had founded and run for years buried drums filled with toxic chemicals. Who wouldn't be? And yet, in that moment, she longed to escape from his embrace.

Now she knew that her marriage was already over. Yet, she hadn't realized that her life was altered forever as well.

Chapter 6

Clare knew that she needed to find a way to deal with her in-laws and put the past behind her. Rising from the bed, she headed into the adjacent bathroom. In the tub, she turned on the taps and stepped under the hot spray of the shower. Within minutes, she felt physically refreshed—but the tightness in her throat remained.

After stepping from the shower, she wrapped a towel around her torso and returned to the main room. As Clare dressed, she planned. She'd start by looking for Trinity at the gas station. After that, well, there wasn't much more she knew to do. For the day, she wore a white T-shirt, jeans and sneakers. Her money was still in her locked suitcase. She removed $40 from the hiding place in her shoe and relocked her bag.

Once she was ready, Clare grabbed her tote bag and

left the room. The door closed and automatically locked. The sun had risen, but the air was still cool. She folded her arms over her chest. The parking lot, a sea of asphalt, stretched out to the road. Beyond that was the gas station. From where she stood, the store looked like a child's toy.

She hustled across the parking lot and stopped at the edge of the road. She looked for any traffic but there were no cars. She took a step forward and stopped. She'd seen something—a flash of metal in the morning light. Turning, she looked back at the ground.

There, at the edge of the parking lot, lay a necklace. She lifted it from the ground. A locket spun in the air. Even before she opened the frame, she knew what she'd find. Instead of a picture, thin strands of hair were tied with a ribbon.

It was Trinity's locket. One of the links had snapped in two.

Clare didn't know why it was in the parking lot, or what had happened to Trinity. But she was determined to find out.

Running across the road, Clare pulled the gas station's door open and stepped inside. It was like nothing had changed since yesterday. The scent of stale coffee and used motor oil still hung in the air. The same shiny garland was still hung across the counter. The same man still stood next to the cash register.

The only change was the countdown calendar. Now it read four days 'til Christmas.

The old man who ran the gas station looked up. "Morning. What can I do you for?"

"I'm looking for Trinity," Clare began. "You know,

from the bar." She jerked her thumb vaguely in the direction of the roadhouse across the street. "Have you seen her?"

"This morning?" the man said. "Naw, she didn't stop by."

Her heartbeat thundered, echoing in her skull. "Where else could she go?"

The man's name was embroidered on the pocket of his shirt. Stu. "Not many places around here. If you want to go anywhere special, you need a car."

That was it. "You think Trinity drove somewhere to get coffee?"

"Not likely," said Stu. "She got no car. And she usually came in here, anyways."

Clare tried to swallow but her throat was tight. She looked out the window. There was nothing to see. Just the same old bar, tattoo parlor and motel. A truck, covered in faded paint, rust and primer, pulled into the convenience store parking lot and parked next to the pump. The driver opened his door and jumped to the ground.

It was Isaac. Her heart began to race again. This time, it was for a wholly different reason.

She turned for the door before she'd planned what to do next. He looked up as she stepped into the sunshine. "Morning," he said, already pumping gas. "You're up early."

Clare glanced in the truck and for the first time, noticed a passenger. It was Ryan. He glared at her from where he sat. Her shoulders tightened with tension. "I was looking for Trinity. She sent me a text saying she was going to get us coffee. That was over two hours ago. She hasn't come back, and Stu hasn't seen her, either."

Ryan opened the door to the truck and sat on the edge of the bench seat. "What'd you say about Trinity? That she's gone? I wouldn't worry about her too much. She might've called some guy and talked him into taking her out to breakfast."

Clare didn't think that was right. Pulling Trinity's necklace from the front pocket of her jeans, she held up the locket. "I found this in the parking lot right next to the road." She examined the chain. "I guess she could've been getting into a car when it broke…"

She looked up at Isaac. His brow was furrowed, and he was watching Ryan. Ryan's complexion turned ashen. It brought back the moment she stood at the window and watched as Isaac and Ryan crossed the parking lot in the middle of the night.

"You think we'll find him?" Ryan asked.

"We can only hope," said Isaac.

What had that been about?

"I have some stuff to mail from Encatador," said Isaac. "The overnight delivery place doesn't open for a few hours. I can go to town now and see if Trinity turns up." Then to Ryan, he said, "You should stay here. Business as usual, right?"

Jumping to the ground, he repeated, "That was the order. Business as usual."

Clare said nothing as Ryan sauntered to the road and then jogged across the street. "Well, I guess I better…" She pointed toward the motel. "You know, get back. Trinity might show up with that coffee she promised."

Isaac returned the nozzle to the pump. "Take care, Clare. And do me a favor. Keep your door locked, okay?"

"They lock automatically, you know that."

"Use the dead bolt and the chain."

His words left her chilled. "Is there something I should be worried about?"

Isaac removed a wad of cash from his front pocket. "Nothing. It's just that you can never be too careful."

Wasn't that the truth.

He stepped past her, his arm brushing against her shoulder. She couldn't explain what happened, but a shock went through her at the feel of his body against hers. She'd never felt anything like it—not even with Kyle.

Then he walked on, and the moment was over.

She watched him for a minute longer before looking back at the line of cinderblock buildings.

"Hey, Clare."

She turned. Isaac held the door to the gas station partially open. "Yeah?"

"You can come with me, if you want."

"To Encantador?" she asked. "Why?"

He shrugged. "It's better than sitting in your room all morning. There's a decent diner and we can grab breakfast. Also grocery store if you need to pick up any food. I have a few errands to take care of, but they won't take long."

"I don't know…" she began.

He pulled the door open the rest of the way. "No problem. Just thought I'd offer." He slipped into the store and let the door close behind him.

Clare walked to the side of the road. She wasn't sure why she'd turned down the offer to go into town. Maybe she'd spent so much time alone recently that she forgot what it was to be around another person. She glanced over her shoulder. Isaac was back in his truck.

There were a million reasons that she should just stay in Mercy. Trinity really might show up. Personally, Clare had secrets to keep. She's shared more with Trinity than she intended. In talking to Isaac, she might give some key detail away. There was also the fact that the more time she spent in public, the easier it became for Kyle to track her down.

Truthfully, there were only a few reasons for her go with Isaac. Clare now had money to purchase food of her own. Even better, she could replace the snacks Trinity had shared. Besides, it wouldn't be *that* bad to spend more time with Isaac—even if every time he looked it her, she felt a spark in her belly.

He turned on the engine and the truck's running lights glowed. Clare waved and he drove toward her. The truck idled as he pulled up at her side and lowered his window. "You need something?"

She swallowed. "Is that offer to ride along still open?"

Isaac had a list of things to do in Encantador, and bringing Clare with him was a distraction he didn't need. Yet, he'd be stupid to ignore the fact that Decker Newcombe had surfaced at the same time Trinity Jackson went missing. The hitman had even made threats towards those who worked for Ryan. Because of that, he didn't like the idea of Clare being alone.

She sat in the passenger seat as his truck rumbled down the road. The town of Mercy became a speck in his rearview mirror. One day soon, he hoped to leave the town for good. Before that, he had to find and catch a killer.

Clare stared out the windshield and he watched her in profile. The curve of her neck. The definition of her chin and nose and mouth.

Without looking in his direction, she asked, "Can I ask a question?"

"Shoot."

"What's the deal between you and Ryan? It just seems to me like…" She stopped and drew her bottom lip between her teeth. "Well, there's a vibe between you two. I know you say he's your boss, but it seems like Ryan's beholden to you."

He sat straighter. Gripping the steering wheel, he turned his eyes back to the road. Ryan Steele was more than beholden. Isaac was the only reason that Ryan was out of jail and without him, he'd go back to rotting in a cell.

He asked, "What makes you think that?"

"He's just, well… What's the word?" She paused to look out the window. "Deferential, I suppose."

Isaac's pulse began to race. He never should've brought Clare with him. She was too curious. Too astute.

"Ryan's a mean cuss," he said. "He's certainly never been respectful of anyone—me, included."

"It's just that he let you give me this job. You set the agenda for the day. It seems like he owes you." She glanced at Isaac. He made the mistake of looking in her direction. Their eyes met and she pinned him with her gaze. Desire, like a lightning strike, shot through him. She asked, "You know what I think?"

He looked back at the road—his jaw tight. "No. What do you think?"

"I think something happened in jail and you saved Ryan."

In a weird way, Clare was right and wrong at the same time. It was best to let her think what she wanted. With an exhale, he rolled his shoulders back. "It's not really something we talk about. So…"

"I won't say a word." Clare put a hand to her chest, as if taking a pledge.

He turned his attention back to the road. A bead of sweat trickled down his cheek. Wiping it away with the side of his hand, he glanced once more at Clare. She was looking out the window.

"What about you?" He glanced at Clare before turning his attention back to the road. "How'd you end up in Mercy?"

Without turning to look at Isaac, she said. "I took a wrong turn."

Isaac guffawed. He couldn't remember the last time he'd laughed out loud. With a shake of his head, he looked back at the road. Sure, Clare had a quick wit but there was more. She hadn't really told him anything about herself. Before he could think of the right questions to ask, he felt that same old shimmy in his seat a moment before the temperature gauge in his car started to climb.

"Damn." He slammed his hand on the steering wheel and eased his foot off the gas. A cloud of steam leaked out from under his hood.

"What's wrong?" asked Clare, a note of alarm in her voice.

He pulled to the side of the road, his tires kicking up a cloud of dust. "Truck's overheating." He should've known better than to take it out so soon after driving around all night. "It's hard to get parts for a vehicle this old. Plus, Mercy isn't exactly a shipping hub."

Clare's tote sat on the floorboards. She lifted it to her lap and looked inside. Pulling out a hair band, she wrapped her locks into a ponytail. "What can I do to help?"

"You? Help?"

"You sound surprised."

He shrugged.

"Why wouldn't I help? The quicker we get the truck fixed, the quicker we find Trinity. Besides, I don't want to sit on the side of the road all day, especially in this heat." She unlatched her seat belt and swiveled in her seat. The tote slipped from her lap and dumped the contents onto the grimy floor mat. He cataloged the contents. Sunglasses. Key fob. Cell phone. A flash drive. A water bottle.

Clare cursed. She bent to pick up her belongings.

Isaac leaned over in his seat. He scooped up the drive.

"Give that to me," said Clare, her voice hard as flint.

The change in her tone from amiable to threatening gave Isaac a jolt. "Sure," he said, holding up the slim metal drive. "Here you go."

She snatched it from his hand with the greedy speed of a thief with a jewel. He had to wonder what was on that drive that was so important?

Silently, she collected the rest of her belongings.

"You know," Isaac began, "that's the second time everything's fallen out of that bag of yours. Ever consider getting something with a zipper on top?"

"You know," she echoed both his words and tone, "I'm a little strapped for cash right now. Getting a bag with a zipper is low on my priority list."

"Maybe if you're a good girl, Santa will bring you a new purse."

She huffed out a small laugh. "Maybe."

"Besides, if you're low on cash, you can sell the bag. I don't know much about fashion designers, but that tote looks real to me. Probably worth something, even at resale."

Clare held the bag to her chest. "I thought about doing just that. Really, I have. Probably would've had no choice but to pawn off my tote if I hadn't gotten the job with you." She let out a long breath. "I've kept it because of what this bag means to me..."

Isaac could clearly imagine some monied dude giving Clare the expensive bag as a gift. Maybe that dude was why she was on the run. Or maybe, he was still out there, and she wanted to get back to him. It drove home the simple fact that he knew nothing of Clare or her life. He liked the way she looked. He liked her company. There was nothing more between them. Period. End of story. He swallowed down the sour taste of frustration. "You've kept it because it was a gift. I get it."

She shook her head. "It's not that at all. I bought this bag myself. At the time, it was more than my monthly rent." She shook her head. "It was a stupid splurge but being able to buy it made me feel like I was finally a success." Clare met his gaze. "Do you know what I mean?"

He recalled the moment that he'd gotten the buy-in from the feds for his plan to catch Decker Newcombe.

At a meeting that made the operation possible, Jason Jones had said, "You've got balls, my man. And you're either a genius or you're a fool." The agent shoved the contract across a wide conference table. The page's edge fluttered with the breeze of movement.

Isaac already had a pen in hand. "I'm a lot of things," he said, signing his name on the appropriate line. His chest was tight with pride. "But a fool isn't one of them. We'll get this bastard and soon."

He turned away from the memory and looked at Clare. The sun, just starting to creep higher in the sky, shone at her from behind. She was surrounded with a halo of light and her features were obscured with shadows.

"I know how you feel." He scratched at the stubble on his chin and let the moment pass.

Sure, he understood Clare's attachment to her expensive tote bag. But she was obviously protective of the flash drive. He imagined that it was part of the reason she was on the run. Even if he'd figured out a small part of her story, there was still so much more about her that he didn't know.

And that mystery was enough of a reason to keep his distance.

For Clare, stopping in Mercy had come with problems she hadn't anticipated. When she'd been by herself, she never had to worry about getting tripped up on a lie. Or worse, accidentally telling the truth.

Then, there was the flash drive. When she was alone in the car, she knew it was safe.

Now, she risked losing it–or worse, facing questions about it if anyone found out about it. If she left it in her car or the room, it might get stolen. Sure, keeping it in her bag wasn't ideal, either. But it was the best she could do for now at least.

Isaac was another problem altogether. He was too damn good-looking. Beyond the looks was the fact that he was charming, smart and insightful. It made him easy to like and easier to trust. But Clare had learned her lesson well. Everyone was capable of deception.

Still, she refused to let the current of life sweep her along. Hugging the bag to her chest, she glanced at Isaac. After weeks on the road, she'd figured out how to fix minor auto problems. "I can help with the car."

"We gotta wait for the engine to cool. Then, the reservoir needs to be refilled." He gave a frustrated sigh. "I can't wait to get rid of this heap of crap."

Sure, the vehicle was old. She patted the dashboard. "This truck is a classic. All it needs is some TLC."

"And that takes money, which I don't have."

She chewed on her bottom lip. Before she married Kyle, Clare hadn't been a wealthy woman. But she'd lived a comfortable life where money was available to cover all her needs, even if she couldn't buy everything she wanted. Life with Kyle had been opulent. Lavish. Excessive.

The minute she left Columbus, her circumstances

changed. Clare's thinking needed to change as well. "Sorry, I didn't mean to imply..." she began.

Isaac waved away her apology. "Just forget about it." He paused. "There's a jug behind your seat. If you want to help, you can grab it for me."

Clare folded the top of her bag over and carefully set it on the floorboard. She turned in her seat and came up on her knees. There, on the floor, was a plastic jug filled with water.

She looped two fingers through the handle and hoisted the water up and over the seat. "Here you go."

"Thanks." Isaac took the jug, not bothering to look her in the eye.

Had he been watching her? Then again, it'd been a while since Clare had gone for a run—much less taken a yoga class or worked out at the gym. Maybe he had taken a peek and hadn't liked what he saw.

Now, that was a humbling thought.

She dropped back to her knees. "You need anything else?"

"Naw, I'm just gonna get this in the reservoir and we can get going."

Isaac opened the door and stepped from the truck. She watched as he walked to the grille. His shirt clung to the muscles in his arms, shoulders and chest. He looked up, their gaze meeting through the windshield. Clare's cheeks warmed and she turned her gaze to the side window.

"Hey," Isaac called.

She looked at where he stood at the front fender.

"Can you pop the hood for me? It's the lever under the steering wheel. Left side."

Clare moved to the driver's seat and pulled back on the toggle. The hood unlatched with a pop. Isaac lifted the hood and braced it on the prop rod. He was hidden behind the hood but still she could hear his curse. "Aww. Dammit."

"You okay?"

"The radiator cap's too hot to touch. Can you grab me something?"

Clare scanned the inside of the truck. True, it was old, but it was clean. Not even a used napkin wedged into a door pocket. She opened the glove box and froze. Atop a pile of maps was a gun, along with a box of ammo.

She told herself that she shouldn't be surprised. It was Texas after all. Besides, given the nature…of business, she supposed, at the bar, it seemed only natural that Isaac might keep a weapon around.

Clare touched the handle with a finger. She expected the metal to be cold and smooth. The gun felt like nothing more than death.

But Isaac was a convicted felon. Weren't there laws about convicts not having weapons? She shook her head. A lifetime of living by the rules had given Clare a headful of thoughts that were ridiculously unhelpful now. Her world was now a dangerous place. In fact, she wondered why she'd never gotten a gun already. Or maybe she hadn't gotten a gun because she didn't know how to use one.

"I think there's a rag behind the seat. It's back where you got the milk jug."

Isaac's voice startled Clare. She closed the glove box.

"Just a sec." She turned and looked over the back of the seat. There, on the floor, was a red bandanna. She pinched the fabric with the tips of her fingers and sat in the seat. "Got it," she called out, while opening the door and stepping from the truck.

The cool air was already giving way to the heat of the day. Clare wondered what the weather was like in Ohio. Most likely rainy and cold. Or maybe there'd be a white Christmas in Columbus this year. Snow wasn't something she'd see in a place like Mercy.

"Here you go." She rounded the front of the truck and held out the bandanna.

Isaac took the cloth. "Thanks."

He bent under the hood and unscrewed the lid of his water reservoir. A hiss of steam escaped. "Damn. Still too hot. If I put in water now, it'll just boil off."

Clare leaned against the side of the truck, her mind returning to the gun in the glove box.

"We got no choice but to wait."

"I was wondering…" Whatever else she wanted to say was stuck in her throat. Maybe her mother had been right, and Clare hated asking for help. She shook her head.

Isaac shoved the bandanna in the front pocket of his jeans. "You were wondering what?"

Clare coughed to clear her throat. "Well, it's just that when I was looking for a rag, I opened your glove box." She paused a beat, forcing herself to speak. "I saw the gun."

"Okay." He narrowed his eyes and watched Clare

for a moment. She wasn't sure what to read in his gaze. Hesitancy? Curiosity? "What about it?"

Maybe asking for a lesson in firearms was a bad idea. Then again, she'd come too far to turn back. Her heart hammered against her chest. "Would you show me how to shoot?"

Chapter 7

When Isaac came to Mercy, he'd made it a rule to never get involved personally with anyone. He should be following that rule with Clare, but he already knew that it was too late to simply be indifferent with her. What's more, he wanted to know why she was hiding in Texas. He wanted to know why she was running.

Clare asking for a firearms lesson brought up a whole other interesting set of questions. Namely, who might she need to shoot—and why?

Even though Isaac did care, he gave an uninterested shrug. "Sure. Why not. We got some time." He walked to the end of the truck's bed. Clare followed. "The first rule of gun safety is this—every gun is loaded. I don't care if you know there aren't any bullets in the firearm. It's loaded." He lowered the tailgate.

Already, she sounded confused. "How can that be? If there are no bullets, then—"

"That's the mindset I want you to have. A gun is a dangerous and deadly tool, and it's key that you to respect that fact from the beginning. It'll help keep you safe when you're using one. Rule two." He climbed into the back of the truck. A metal box was wedged behind a wheel well. He lifted the lid and paused. "Never take out your gun if you don't intend to use it. Got it?"

She dutifully repeated the rules.

He nodded at her words and lifted the lid of the metal box. Taking a knee, he rooted around inside, tossing several empty soda bottles into the bed of the truck. Slamming the lid shut, Isaac collected the bottles and stood. He walked the edge of the truck and jumped to the ground. He landed right next to her, and a shiver of desire ran down his spine. Clare really was a beautiful woman. Her fingers were long and graceful. What would it be like to have her touch him? To explore her in return.

"Here, hold these." Laced between his fingers were the empty bottles. "We'll use these for target practice."

Clare took the bottles.

"Now," Isaac continued, "we need the gun and the ammo. What's the first rule of firearms?" Walking to the passenger side of his truck, he looked over his shoulder as he spoke. Her legs were firm, and the swell of her hips filled out her jeans nicely. Another image stole into his mind, one of arms and legs tangled in sheets. Or of her thighs parting as his hips drove forward. His mouth went dry, and he looked away.

She repeated his earlier warnings. "A gun is always

loaded. Followed by rule two and that's to never take out a gun unless you plan to use it."

He heard her words and nodded, but his mind was still filled with his fantasy. True, it'd been months since he'd last slept with a woman. Maybe it was a simple physical need that drew him to Clare.

Then again, he'd seen plenty of good-looking women pass through the bar in Mercy. And well, his pulse didn't race *veins around* any of them at all.

Isaac stood at her side. In one hand, he held the gun. In the other hand, a box of bullets. "I stowed your bag behind the seat. Hope that's okay."

"Yeah. That's fine."

He nodded and slipped the gun into the waistband of his jeans near the small of his back. After locking the truck's door he asked, "You ready for your first shooting lesson?"

Clare walked next to Isaac. It took less than five minutes for him to find a flat-topped rock, that was about three feet high.

"This will work," he said, setting the bottles in a row.

She watched him walk back to where she stood. "Now what?"

"I always want you to be cautious around guns. But if you take out a firearm, it's because you plan to eliminate a threat. Aim for the center mass." Isaac used his finger to outline a circle on his torso. All the while, he kept his gaze on Clare's face as he spoke. He was making sure that she was paying attention to what he said, and what's more had, absorbed the information. She didn't mind that he was being so careful while teaching her how to use a firearm. But again, his background as a convict didn't seem to meld with his caution. "Got it?"

"Got it." She paused. "Where'd you learn how to shoot?"

"Aww, darlin'," he said, his drawl becoming thick. "I learned how to handle a firearm from a young age."

Was that really true? Or was there more to his story? Before she could wonder, he held the gun on the flat of his hand. "This here is what's commonly called a handgun. Officially, this is a Glock 19. It's not a big gun, but it can punch a hole through a person at one-hundred paces. The magazine holds ten bullets and there's one in the chamber."

"Eleven shots," she said.

Isaac smiled. "Glad that you're paying attention." He pointed at the gun again, going over each part, from the grip to the magazine, making sure she could familiarize herself with each.

"If you're going to shoot, you're going to have to know how to reload a gun." He pointed to a black button on the left side of the firearm's grip. He pressed it with his thumb. The magazine slipped free. He handed it to Clare. "That's the magazine release." Next, he pulled back on the slide and bullet was ejected from the top of the gun. He handed that to her as well. "And that's the ejector port."

Next, he pulled back on the slide and exposed the ejector port once more. "This is the slide release lever, and it locks the slide into place and open. You can see into the magazine well." He held up the weapon so Clare could see daylight at the other end of the gun. As he spoke, Clare had to admit, that his precise lessons weren't what she expected from an ex-con. Isaac was definitely proving to be quite a puzzle—it's just that she didn't know how all of the pieces fit.

He concluded, "Now you know that the firearm is empty."

He spent a minute loading the firearm. The magazine was returned to the well. He released the slide and chambered a round. Then, he released the magazine a second time and took the extra bullet from Clare. "When you add the final bullet, it's called topping off." Holding the fiream by the grip, he held out the gun to her. "Now it's your turn."

She slipped her hand over his as he passed the gun on to her. Clare's breath caught in her chest. It was more than holding a deadly weapon. It was Isaac. He was large man—muscular and solid. His shoulders were broad, and his arms were well-defined. Having him so close both excited and intimidated her.

He let go of the gun and the weight of the firearm pulled her arm down. "It's heavier than I imagined."

"If you spend a lot of time handling weapons, you'll get used to it."

They spent the next few minutes working together to load and unload the gun. Eventually, Clare knew all the steps by heart.

Isaac said, "Firing a gun is easy. Point and shoot. Hitting a target, now that's the tricky part."

Clare turned to look at the bottles lined up in a row. They were impossibly small from this distance.

"See this." He pointed to a small piece of metal that stuck out from the barrel. "That's the sight. You line that up with your target and pull the trigger. Got it?"

"Line the sight up with the target. Pull the trigger. Got it."

Gripping the gun in one hand, he pointed the barrel to the ground. "Take it."

Isaac chuckled. "Unless you're using a gun all the time, your arm and wrist will fatigue quickly. In the end, it'll mess up your aim. So, you'll have to compensate."

"That's a lot to keep in mind."

"Sure, but using a gun is serious business." He pointed to the soda bottles. "Just remember what I told you and fire."

Clare lifted the gun. Her wrist wobbled.

"Tighten up everything." Isaac ran his hand over her forearm.

Her pulse raced at his touch, but she squeezed the muscles in both arms from wrist to shoulder. The gun steadied in her grip. The sight, a red piece of metal stuck up from the barrel. She touched the red tip to one of the bottles and pulled the trigger.

The blast of gunfire filled the silent desert. The scent of gunpowder wafted on the breeze. The gun bucked in Clare's hand, sending a shock wave through her body that she felt in her chest and her teeth. A cloud of dust erupted in front of the rock.

The dust settled and all the bottles were still standing.

"Damn," she cursed, passing the gun from one hand to the other. Her palm throbbed and she shook it out. "What'd I do wrong?"

"You can't expect to be an expert after firing one bullet."

"Is that another rule for me to remember?"

"Life advice," Isaac said. "There was this one time I

was teaching a young man how to shoot…" His words trailed off and he scratched the side of his ear. "Anyway, everyone always thinks it's easier to be a marksman than it really is." He paused a beat. "Try again."

Clare lifted the gun, taking care to line up the sight with a bottle. Inhale. Exhale. Pull. Fire. Once again, a cloud of dirt and gravel shot up into the air. As the dust settled, she saw that the bottles still stood in a row. Sure, she wasn't surprised, but she was still disappointed. "Dammit. What am I doing wrong?"

"You aren't doing anything wrong, but I can help you get a little closer to right. Lift your gun and aim at the last bottle."

She did.

Isaac moved in behind her, close enough that his chest touched her back. He bent down so his cheek was next to hers and she could hear his breath. "Lift your arm a little." He placed his hand near her wrist and applied the whisper of pressure. "You want the sight on top of the target, not beneath it."

The bottle was hidden behind the sight. Yet, with Isaac so close, it was hard to concentrate on anything beyond the feeling of his body next to hers.

"See what I mean?" he asked.

She looked at the sight and covered the bottle with the red metal line. "I think so."

He put pressure on her arm from the bottom. "Make sure you keep the gun level. Now fire."

Hooking her finger around the trigger, she pulled back. The gun jumped in her hand as the rock exploded into bits of dust. The bottle still stood upright. She lowered the gun, letting the weight of the weapon pull down on her shoulder. "I missed again."

He squeezed her arm. "Not too shabby for only firing a gun three times." He stepped back. "Try again."

Clare rolled her shoulders up, back and around. She stared at the bottle, imagined the bullet punching a hole through the plastic. Lifting the gun, she covered the target with the sight. Inhale. Exhale. She squeezed the trigger. The boom of the gun's blast rolled out over the plains as the bottle shot up into the air.

"You did it," he whooped. "I knew you could. Try again. See if you can hit another bottle."

She aimed and pulled the trigger. The crack of a whip echoed over the plains as the bullet kicked up a cloud of dust. The bottle still stood. She inhaled. Exhaled. Setting the sight on the target again, she fired. Shredded plastic jumped off the rock as the bullet ripped through the empty bottle.

"Great job," said Isaac. His enthusiasm made her smile. "You're a great natural shot, but make sure to practice whenever you get a chance."

"That was a combination of excellent teaching and beginner's luck." She held out the firearm. "I want to see you shoot."

Isaac took the gun from her hand and worked his jaw back and forth. "The engines probably cooled enough that I can add water by now. You ready? Or you want to try and shoot again?" He offered her the butt-end of the gun.

She waved the firearm. "I'm good."

Isaac nodded toward the rock. "I'm gonna get the bottles. No sense leaving garbage out here."

"No littering. Now, that makes you a man after my own heart."

He stared at her. "Huh?"

"You won't litter. I went to school for environmental engineering. Just a little conservation joke." *And apparently not a very good one.* Her face burned. "I can help." She hustled past Isaac and scooped up the bottles that were still standing.

Isaac had shoved the gun into the waistband of his jeans again. She leaned her hip on the rock and watched as he gathered the bottles that had been shot. He looked up at her and smiled. Just seeing that smile warmed her insides.

Then again, he never answered her question about where he'd learned to shoot. It wasn't an accident. He'd obviously ignored her. She was determined to find out more about the man who it her up like a freaking Christmas tree.

They began to walk. "You never answered my question earlier, about where you learned to shoot so well. Why's that?"

He leveled his gaze at her. "Why's it matter?"

She swallowed, not sure what to say next. "It's just that I'm out here in the middle of nowhere with a guy I don't know anything about. Suddenly, I learn that he's a master marksman. I have a right to be curious."

Isaac continued to stare at Clare. "No, you don't. Besides, you were the one who wanted the shooting lesson."

He was right. She had asked for his help. In the distance, sunlight winked off the truck's windshield. Clare trudged toward the waiting vehicle. Isaac walked at her side.

At the truck, he lowered the tailgate and jumped into the bed. "Hand me those bottles."

She did. He placed all the plastic back into the metal box and shut the lid. Then, he jumped to the ground. "Imani Omar." Isaac slammed the tailgate closed.

"Who's that?" Clare asked. "The person who taught you how to shoot?"

"Nope. She's the first girl I ever kissed. Prettiest girl in the seventh grade. Beautiful, brown eyes. Long nails that she kept pained bright pink. She smelled like vanilla and tasted like strawberry syrup. I think it was her lip gloss."

"Why're you telling me about a girl you kissed when you were a kid?"

"No, Imani wasn't a girl. She was *the* girl. I'm not telling you about how I learned how to shoot because that's not a story you need to hear." He rested his hand on the top of the tailgate and shrugged. "When you asked me about my firearms instructor and I wouldn't answer, you started to worry that I was untrustworthy."

He wasn't wrong. She shrugged. "So instead…"

"Instead, I decided to tell you about Imani. She's more important, anyway."

"Because she was your first girlfriend?"

Isaac shook his head. "Girlfriend? No. Especially not after the kiss."

"Why's that?"

"I'd rather not say."

"You were the one who brought her up. You can't start a story without finishing. It's not fair."

"Well, I was an inexperienced kisser."

Clare asked, "Isn't everyone inexperienced at that age?"

"Trust me, I was bad."

Isaac slapped the back of the truck and walked to the front grille. Clare followed. The hood was still up. The jug filled with water sat on the ground. "Now you've got me hooked on your story. How bad were you at kissing?"

"Let's just say I didn't have an understanding of technique." He lifted the jug from the ground and took off the lid, pouring water into the reservoir. "I definitely didn't know how to French kiss, and she taught me everything I needed to know. At that age, anyway."

Clare laughed out loud. "I think I get it."

She waited as he screwed the lid back in place and slammed the hood shut. "Let's get out of here."

Clare stepped away from the truck at the same moment Isaac turned. They collided and she pitched back. She knew she was going to fall. Before she went down, Isaac caught her in his arms.

Her hands were pressed against his chest. His heartbeat was strong under her palms. Without thinking, she brushed her mouth against his. His lips were strong, and he tasted of citrus.

Then, Clare started thinking too much. She stepped back. "I shouldn't have done that. I don't know why. I mean, I do. You're handsome, and you were holding me, and it just seemed like the thing to do. If you're offended, I'm so sorry…"

"I'm not offended. You don't need to be sorry. It was nice."

Well, nice was something. "Okay, so long as we understand each other." What kind of understanding they had, she wasn't sure.

"Hey, Clare?" He reached for her. His touch was alluring, and she didn't move away. He pulled gently on her hand. She let herself be drawn closer, and as his forehead touched hers, their gazes met. "Okay?" he muttered, his lips nearly against hers.

It felt like torture, when all she wanted was his kiss. Again. "Okay," she whispered as his mouth took hers.

This time, it felt less gentle and more like an exploration. He pressed his tongue into the seam between her lips and she sighed, opening herself to him. Pressing her body against his, she melted into the embrace. Isaac wrapped his strong arms around her waist and held her tighter. The kiss became hungrier and deeper. His hands traced her side, her stomach, her breasts. She ran her fingers through the short hair at the nape of his neck and the heat of his skin scalded her hotter than the Texas sun.

"Oh, Isaac." Clare was dizzy with lust and longing. But she needed to stop now because in a minute she'd lack the fortitude to walk away.

Breathless, she pushed Isaac's chest. "You've obviously gotten better at kissing since the seventh grade."

He gave a quiet chuckle. "That's good to know at least."

Her head still swam and her legs were weak. She reached for the door handle to keep herself steady. "We better get going. You have errands and I'd like to look for Trinity." After pulling open the door, she climbed onto the seat and got settled. Yet, her mind raced as she wondered what the hell should happen next...

Get a hold of yourself, Clare. You're a grown woman.

Sure, she wanted to believe that. But she knew that she was lying—because that had been a hell of a lot more than *just a kiss*.

And if she didn't forget it—and remember why she was in Mercy—it could only lead to trouble.

Decker Newcombe drove through the side streets of Encantador, one hand holding the steering wheel and the other resting on the book he'd stolen from the library. *The Complete Guide to Jack the Ripper.*

He'd killed the redhead to send a message to Ryan Steele. As life leaked out of the woman, he knew that the money wasn't as important as his legacy. His heritage was murder and terror. But he didn't want to die in obscurity, like his infamous ancestor.

Hell no, that wouldn't do for him.

He'd never settle for the hollow notoriety that came with being an unknown killer. He wasn't a shadowy bogeyman. If it weren't for DNA found on the clothing of a victim, Jack's true identity would've forever remained a mystery.

Wrapping his hand tighter around the steering wheel, Decker looked for the perfect place to watch and wait. He found it in an abandoned municipal lot that was surrounded by the rear entrance to a strip mall. It was 10:15 a.m. A dollar store sat between a laundromat and an Asian restaurant that was only open for dinner. There was also a grocery store that wouldn't open for another forty-five minutes. He scanned the roofline of the buildings and above each door for cameras.

There were none.

Slumping low in the seat, he reached for his book. After opening the covers, he scanned the table of contents. "Chapter Three: Victims of Jack." Page 87.

He read:

> *Throughout the fall of 1888, Jack the Ripper was believed to have committed five grisly murders. Also known as the Canonical Five, there were eerie similarities between each of the killings. First, all the victims were women. Second, they all worked as prostitutes in London's Whitechapel neighborhood. Finally, each woman was disemboweled after her death.*
>
> *Their entrails were never found.*

Decker set the book on the passenger seat. Pulse pounding against his skull, he gripped the steering wheel tight. His mouth was dry. What would it have been like all those years ago? London streets so dark that it'd be impossible to see a hand in front of a face. Or a knife at a neck. Had his ancestor hidden in shadows and waited for his prey?

Or had he spoken to his victim before slitting her throat?

Drawing in a deep breath, he finally knew what he wanted.

The scent of decay and death already filled the car. Turning his gaze to the rearview mirror, he glanced at his closed trunk. Even though he couldn't see it, he knew that the body of the redhead was still there, waiting for Decker to make his mark.

One day soon, the world would fear his name, too.

Chapter 8

Clare glanced out the window as the truck passed a large wooden sign. In blue script were the words *Welcome to Encantador: A Charming Place to Live. Population 2,872.*

A single street led through the middle of town. Both sides of the road were lined with businesses. A doctor's office. A post office. A diner that served breakfast and lunch sat across the street from a bar that only served dinner and alcohol. Like arteries off a vein, side roads led to and from neighborhoods. Houses, surrounded by green lawns, sat behind picket fences.

"Looks like a nice town," said Clare, as Isaac pulled the truck next to the curb.

Isaac gave a noncommittal grunt. "Guess so." After turning off the engine, he pocketed the keys. Pointing, he said, "That's the best place to look for Trinity."

The diner, Over Easy, sat in the middle of the block. The picture of a snowy field and happy snowmen had been painted across three windowpanes that overlooked the street. A paper cutout of Santa hung from the front door.

Following Isaac, she stepped into the diner. The dark and nutty aroma of coffee greeted her, along with the spicy-sweet scent of baking cinnamon. Her stomach gurgled, a painful reminder that she'd skipped more than her morning coffee—but breakfast as well.

She was also developing one hell of a headache, the result of no coffee—which she'd basically lived on for months on the road—and the burning Texas heat. Now that she thought about it, she hadn't even had much water this morning. No wonder this place smelled so good.

He stopped on the threshold and scanned the room. "Trinity's not here."

She followed his gaze. Half a dozen booths lined one wall. A narrow counter with fifteen stools sat between the booths and the kitchen. All the stools were vacant, and only half the tables were filled. Trinity was definitely not one of the customers.

Swallowing, she asked, "If she's not here, where else could she be?"

"Maybe she stopped by earlier and left. Let's grab a seat," said Isaac, leading the way to the counter. "The server might know."

Clare sat on a stool. Isaac took the seat beside her. Both places were already set with silverware wrapped in a paper napkin. An upside-down coffee cup rested in a saucer.

An older woman with short gray hair stood behind the counter and approached as they sat. "Morning, folks." Her name tag read Mae. Flipping over the coffee cups, she continued, "Want a fill up?"

"Please," said Isaac.

"High-test or low-octane?" the server asked, comparing coffee to gasoline.

Isaac looked to Clare, waiting for her order.

"I'll take caffeinated," she said.

"Make that two."

"Anything else?" Mae asked.

"The cinnamon rolls smell good," said Isaac before asking, "They fresh?"

Mae filled Clare's cup with coffee from a glass pot. "Of course, they are. Came out of the oven a few minutes ago." She filled Isaac's cup.

Once again, he looked to Clare. How long had it been since someone actually showed her any consideration, even if it was just to let her order first? Obviously, there were the two months since she left Columbus. But honestly, it had been longer.

Sure, on paper, Kyle had been the perfect husband. Smart. Good-looking. Successful. But when it came down to it, there were problems in the marriage even before everything went to hell.

"Hon? Y'all want a cinnamon roll?" Mae asked, drawing Clare from her thoughts.

Clare's stomach growled again. "Yes." After a beat, she added, "Please."

Isaac said, "Make that two."

Mae nodded and turned toward the glass and chrome pastry cabinet. Clare reached for a bowl filled with packets of sweeteners. After emptying two sugars into her coffee, she stirred and then sipped. The drink warmed her from within and she gave a contented sigh as the caffeine hit her brain.

"The first sip is always the best." Isaac held his own cup, lifting it slightly as if they were toasting with champagne flutes.

"You think the coffee's good, wait 'til you try these," said Mae, setting two plates on the counter. Fat cinnamon rolls, covered in icing, filled each plate. "Enjoy."

Clare reached for her silverware and unwrapped the napkin. After cutting off a piece, she stabbed it with her fork and took a bite. Spicy sweetness filled her mouth. "Wow," she said around her bite. "That's delicious."

Mae beamed. "Glad you like it. It's my momma's recipe."

Isaac had already finished half his cinnamon roll. "Compliments to your mom," he said, taking another bite.

"Well, she's been gone for nearly thirty years, but I'll tell her when I see her in Heaven." Mae filled Isaac's cup with fresh coffee. "What brings you two to town? You folks visiting family for the holidays?"

Isaac took the last bite of his roll and scraped his fork through the icing on the plate. "We're looking for a friend of ours. We think she might've stopped by this morning."

"Maybe I can help. What's she look like?"

"Redhead," said Clare, a bite halfway to her mouth. "She's tall, too."

"A tall woman with red hair," Mae echoed as she shook her head. "Can't say that I've seen someone like that, but the breakfast rush was especially busy today. Maybe she was here, and I just don't recall."

"Oh, trust me." Isaac pushed his plate back. "You'd remember Trinity. She's got a few pretty elaborate tattoos. One like a tiger on her arm. A pink python on her leg."

Mae shook her head. "I definitely didn't see anyone like that."

"Any place else that might've been open around half-past seven?" Clare cupped her hands around her mug of coffee.

"Just us." She glanced over her shoulder. A wall clock sat above the door to the kitchen. It was almost eleven o'clock. "The grocery store opens soon. She might be headed over there."

Isaac nodded. "Thanks."

With a coffeepot in hand, the server came from behind the counter and moved to a table.

"So…" Clare wasn't sure where to lead the conversation. She refused to bring up the kiss, even though her lips still tingled. Still, she was curious about Isaac. "What's your story? You met Ryan in jail. Then came looking for a job when you got out. What was going on in your life before all that happened?"

He gave her that smile. "Me? I thought I told you. I'm a Texas boy, born and raised."

Clare ignored the fluttering in her chest. "How long have you been in Mercy?"

"About a year."

"A whole year?" Clare couldn't imagine spending that much time in a place like Mercy, Texas. Then again, she might not have another choice. She took a bite of

her cinnamon roll and thought about her future. Before
she could plan for anything beyond today, she needed
to deal with her past—Kyle and her in-laws included.

Mae returned. "Anything else I can get for you two?"

Clare had eaten the entire roll. "I'm good."

Isaac got to his feet. "Thanks for your help." He
pulled a roll of cash from his front pocket and set a bill
on the counter. "That should cover everything," he said.

"You don't have to pay for me," Clare began.

He stopped her words with his smile. "It's not every
day I get to take a beautiful woman out for coffee." His
Texas drawl was thick, and his voice made her toes tin-
gle. "Come on." He held the door open for Clare to pass.
"Let's see if the grocery store is open and ask about
Trinity before it gets too busy."

As she walked past, her shoulder brushed against his
chest in the cramped doorway. At least by now she'd
had enough accidental physical contact with Isaac that
she knew what to expect. The little hiccup to her pulse
as her heart began to race. The warming of her skin at
the exact point of contact. She also knew that she'd be
able to feel his touch on her skin for hours more.

The grocery store looked as though it had been built
not long after World War II ended. It consisted of one
level—all red brick, glass and metal—and filled half
the block. Wide windows looked onto the street and held
posters advertising weekly specials. A set of glass doors
opened automatically. A wave of frigid air washed over
Clare. She hugged herself tighter and followed Isaac
inside.

A teenaged girl in a blue smock stood next to the entrance. "Morning. My name's Adeline." She held out a paper flier. "Care to see our specials?"

"We're actually looking for someone," said Isaac. "A friend of ours. Tall woman. Red hair, lots of tattoos."

"When would she have stopped by?" Adeline asked.

"This morning," said Clare.

The teenaged greeter's smile faded as she shook her head. "Nobody's been in the store who looks like that."

"You sure?" Isaac pressed.

"Sure, I'm sure. I've been right here since we opened."

Clare couldn't help it; her shoulders slumped with disappointment.

An older man with silver hair and a thin mustache approached Adeline. He wore a tie in the same shade of blue as the smock, black trousers and a white button-up shirt with short sleeves.

"Adeline, I need you to help Greg in the back. I'll take care of handing out today's ad."

"Yes, Mr. Yoshida." Adeline handed over the stack of papers, then glanced at Clare and Isaac. "Uh, these people could use some help, I think." She quickly headed to the back of the store.

Mr. Yoshida tapped the sheets on a window ledge, until all edges were in a line. "Morning, folks." He smiled. "Anything I can help you with?"

"We're here looking for a friend of ours. Female. Tall. Red hair," said Isaac. "She would've come in right as you opened."

"Hmm," hummed Mr. Yoshida. "I haven't seen anyone like that in the store. Or in town all morning, really." He paused. "Why are you looking for her, anyway?"

"She's my roommate," said Clare. "This morning she

went out, texted that she'd be back within a few minutes and hasn't come back for hours." Her words trailed off. "Well, I'm just worried is all."

Mr. Yoshida kept the same smile on his face, but his brows came together in a look that was both friendly and troubled. "I can see why you'd be concerned. Tell you what, I'll keep an eye out for your friend."

"Trinity," Isaac said.

"Okay. Trinity. If she shows up, I'll tell her that you've been by and ask that she call to tell you she's okay. How's that sound?"

"Much obliged," said Isaac, his Texas drawl thick once more.

The doors opened. A woman, carrying a dark-haired toddler, walked through the door.

"Ms. Erikson," said the store manager. "Nice to see you this morning. Here's a flier with all our specials…"

Clare, Isaac and their search for Trinity was all but forgotten.

The scent of cooking meat filled the air. It was so much like what she'd smelled the last night she's spent in Columbus with Kyle. After her discovery of the memo outlining the secret burial of toxic chemical, they'd walked from the corporate offices of Chamberlain Plastics Manufacturing to the Dublin Link. The pedestrian bridge connected both sides of the Scioto River. Each bank was filled with newly erected luxury apartments, chic boutiques and restaurants.

Clare leaned against the railing as the wind whipped through her hair. She held her tresses in one hand and watched her husband. Kyle stood at her side and stared at the water as it flowed. Kyle was the first to speak. "I guess it'd be wrong of me to ask..." He blew out a breath and shook his head. *"Never mind. It'd be wrong."*

Even then, she knew what he wanted. Yet, she'd said, *"Ask."*

"Is there any way we can just ignore the whole thing? I mean, it was years ago. Laws were different back then, weren't they? Besides, I bet my dad didn't even know how toxic those chemicals were."

She'd read the memo. She understood—same as Kyle—that his father knew he'd broken the law by burying the drums of toxic sludge. And worse, he knew the chemicals were dangerous, knew the damage they could cause. *"We can't,"* she said. *"And you know why."*

Kyle scoffed, showing a side she'd almost never seen before—especially not directed at her work. *"You can't really think one report will make a difference in a decades' old mistake that nobody seems to know about."*

"First, it's morally wrong to ignore this. People are going to get sick if they haven't already, and part of my job is to look into that. And second, we know. To ignore the problem makes us complicit, Kyle."

"This will kill my dad. It'll ruin his reputation. Destroy the family business." Kyle shook his head. *"He's going to hate me."*

Clare couldn't help but feel sorry for Kyle. True, her father-in-law was a tough bastard. She placed her hand on his arm. *"We'll get through this, together. Besides, I used to work for the EPA. If the company comes forward now, the government will go easier on the business."* Finally, she had a way to be useful to Kyle and his family. *"I know how to best negotiate a settlement. Your dad might not get that much time in jail..."*

"My dad in jail?" he spit. *"There's no way I'm going to let me dad get arrested."* He drew in a shaking breath. *"I'm sure this is hard for you to understand, Clare, since you don't have a family name to protect."*

A family name? *"Don't you dare make this about me. What I'm talking about is taking responsibility and protecting the community."*

"No, you're right." His tone was conciliatory. Kyle stepped away from the railing, letting her hand from his arm. Without looking in her direction, he began to walk. *"Let's go. I have a lot of thinking to do."*

The memory faded. Clare's stomach cramped painfully as her breakfast roiled. "I gotta get out of here," she said, bolting for the door.

Turning, she jogged outside. The sun was bright, and her head began to pound.

Isaac stood at her side. "You looked a little sick in there."

"I'm fine." She tried to smile.

The thing was Clare was far from fine. Her last day in Columbus haunted her even now. Yet, she had to do more than escape from the ghosts of her past. She needed to decide how to deal with her problem. Because until she did that, Clare would never have a future.

Clare and Isaac stood on the street. The queasy feeling that gripped her in the grocery store had passed, yet she was exhausted. Maybe she shouldn't have been so quick to come with Isaac to find Trinity.

Isaac said, "I need to send a package by express mail to San Antonio. You can come with me if you want. Or hang out for a bit."

"You go. I'm fine." But was she? After months of being by herself, she loathed the idea of being alone. "I promise, I'll be okay on my own."

"I know you'll be okay. In fact, you might be one of the most capable women I've ever met." He lifted his hands in surrender.

She smiled again. The expression was starting to fit once more. Drawn like a magnet to steel, she took a step toward him. His scent—musky and male—enveloped her. "That's a nice compliment."

"You need to quit calling me that," he said, his tone teasing.

"If you aren't nice, then what are you?" she asked. "A hero?"

"To tell the truth, I'm nobody's idea of a hero."

His voice was dark and smoky, like a good wine, and she was drunk on his words.

"I..." she began, not sure what to say next. She'd kissed him once and she wanted to kiss him again. "I..."

Her words were cut off as a scream pierced the quiet morning. The sound was almost feral, and full of terror. Clare froze as her blood turned cold. The scream continued, echoing off the buildings.

Isaac scanned the street. "What the hell?"

"I think it's coming from over there." She pointed a shaking finger at the narrow alleyway that ran alongside the grocery store.

Squeezing her shoulders once, Isaac said, "You stay here."

"What? Why? Where are you going?" Her words didn't matter. He'd sprinted toward the sound. Then, the screaming stopped. The silence was worse than the noise.

She glanced up and down the street. Doors to businesses and offices were opening. People stood on the sidewalk, shading their eyes with their hands. They looked to one another, all confused about the scream that had shattered the silence.

"What was that racket?"

"Where'd all the noise come from?"

"Everyone okay?"

"Did anyone call Sheriff Cafferty?"

Clare looked toward the gap between the two buildings, her eyes retracing the path Isaac had taken. He still hadn't returned.

Indecision pinned her to the concrete. Yet, she forced herself to move, one step at a time, toward the alleyway.

From where she stood, Clare could see Isaac. The muscles in his neck were tight. His back was damp with sweat—she could tell because the fabric of his shirt stuck to his skin. Isaac cursed and ran a hand through his hair. Even from the end of the alleyway, she could tell that he was looking at something on the ground.

Mr. Yoshida, the grocery store manager, stood near the grocery store's rear door that led to the alleyway. Next to him, Adeline sobbed.

"What is it?" a man asked.

Clare took another step. "I'm not sure."

She made it to the end of the alleyway and finally got a look at the scene—and immediately regretted it. At Isaac's feet lay a body—or what was left of it. The first thing Clare saw was red hair, matted with blood. The eyes stared at nothing. The mouth was open as if death came in the moment of a scream. She sucked in a breath. Isaac turned and the look in his eyes said it all. He rushed to her side, trying to put himself between her and the gory scene.

She began to tremble.

"Don't look," he said. He took her face in his hands and met her gaze. "Clare, *please*. Just…don't look!"

It was too late. Clare had seen enough to know the truth. The pile of bone and blood and gore lying in the alleyway was Trinity. Or rather, it had been Trinity.

"Isaac… I… I don't understand." Clare was suddenly freezing, and she began to tremble. Her eyes were dry. Her throat was tight. She wanted to cry, but the tears refused to come. "What in the hell happened? She was fine when she left this morning!"

Isaac's expression was grim. "I have no idea. But we're damn well going to find out."

Chapter 9

Sheriff Maurice "Mooky" Cafferty dropped his foot onto the accelerator and his police cruiser shot down the road. Lifting the mic from his in-car radio, Mooky pressed the talk button. "Dispatch, this is Sheriff Cafferty." He drew in a deep breath. "Repeat what you just said."

"Shane Yoshida, down at the grocery store, found a body in the alley, next to the dumpsters." The 9-1-1 operator's voice broke on the last word. She continued, "It's a woman, and he says that she's a bloody mess."

The single word rattled around in his mind. *Body.*

There'd been a killing in his town. His stomach started to burn. Reaching between the seats, he found the bottle of antacids and flipped open the top. There were only three tablets left, and he poured them all into his mouth. Chewing furiously, he swallowed and tossed the empty bottle aside. Bringing the mic back to his mouth, he depressed the talk button. "He say anything else? Did he recognize the victim?"

"Don't think so, Sheriff."

"Anyone there?"

"I called in Todd and Kathryn," said the dispatch operator, mentioning the names of the two deputies on duty. "They're on their way. ETA is two minutes."

"Ten-four," he said. "I'm right behind them."

After hooking the mic back onto the radio, Mooky flipped two switches. Immediately, the lights atop his car began to flash and the siren started to wail. He dropped his foot onto the accelerator. The car shot down the road, pressing him into his seat. Ahead, he saw the grocery store and the road—clogged with onlookers. The burning in his stomach combusted into an inferno.

Laying the heel of his hand on the center of the steering wheel, he let out two quick bursts from his horn. The crowd slowly parted. Mooky turned off the siren as he parked his cruiser across the end of the alleyway.

Todd Travers, the newest addition to the department, came up to the cruiser. As Mooky opened the door, he asked, "What've we got?"

"It's bad, Sheriff. Real bad." He worked his fingers through the belt loops on the uniform trousers. "I ain't seen nothing like it."

Kathryn Glass, a ten-year veteran of the department and the chief undersheriff, stood in the middle of the alleyway. She wore dark sunglasses. The lens reflected the swirling lights on the roof of his car. Her arms were folded and her shoulders stiff. Behind her, a tarp lay on the ground.

"That her under the canvas?" he asked Todd. "The victim?"

The younger officer pulled on the belt loops so hard that Mooky feared the seams might rip. "Uh-huh."

Mooky had been with the department for almost twenty-years, and half of those as the sheriff. He'd seen a lot—but he also knew how violent deaths could affect police officers. He'd speak to Todd later and remind him that counseling was available if the images stayed with him awhile. Hooking the arm of his sunglasses to the front of his shirt, he said, "Secure this location. Get everyone off the street and set up a barricade at each end of the block. Barricade the other end of the alley, too. Can you do that?"

The young deputy swallowed. "Yes, sir."

He gave a quick squeeze to Todd's shoulder. Turning, he scanned the crowd again. He recognized most every face—except two. There was a big guy and a blonde woman, who was crying.

He strode down the alley. From twenty paces, the stench of decay hit him like a brick wall. Hand covering his mouth, he called out, "What've we got, Kathryn?"

"A mess." She hitched her chin toward the heap on the ground. "Come see for yourself."

Mooky knelt next to the tarp and lifted the corner. One glance was all he needed. Bile rose in the back of his throat. But he'd be damned before he puked at a crime scene. Coughing, he looked away. He cataloged everything he'd seen. Red hair. Blue lips. Exposed and sliced flesh. Eyes that saw nothing. And yet, in her frozen gaze, he'd seen terror.

He shuddered to think of the last thing she'd witnessed.

"You recognize her?" Mooky asked as he stood.

"Never seen her before in my life."

He dusted his hands together and looked back at the end of the alleyway. His car was still parked but the crowd was no longer visible. At least Todd was doing his job. "Who found the body? Dispatch said that Shane Yoshida called in."

"One of the employees found her when she brought out some trash. A college student home for the holidays. Her name is Adeline." Kathryn paused. "They're all inside. Adeline was pretty shook up by what she saw."

"I can imagine." Mooky had been shaken as well. "I'll go interview them. You call the medical center and have them pick the body up."

A metal door was set into the wall at the back of the store. It'd been propped open with a brick and Mooky stepped into the stock room. To his right, he saw the office. The door was open and from where he stood, he could see a metal desk, two filing cabinets and three chairs—all filled. The store manager came out to greet the sheriff, clearly shaken. "Thanks for getting here so fast, Sheriff."

"Sorry to see you under these circumstances, Shane." Mooky paused at the threshold. Aside from the manager, there were two females. One was Shane's wife, who was also the bakery manager. Mrs. Yoshida held the younger woman's hand, trying to comfort the shaken teenager. He turned to the girl now. "I haven't seen you since you were just a kid, Adeline, but I played football with your daddy." He took a small notebook and pen from the front pocket of his uniform. "Can you tell me what happened? How'd you find the body?"

Adeline drew in a shaking breath. "Well, Mr. Yoshida told me to help in the back. The stock workers needed the broken-down boxes put in recycling and I went to take them out. I saw her as soon as I opened the door." She let out a shuddering breath. "I guess I just started screaming and everyone came running."

"Did you get a good look at the woman?"

Adeline shook her head. "I just saw the body and the cuts and that's all." Her voice began to tremble.

"Who covered her with a tarp?" Mooky asked.

"That was me," said Shane. "It seemed like the decent thing to do. Plus, a crowd was gathering." He lifted his shoulders and let them drop, his face pale.

"Then what about you? Did you get a good look at the woman's face? You ever see her before?"

"No. Never." He paused. "But…"

"What?" Mooky coaxed.

"There were two people looking for someone that matched the woman's description. A man and woman. He's a big guy. She's a blonde."

The acid in Mooky's gut spewed like a volcano. He'd seen those two himself, standing at the edge of the alleyway. Now all he could hope is that he could find them before it was too late.

Clare pressed her eyes closed, but the image of Trinity's flayed body, sprawled on the ground, was burned into her brain. Purple bruises circled Trinity's neck. Her clothes were torn and covered in gore. The flesh in her chest and abdomen were cut.

She drew in a shaking breath and counted. One. Two. Three. As she exhaled, a sob escaped.

A sheriff's deputy had cleared the street and she now stood behind a wooden sawhorse at the end of the block. Isaac still held her shoulder. "It'll be okay," he whispered into her hair. "I promise."

How was that even possible, though? After what she'd seen, Clare found it hard to believe Isaac's words.

Clare groaned. "Her poor daughter. Does anyone even know how to get a hold of her ex?"

Isaac said, "I can get a number."

"Excuse me." A man with a brown crew cut and a tan sheriff's uniform strode down the street. A pair of sunglasses covered his eyes, yet she had the uncanny feeling that he was looking directly at Clare. "Can I speak to you for a minute?"

Pressing a hand to her chest, Clare mouthed the word. "Me?"

"Yes, ma'am," said the cop. He maneuvered around the end of the barricade. "I'd like to speak to both of you."

Clare's hands began to tremble. Shoving her palms under her armpits, she nodded. "Sure."

The man removed a business card from his pocket and held it out. "My name's Maurice Cafferty. I'm the sheriff for this county."

Clare accepted the card. Numbers for both his office and cell phone were listed. She handed it to Isaac.

Isaac asked, "What can we do for you, Sheriff Cafferty?"

"The folks in the grocery store said you came in this morning."

"So, what if we did?" Isaac asked. "Nothing illegal about going to a grocery store."

Isaac was avoiding answering the sheriff's questions. Was it because he'd been incarcerated? Or was there more? She hadn't asked him about his midnight road trip with Ryan. Yet, she suspected there was more to Isaac's story than the few details he'd shared so far.

The sheriff said, "Listen, I don't want to play games with you. We can either have a friendly chat here. Or you can come to my office and answer my questions more formal-like."

Isaac sighed. "What can we help you with?"

"Just answer the question," said the sheriff. "What were you doing in the grocery store?"

Trinity deserved justice. If Isaac wouldn't tell the sheriff what they were doing, she would. "We're in town, looking for a friend."

"That friend have a name?" The sheriff removed a small notepad from the breast pocket of his uniform, along with a pen.

"Trinity," said Clare.

"Trinity what?" the sheriff asked, his pen pressed against the paper.

Isaac said, "Her name was Trinity Jackson."

The sheriff wrote it down, then looked back to Clare. "What about the two of you? You have names?"

She could hardly ignore the investigation of anyone's murder. It didn't matter whether she knew her last name or not. Yet, she didn't want to get involved with the police—not while her ex-husband was still out there, somewhere.

Had the past several weeks of running just come to

nothing? Because if Kyle could find her in a place like Mercy, where else could she hide?

The sheriff ask for Clare's driver's license. She wanted to refuse. The minute he scanned the bar code on the back, her name would end up in a computer system. From there, it was just a matter of time before Kyle figured out that she was in Texas.

Her eyes burned. She loathed the idea of running again, but she had no choice. As soon as she could, she had to get back on the road. But if Clare could be found in a place like Mercy, where else could she hide?

"A report will show up in my office," Sheriff Cafferty said. "Until then, let's start over with the person you're looking for." Pen perched on his notepad, he asked, "Description of your friend?"

"Female," Isaac began as he listed the basics. "Tall, maybe five feet ten inches. Red hair. Lots of tattoos. There's a tat of a pink python on her leg."

The sheriff scribbled on his notepad. "Now we're getting somewhere. Why were you looking for her?"

She felt the pull to flee, like a tether around her middle pulling her toward the open road. But she couldn't leave now, even if she wanted to go. Besides, Trinity had been kind and Clare owed her for the kindness. She answered the sheriff's question. "She's been missing."

The sheriff lifted his brows as he wrote. "How long had she been gone?"

Clare swallowed, already knowing how her answer was going to sound. "Since a little before six o'clock."

The sheriff jotted a note in his book. "That's last night, right? Or, do you mean yesterday morning?"

"No." Clare shook her head. "This morning."

Sheriff Cafferty stopped writing. "She's been gone since six o'clock this morning," he repeated, his tone filled with incredulity. He checked his watch. "Well, that's only a few hours. Did you have reason to think she was in trouble?"

"She texted me that she was going to grab us a cup of coffee. When she hadn't showed up after a while, I went looking. I found a necklace—one that she loves—near the road." She paused. "One of the links was broken."

"I assume you know that the body of a redheaded female was found in the alleyway behind the grocery store. I've reason to believe that she's your missing friend. I need someone to identify the body and for now, you two are the best I've got."

Clare had already seen the corpse, yet a wave of emotion washed over her. Her eyes burned and her throat was tight. She tried to speak but the words were caught. She could only manage to nod her head.

The sheriff put the notepad and pen back in his pocket. Rocking back on his heels, he continued. "I'd also like for you both to answer some questions at my office."

"What kind of questions?" Isaac asked.

"I want you to help me understand why two people show up in my town and start looking for a woman who really wasn't missing but was already dead."

Clare took a step back. "Are you saying that you think we're involved with what happened?"

She didn't need to ask the question because she already knew the answer. What's worse, this wasn't Columbus, Ohio. There were no traffic cameras on every corner to chart their drive from Mercy to Encantador. Hell, there were barely traffic lights at all. They had no way to prove when they actually arrived in town or even to prove that they had nothing to do with Trinity's murder.

The floor-to-ceiling windows of Chamberlain Plastics Manufacturing overlooked downtown Columbus. Kyle Chamberlain sat in his corner office. The Scioto River, almost serpentine in its movement, shimmered with the light.

Walking to the sideboard, he picked up a bottle of fine Tennessee whiskey. The same questions he'd been asking himself for months occupied his thoughts. Where was Clare? What happened to the flash drive? And what did she plan to do with the evidence? Two months of hearing nothing and waiting for a story to break in the media, putting their family business—indeed, their family—in the harshest of spotlights was starting to show on Kyle. He'd lost hair and gained weight. What's worse, his father's fury hadn't faded.

After pouring two fingers from the bottle, he tossed back the drink in a single swallow. The liquor exploded in his gut like a bomb, and Kyle's limbs began to relax.

A voice came from the door. "A bit early in the day for a drink, don't you think?"

Kyle glanced at his father. It was hard to look at the old man and not see his own future. "My wife is gone. And we have no idea when she might use the information that she took to expose the company. Days like today are why God invented alcohol." Kyle poured another drink.

"She's your ex-wife." His father lifted a single brow. "And you know that."

Kyle certainly did know that Clare had left him. Divorced him. Guilt hit him like a fist to the gut. In the tug-of-war on whether to release the memo or keep it hidden, he'd chosen his father over his wife. Sure, Kyle had been raised to believe that family loyalty was supreme. But with Clare gone, he wasn't so sure. He threw back his second drink.

His father asked, "Any news from the private detective?"

"Nothing. Apparently, she disabled the GPS tracking on her car, turned off her phone and hasn't used a credit card since the day she left." His father knew all those facts, as well as that the family had spent a small fortune trying to locate her. Kyle's phone pinged with an incoming text. He glanced at the screen, blinked, refocused. "I'll be damned."

"What is it?"

"The PI just send a message. He said that Clare's name was run through a police database."

"She's back in Columbus?"

"I don't think so." Kyle scrolled through the message. "The search took place in a town called Encantador, Texas." He poured another drink. "I'll pass this along to the PI."

"That's the problem with you." Taking the glass from Kyle's hand, his father dumped the whiskey into the wastebasket. The medicinal scent of booze wafted through the room. "You never do anything on your own."

"You can't be suggesting that I waste my time following up on this myself."

"Suggesting? No. Telling? Yes."

Kyle mentally scrambled for a way to avoid the task. "What if she just got a flat tire and has already moved on?"

"Then you better find her before she disappears again."

"Me?" Kyle asked. "What am I supposed to say to Clare?"

"You force her to see things our way. And you get the evidence back."

"And if she refuses?"

His father met Kyle's gaze. The look sent a chill down his spine. "Make sure that she can't."

The Sheriff's Department sat at the edge of town in a converted warehouse. The whole property was surrounded by a chain-link fence and topped with coils of razor wire, so Isaac guessed that beyond the office space for the sheriff and his deputies, there were facilities to hold prisoners as well.

Isaac sat in a windowless interrogation room that was barely big enough to hold the wooden table and four seats. Isaac sat in one of the chairs, with Clare at his side.

Back when he was a cop, he never would have put two suspects into the same room and let them wait. It gave people a chance to talk and decide on the story they planned to tell. He couldn't help but wonder about Sheriff Cafferty. He could be playing a game with Isaac and Clare. The room might be filled with electronic surveillance. At this moment, was the sheriff watching them both while waiting to see what they said to one another?

Or was the small-town sheriff not used to investigating serious crimes, and therefore had no idea how to deal with serious criminals?

For the sake of Trinity, Isaac hoped it was the first but feared it was the latter.

Either way, he didn't need to worry about Clare saying anything incriminating. They'd been settled in the interview room for more than ten minutes. In all that time, she'd done nothing but stare at her hands.

"Say something," he said, his voice low. Then again, if the room were bugged or a camera was hidden in a vent, there was no reason to whisper.

She shrugged. "What is it you want to hear?"

He tried again. "It'll be okay."

"If you say so," she said, unconvinced.

After shaking her head, she looked back at Isaac. "What's going on in Mercy?"

Now, that was a loaded question and something that Isaac couldn't answer. Yet, it was impossible to miss the challenge in her tone.

"I don't know what you're talking about," he lied.

"Can you cut the crap, just for a minute?"

"Excuse me?" he asked, his anger flaring.

For a split second, Isaac realized that Sheriff Cafferty might be a genius to have left Clare and Isaac alone for so long. With tensions high, people began to turn on each other. Vengeful subjects might be more willing to talk to the police than ones who were simply scared.

Clare gritted her teeth. "Stop lying to me. I know there's more going on in Mercy. I know there's more to your story as well. So, don't pretend like you care about me or how I'm doing. You're in this up to your neck."

"What makes you so damned certain?"

"I saw you leave the motel last night. You and Ryan. Where'd you go? Is that what got Trinity killed?"

Clare thought he was somehow responsible for Trinity's death. Was his growing attraction—hell, his desire—for Clare enough for him to care what she thought of him?

The answer came to him quick and clean. *Yes.*

But was he willing to blow his cover, just to prove that he had nothing to do with a murder?

That answer wasn't as easy to find. In his own indecision, there was a danger to both himself and his case. "You've been asking me a lot of questions. Maybe it's time for you to answer a few of your own. Who are you, really?"

"Transferring your anger will change nothing," said Clare. "You can accuse me all you want, but you've been lying to me from the beginning." She went back to silently staring at her hands.

The sheriff and a female deputy slipped into the small room. Without preamble, they sat on the opposite side of the table. Both set pads of paper and pens before them.

"Mind if I record this interview?" Sheriff Cafferty asked.

A younger deputy, a male, squeezed into the tight space. He held a small video camera. A tripod was tucked under his arm.

"Be my guest," said Isaac.

The deputy set up the video equipment and left. The green record light glowed on the camera.

How many times had Isaac been in a room like this? It was too many to count.

Yet, today was different. Now he was the one being questioned.

The sheriff ran down the basics of the case and asked them to state their names for the record.

Isaac paused just long enough to wonder how much he'd be forced to share. He glanced at the camera before looking at the sheriff. "My name is Isaac Patton." At least he hadn't used an alias in his cover story. Then again, one of the rules of working undercover was to make it real life as much as possible. It made the operative less likely to make a mistake. To keep Isaac's past with the San Antonio PD secret, much of his personal history had been removed from the internet.

"And you?" The sheriff pointed to Clare with his pen.

"Clare." She paused and cleared her throat. "My name is Clare Chamberlain."

"Where you from?" Sheriff Cafferty paused as he wrote on his notepad. "Originally?"

"San Antonio," said Isaac, again thankful that his cover story matched as much of his actual background as it did.

"And you?" The sheriff pointed to Clare.

Clare shifted in her seat. "Columbus, Ohio," she said, her voice a whisper.

The sheriff made a note. Setting the pen aside, he leaned back in his seat. With a loud exhale, he folded his arms across his chest. "Encantador is a peaceful town. The folks who live here mostly abide by the law." He pinched the bridge of his nose, inhaled and started again. "We're not used to seeing this kind of crime committed in our town. So, I'm gonna level with you both. I don't like what I see."

Clare asked, "What is that you see, and don't you like?"

"The few facts you've given me don't pass the smell test. You both say that you came from Mercy this morning because you're worried about this missing friend. Yet, she'd really only been gone for a few hours, which, to be honest, isn't legally considered missing. Then she turns up here, deader than a doornail." He paused again. "Here's what I'm thinking. You two had something to do with her death and you left her body in that alleyway. Then, you come back to town and start asking questions." He hooked air quotes around the last two words. "You're thinking is probably something like this—nobody'd suspect the concerned friends." He reached for the pen and pressed the nib into the pad of paper. Ink leeched into the fibers. "Care to tell me if I'm wrong?"

Sure, the sheriff was wrong. Which left Isaac with a decision to make. Did he stick to his cover story or did he tell truth?

Chapter 10

Sheriff Cafferty had all but accused Clare and Isaac of killing Trinity. He cast a glance at Clare. Her eyes were wide. Her brows were drawn together, and her lips were pressed into a colorless line. He knew she was worried, and she should be.

"There're a few problems with your theory, Sheriff," said Isaac.

"Enlighten me."

"There's not a lot to the town of Mercy. It wasn't hard to figure out that Trinity was gone." He sat back in his chair. "Clare found her broken necklace in a parking lot. It was enough to make us concerned, because Trinity never took it off. Ever." Isaac leaned forward. "You've been up front about your suspicions. But I gotta tell you. You're wrong to make up your mind already."

"Okay, so if I shouldn't make you two my prime suspects, who should I have in mind?"

The notion of giving away a year's worth of work left him ill—especially since Newcombe had finally made contact. Yet, Isaac couldn't exactly hinder a murder investigation. And finally, there was Clare. He still didn't know much about her situation, but she was obviously running from something.

Or someone.

He couldn't—no, make that wouldn't—let her be suspected of murder. "For the past year, I've been working undercover in Mercy. I'm on assignment trying to find Decker Newcombe. He's a hitman who killed a district attorney in Wyoming."

The sheriff gave a grunt of disbelief. "I'm supposed to believe that you're working undercover?"

"It's the truth."

"Now, you know I'm not going to take you at your word."

"I figured as much." He exhaled. "Go ahead and do a search for Decker Newcombe. You'll see that he's wanted for the murder of Jacob Loeb, the DA from Pleasant Pines, Wyoming." Isaac paused as the sheriff removed his phone from a holster on his hip. As the sheriff typed with his thumbs, Isaac continued, "My gut told me that Newcombe would reach out to Ryan Steele at some point. Steele is one of his old contacts. I came up with a plan. The feds bankrolled all of Steele's businesses, including the bar he owns in Mercy. Then, I posed as an employee at the bar, hoping Newcombe would make contact."

The undersheriff leaned forward. "Everything you said about Newcombe's past checks out. Still, it don't mean I can verify a word you say. You could've done an internet search, same as me."

Now was the time for Isaac to prove his bona fides. "Who do you know with the FBI? Anyone out of the San Antonio office?"

Glass and Cafferty exchanged glanced.

"We can find a name if you give me some time," she said.

Isaac said, "Take all the time you need. I'm not going anywhere soon."

"Damn right, you won't. This door locks from the outside." The sheriff rose to his feet. Undersheriff Glass stood as well. "You both just wait here. I'll be back in a minute."

Without another word, both officers left the room.

Then, the room was silent. He kept his gaze on the table, yet he could feel Clare watching him.

He glanced at her from the side of his eye.

The single look was all the invitation that Clare needed to speak up. "You lied to me."

Whatever he'd expected her to say, *that* had definitely not been it.

He wasn't going to be chastised—especially since she was part of the calculus to blow his cover. "What was I supposed to say to you? Someone who, oh, by the way, is a complete stranger. And who is clearly carrying some big secrets of her own."

"I'm not saying that your investigation isn't important." Clare inhaled. Exhaled. "Or even that I have a right to know everything—or anything—about you. It's just that after we found Trinity's body, you owed me the truth."

Did he? Isaac wasn't ready to admit to anything—at least, not yet.

"What about you?" he countered.

"What about me?"

"You've been far from honest with me about your past. What really happened in Columbus?"

She hesitated. "Nothing."

She was lying and they both knew it. Then again, why should she trust him? He'd hardly been forthright with her. He supposed now was the time for all the BS to end.

"Alright," he said with a sigh. "After college, I joined the San Antonio PD. They figured out I was a good shot and put me on SWAT. My training agent was a guy named Miguel. He was the one who honed my sharp-shooting abilities. He drove home all the rules of firearm safety. We ran together every morning. He invited me over for cookouts on the weekend and his kids called me Uncle Isaac." A stab of emotion struck him in the chest. The severity of the residual pain surprised him. Clearing his throat, he continued, "One night the team got tasked with a raid in an apartment complex. Our subject was the member of a street gang. He got a tip that we were coming. The rest of the gang members turned the complex into a shooting gallery." The memory crashed down and he slumped in his seat. "Anyway, Miguel and I were close to the subject's apartment. Just a short hallway between us and them. We were told to wait for backup. The funny thing was—Miguel wanted to rush in. I insisted that we wait. Those few minutes gave the gang time to regroup." He cleared his throat. "We went in, and Miguel caught a bullet in his throat. He bled out on the floor as I applied pressure to his wound."

"Oh, Isaac." Clare drew her lip through her teeth. Before she could say anything else, the door opened. Sheriff Cafferty stepped into the room. He held a small square of yellow paper, the sticky strip on the back was adhered to his finger. "I got a name and number for the SSA at the San Antonio Field Office."

"Jason Jones."

"That's the one."

"Call him. Ask about me. Tell him there's been a homicide and you want to know if I'm a guy you can trust."

After dropping into one of the seats, the sheriff placed his phone on the table and entered the number. He turned on the speaker function and the call went through.

A familiar voice answered after the third ring. "This is Agent Jones."

The sheriff leaned toward the phone. "Hi. This is Maurice Cafferty, sheriff out of Encantador in Texas. I've had a recent homicide and a name has come up. Isaac Patton."

Jason cursed. "Is he your victim?"

"No. In fact, he's alive, well and sitting right across from me. I've got you on speakerphone."

"What've you gotten yourself into?" he asked.

Isaac smothered a grimace behind his hand. "Nice to hear your voice, too."

"Glad that you're on this side of the grave. But you didn't answer my question. What's going on?"

"There's not much that would get me to break my

cover, but one of Steele's employees was murdered this morning."

Jones asked, "Any suspects?"

"Aside from me?" Isaac looked the sheriff dead in the eye. The other man had the decency to look away. "Not really."

"Murder isn't a federal offense," said Agent Jones. "Why bring me into the case?"

"It's more to verify Mr. Patton's identity," the sheriff added. "Is he someone I can trust?"

"He's a pain in the butt," said Jason. "But yeah, he's trustworthy." The fed continued, "Is my package on the way? IT is ready."

"I haven't had a chance yet." Isaac tamped down his annoyance. What part of *he'd gotten involved in a murder investigation* didn't Jason understand?

"Get it done," said Jason and then, "You need anything else from me, Sheriff?"

"Thank you, Special Agent. I'm set for now." Reaching for the phone, the sheriff ended the call.

"Satisfied?" Isaac asked.

Leaning back in his chair, the sheriff cradled his head in his hands. "I suppose so."

Turning to Clare, Isaac said, "Like you heard, I still have some business to take care of here. After that, I can give you a ride back to Mercy."

"You forget something?" the sheriff asked.

Was the guy really still going to threaten Isaac and Clare with a murder charge?

Gritting his teeth, he asked, "What's that?"

The sheriff sat forward "The body. I need someone to identify the victim."

* * *

The Encantador Medical Center was a two-story building of redbrick located a few blocks from the sheriff's office. The main floor contained a walk-in medical clinic. A hospital with six beds was located on the upper level. The morgue, located in the basement, was a windowless room with the same tile on the floor and three of the four walls. A metal counter bisected one wall. An empty stainless steel table sat in the middle of the room. The sheriff stood next to the sink and scrolled through his phone.

The fourth wall, on the far side of the room, was filled with large stainless steel doors—four across and three, top to bottom. Clare had seen enough movies to recognize them as coolers where bodies were stored. Trinity was certainly behind one of the doors.

A sudden chill gripped her, and she gave an involuntary shiver.

Isaac stood at her side and leaned in close, the heat from his body was warm and soothing. "You don't have to be here," he whispered, his words washing over her shoulder. "I can do this by myself."

Glancing at the door, Clare had a momentary fantasy of sprinting from the room. There was no shame in not wanting to look at a dead person. Yet, she shook her head. "I owe it to Trinity to see this through."

"You've done plenty for her, you know. If you hadn't found her broken necklace, neither one of us would have come here. It would've taken weeks to identify her body."

Was Isaac right? Clare thought not. First, there'd be media reports about the murder and the unknown victim. Someone from Mercy would've recognized Trinity from the news. "I bet that you would've nosed around the investigation." She gave a quick smile to show that she was teasing.

She still wasn't sure how she felt about Isaac after confessing that he was a cop and not a criminal. Did she like him more—or less? At least with the old Isaac, she thought she knew him. This new guy was filled with secrets.

The door opened and a dark-haired woman in a white lab coat crossed the threshold. Embroidered above the breast pocket were the words: Shelia Garcia, MD

"Thanks for coming over, Sheriff," said the doctor. "I haven't had time to do anything other than scan the report." She grimaced. "Sounds pretty gruesome."

"Worst damn thing I've ever seen," said the sheriff.

Dr. Garcia approached the sink. Using pedals on the floor, she turned on the water and began to wash her hands. Looking over her shoulder, she made eye contact with both Clare and Isaac.

"This is Isaac Patton and Clare Chamberlain," said the sheriff, obviously understanding the doctor's glance as a question that needed answering. "They both knew the victim and are here to do an ID."

"Alright, then." Moving to the end cooler on the middle row, the doctor opened the door. She pulled out a drawer, along with a blue sheet that was draped over a form. "If you both can come here?" Dr. Garcia asked.

Clare and Isaac took up places on the opposite side of the drawer.

The doctor folded the sheet down, just so the head, neck and shoulders were visible. The skin was white. The lips blue. The eyes were closed, yet one was swollen and bruised. The tail from a tiger tattoo was visible on the upper arm. The features were unmistakable. Clare swallowed. "It's her."

"You sure?" the sheriff asked.

Isaac answered, "Positive."

"Do you have contact information for her next of kin?" The sheriff held his pad of paper and a pen.

Isaac shook his head. "I can find the information once I get back to Mercy. Or I can call Ryan now."

"Give it a minute before making the call," said Sheriff Cafferty.

Clare's chest hurt as she thought about Trinity's daughter and the sad fact that the little girl would never get to know her mother.

"Okay, then." The doctor reached for the sheet, ready to cover the face once more.

"Wait," said Clare, not even sure of why she'd spoken. Something was wrong. What was it?

The doctor froze, cloth in hand.

Moving closer to the body, Clare pointed to the throat. An ugly dark line ran straight across her neck. "Bruises? Is that the cause of death?" she asked. "Strangulation? I only saw a little bit of Trinity in the alley, but it looked like she'd be stabbed, too."

Isaac said, "There wasn't a lot of blood on her clothes. That means that she was cut postmortem."

The doctor drew her brows together and pulled the sheet to Trinity's ankles. A jagged seam ran through her sweatshirt and the front of her jeans. They had been pulled back together for transport, but the fabric had black stains and was stiff with dried gore.

"But there's blood…" Clare began.

Dr. Garcia spoke as Clare's words trailed off. "Not as much as I'd expect to see if her heart was beating when she sustained these injuries."

Clare's confusion must've shown on her face because the sheriff picked up where the physician left off. "If she still had a pulse, blood would've gotten everywhere. Think of a fountain."

The image of a blood fountain left Clare lightheaded. Yet, she tried to put the pieces together to form a timeline for Trinity's death. "You think that she was strangled, then stabbed and cut after she was dead?"

"I have to do an autopsy first," the doctor began. "But that'd be my initial assessment, yes."

"What'd you think the killer used to strangle her?" Sheriff Cafferty asked. "His own hands?"

The doctor bent closer to Trinity. "Not his hands. The bruises are uniform all the way around. With fingers, there's different amounts of pressure, so the bruising isn't consistent all the way through."

The sheriff asked, "She strangled with a cord?"

It was Isaac who answered. "Cords are thin. This was something wider—maybe a belt."

The doctor looked at Trinity's hands. She used a pen to point to the ring finger. "See that?" The nail was ripped away. "She fought. If we're lucky, we'll get some of the killer's DNA." She swiped around the nail with a swab before sealing the swab inside a vial. "Since this is a definite homicide, I'll let you send this to the crime lab." She set it on the counter. "They can at least identify DNA that doesn't belong to the victim."

The doctor continued talking. "Let's see what else we have." She slipped on a pair of surgical gloves and held out a box of surgical masks for everyone to put on. After putting on a pair protective glasses, she continued, "Of course, anything I note here might not jive with my final findings." She peeled back the sweatshirt and jeans, exposing Trinity's chest, torso and hips. There was a deep gash that ran from under her rib cage downward to her pelvis. Several other lacerations bisected the first. The flaps of flesh exposed muscle and bone.

The floor under Clare's feet seemed to tilt. She feared that she'd lose her footing—or worse yet, her breakfast.

Yet, there had been something about Trinity's wounds. Something almost…familiar.

Isaac's cover was blown and there was no going back. Since he couldn't retreat, that left only one direction—forward.

The sheriff wasn't a bad guy, per se. To Isaac, he seemed like a good cop who genuinely cared about his community. Moreover, he took his duty to protect and serve seriously—even if there was a bit more bluster in his personality than Isaac actually liked.

The doctor continued to examine the wounds. "The blade is smooth—as in, not serrated—and about five inches long."

"A hunting knife?" Isaac suggested.

The doctor shrugged. "Possibly. Or even a strong kitchen knife." She paused and bent closer to Trinity's middle. "What's going on here?"

"What's going on where?" Clare echoed, her voice an octave higher.

"The abdomen doesn't look right." Dr. Garcia drew her brows together. "It's almost concave." She picked up a set of surgical clamps and held on to a flap of skin. Pulling up and back gently, she exposed organs and tissue. The doctor gasped and jumped back as if the clamps had become hot to the touch. They hit the floor with a clatter.

The doctor drew in several long breaths. She picked up the discarded clamps from the floor and tossed them into the sink with a clang. For a moment, the room was silent. With a shake of her head, the doctor continued, "This woman has been more than cut open, but several of her organs have been removed."

"Removed?" the sheriff echoed.

Dr. Garcia confirmed the worst. "Trinity was disemboweled."

Isaac went cold. "You have more than a murderer in your town—but a deranged killer." From everything he knew of Decker Newcombe, the hitman only killed for profit, not pleasure. Still, what were the chances that two killers were in the same area? He had to get in touch with Jason and pressure the fed to get more resources on the case.

"Now, if you don't mind, I have an autopsy to perform." The doctor slipped the swab and tube into an evidence bag as she spoke. After a beat, she held out the vial with the DNA sample. "Go straight to the lab, Cafferty, and drop this off for me."

"Yes ma'am," said the sheriff, taking the evidence bag.

That was their cue to leave.

The hallway—floor and wall, both—were covered in the same white tiles as the morgue. The sheriff leaned against the wall and shoved his hand into his uniform pocket. "Where are those damned antacids," he mumbled before continuing, "You said you could get me a name and number for a next of kin?"

Taking out his phone, Isaac placed a call to Ryan. He actuated the speaker function as the phone began to ring.

Ryan answered, "Hey, pal."

There was no way to soften the news of a murder. He said simply, "We found Trinity's body."

"Aww, hell. What happened?"

"I'll save you all the details, but it was bad. I've got you on speaker. The sheriff and Clare are here with me." He paused. "I need a name and number for Trinity's ex. The sheriff's gotta let him know."

"Give me a minute." In the background, Isaac could hear the clicking of fingers on a keyboard. He imagined that Ryan was accessing an employee database. Despite the fact that Steele was only running a bar and tattoo parlor as bait, he was actually a decent businessman. "I got it here. You ready?"

The sheriff had a pad of paper and pen in his hand. He said, "Go ahead." Ryan gave the information, which Cafferty wrote down. "Thank you so much."

Ryan said, "Let me know if you need anything else. And, Isaac, is this connected to our other *friend*?"

Decker Newcombe was no friend of Isaac's, yet he understood the cryptic question. "We might have a lead. I'll keep you posted." He ended the call as another thought came to him. He said to Cafferty, "You have some DNA from the killer found under Trinity's nails."

"Possibly," said the sheriff, clarifying. "We'll know in a day or two once the tests have been run."

"Let me know what you find." Isaac gave the sheriff his cell phone number. If Decker was responsible for Trinity's death, they'd connect him by his DNA. It was the kind of information that Jason would need to keep Isaac's case open.

"One more thing," said Clare. From the front pocket of her jeans, she pulled out Trinity's locket. "This was hers." She nodded her head to the door of the morgue. "I think she'd want it given to her daughter. Can you pass it on for me when you talk to her ex-husband?"

"I'm happy to oblige." Cafferty took the necklace and placed it the breast pocket of his uniform. "How much longer are you staying in town?"

Isaac had to send the phone to the FBI's office in San Antonio. All the same, he didn't want to be away from Mercy for too long. Decker was close, and Isaac was determined to find him. "We'll be here for a little longer."

"I'd like it if you can stay for a few hours. I'm going to call in the state police. They might have questions about the victim that only you can answer."

He wanted to argue. But what was the point? The sheriff could order Clare and Isaac to stay in town. Besides, staying in Encantador would give Isaac a chance to ask a few questions himself—like if anyone had seen Decker. Maybe he'd get lucky, and someone had noticed something important. And if not? Well, then his luck had run out.

Chapter 11

After spending time in the dark basement, the midday sun was blinding. Heat rolled off the pavement. Clare stopped at top of the steps, suddenly lightheaded.

If Clare had just gone with Trinity, maybe her friend would be alive. Or maybe Clare's body would've been dumped in the alleyway. She gripped the railing to keep herself steady.

Isaac's hand was on her elbow. "What's going on?"

"I'm fine." His touch left her breathless and her flesh tingling.

"You're probably just hungry." He looked at his phone. "We didn't have much of a breakfast and we missed lunch."

Clare hadn't noticed her empty stomach until Isaac mentioned food. Her middle gave a grumble. "Maybe."

Isaac gave her that smile that left Clare weak in the

knees. "C'mon. I'm know that I'm starved. You look like if you don't eat soon, you'll pass out."

"Gee, you really know how to flatter a girl."

"Being blunt seems to be a side effect from working undercover for so long." He shrugged. "Let me take you out to lunch because honestly, you aren't going to find food this good in Mercy, even though the bar is the only place to eat—or any place else nearby."

The short walk to Isaac's truck gave her time to think. She needed to eat, but more than that, she realized, Trinity's murder was a turning point for her.

Sure, she'd been running for months, always thinking she had to solve her problem on her own. Clare recalled what her mother had said this morning. *You've always been so independent. Even as a little girl. Me do. That was your favorite phrase.*

Maybe that had been her problem from the beginning. Clare never let anyone help.

They reached the truck, and without a word, Isaac unlocked the door, collecting an evidence bag with a phone inside from under the driver's seat. He tucked that into a paper bag that was stashed with the evidence bag. He was obviously working on something big if he had a direct line to a supervisory special agent with the FBI. He'd been working undercover for a year. Isaac was the perfect person to ask for ways to deal with her former in-laws.

If she could work up the nerve.

He slipped his Glock 19 from the glove box and tucked it into the waistband at his back. Untucking his shirt, he covered his firearm with the hem.

"The delivery service is over there." He held the bag

and pointed across the street. They waited for traffic to pass before crossing the road.

Clare paused on the sidewalk. "I'll wait here."

It took Isaac only a few minutes to send his package and return to where she waited. By then, she'd made a decision. "Can we talk?"

"Let's go to the restaurant." Isaac started walking down the sidewalk. Clare stayed at his side. "We can find a corner table and talk there."

He stopped in front of barbecue place. A cartoon cow and pig were painted on a large set of windows. Stenciled beneath were the words *Phil's. Best Damn BBQ in the Lone Star State.*

Next door, the Saddle Up Inn, sat behind a parking lot. On the other side of the restaurant was a florist.

Isaac pulled the door open, and she crossed the threshold. After everything that happened over the past few hours, Clare shouldn't have been hungry. Yet, her mouth began to water as the savory scent of roasted meat rolled out of the restaurant. "Smells better than good."

"Just wait till you taste the food."

A man with a mustache, beard and a bald head stood behind a cash register and looked up as Clare approached. He wore a bolo tie, white shirt and a name tag that read Phil. "Howdy, folks," he said. "Just the two of you?"

"Yes," said Clare.

Phil took two menus from beneath the counter. "Right this way."

Wood, gray with age and weathered, covered the walls. More than a dozen tables, with red-and-white-checked cloths, filled the middle of the room. Thankfully, there were no other patrons.

As Clare sat, Phil said, "Heck of a day. Did you hear that a body was found in the alley behind the supermarket?"

Clare and Isaac glanced at each other as Isaac took a seat and asked, "Really? What happened?"

Clare assumed he was looking for news being churned through the town's rumor mill.

"Well, I've been hearing that it was a pretty grisly scene. They didn't just die. They were slaugh—" Phil stopped himself. "But don't let me put you off your meal. Care for some tea?"

Of course, Phil meant sweetened iced tea—the only thing that was served in the South. But that was fine with Clare. It was the perfect cool drink that would also give her a jolt of energy, which she lacked. "Please," she said.

Isaac added, "Make that two."

The proprietor disappeared into the kitchen to fetch their drinks.

Eyes on the menu, Isaac began, "You said we needed to chat. What about?"

Looking down at the menu, she saw nothing. "It's about what happened to me in Columbus."

For a minute, he was silent. Finally, he said, "Okay. I'm listening."

Her throat tightened like a fist, making it hard to speak or even breathe. "I found something I shouldn't have. Something so damning that people would kill to keep me quiet."

"Who?"

"My ex-husband." Sure, she'd decided to trust Isaac. But she needed more than a confidant. "I need help." She paused, choosing her words carefully. "And you have certain knowledge. Skills."

"I'll do what I can," said Isaac. "But you need to tell me everything."

Without another thought, she found the burner phone that she'd picked up after leaving Ohio. Holding it to her chest, she said, "My husband's family is wealthy. Seriously rich, and powerful. They have connections in state government and even in DC. They own a company that manufactures plastics. When we met, I was with the EPA in Northern Virginia working on the hazardous waste compliance program. When we got married, I tried to get an interagency transfer, but my position was already filled in Ohio. I taught some classes at the university part-time. Budget cuts reduced my department, and I was let go. For the first time in my adult life, I didn't have a job. But I didn't need money, either. Since I'd worked hard my whole life, being able to relax seemed, well, nice."

"I'm guessing it didn't last long," said Isaac.

Before she could say more, the kitchen door opened.

Phil approached with two glasses of tea on a tray. "Here you go." He set both on the table, along with small paper napkins. "I just checked with the cook. Jorge recommends the brisket sandwich."

"Sold," said Isaac. "Give me fries and a side salad."

"I'll take the same," said Clare, thankful for the easy decision. "No fries for me."

"Are you sure?" Phil asked. "They're pretty darn good, if I do say so myself."

"I'll steal a few from him." Using the end of the menu, she pointed to Isaac.

"Alrighty, then. Be back in a jiff with those sandwiches." He didn't bother to write down the order.

She waited until Phil was in the kitchen to pick up the narrative where she'd left off. "It wasn't long before I got bored and offered to help at the family business. After all, they manufacture plastic and there's a lot of environmental regulations to follow. I'd never worked for industry, but after years of working on hazardous waste regulations with the EPA, I definitely knew how to keep the company in compliance." She gave a quick laugh at her own ignorance, although it hadn't been funny how she completely trusted her ex-husband. "Kyle turned down my offer. He said they already had an internal department that handled environmental compliance."

"That wasn't true?"

"He was being honest to a point. I also think he realized how dangerous it was to let someone from the EPA have access to all the company's files." She sighed. After powering up the phone, she opened the photo app. "He encouraged me to volunteer in the community. I got involved with an organization that turned unused plots of land into parks. It was fulfilling, until I found these."

She opened the first picture and handed the phone to Isaac. "This is a form from about twenty years ago. Two-dozen containers of cadmium and chromium, heavy metals that are used in manufacturing plastics, needed to be disposed of properly. Chromium needs to be incinerated. Cadmium has to be mixed with hydrochloric acid, sulfuric acid and nitric acid to break it down. That's the law, but it's expensive." She took back the phone and opened the next photo. "Then, there's this." The trail of memos was easy to follow. They all outlined the decision by Kyle's father to bury the chemicals on a plot of undeveloped land. "That piece of land was where we wanted to build the next park."

Isaac leaned back and cursed. "That's pretty damning evidence."

"I agree. I showed Kyle. I assumed that he'd want to make it right."

"He didn't."

Clare shook her head. Her eyes burned but she refused to cry anymore. She'd made her choice when she stole the documents and left Ohio, knowing what her fate could be. But the risk was worth it if it meant she could find a way to expose the company—and protect herself. "Those heavy metals will eventually burn through the drums and leech into the soil. Once the water is contaminated, there would be an elevated risk for issues like increased renal failure and other kidney diseases in the population, especially children. Cancer rates—especially kidney and liver—would be likely to rise. I said that the authorities had to be notified. Kyle said it would ruin his father and the company." She let out a long breath and shuddered. "In the end, he agreed with me. I went to bed that night thinking everything was okay. But something woke me, and I overheard him talking to his father on the phone."

The tile was cold beneath her feet. The hallway was dark, save for a seam of light at the bottom of the door to Kyle's office. Clare, clad in her robe, held her breath and listened as Kyle spoke to his dad.

Her father-in-law said, "I told you from the begin-

ning that marrying one of those environmental types was a bad idea." The words wounded Clare. Kyle Sr. always seemed to like her. Obviously, it was just an act. "I told you that she was going to cause us problems and that you shouldn't defy me. But you swore her love for you was strong and that you could handle her. And here I am now, having to say 'I told you so' but it's our livelihood and reputation on the line."

"It's a little late to chastise me now." Beyond the voices in the room, Clare could hear the tinkling of ice on crystal. She imagined that her husband had poured himself a whiskey. "The proverbial cat is out of the bag. We have no choice but the deal with the situation."

"The hell we don't have any choices," her father-in-law said, his voice colder than the ice in Kyle's drink. "By tomorrow afternoon a tragic accident will solve all our problems..."

Back in the restaurant, with the bright Texas sun beating down on the sidewalk, Clare spoke. "I listened while Kyle and his dad planned my murder to keep me quiet. After Kyle left for work that morning, I printed off the documents and saved them to a flash drive as well. Then, I packed a bag. I took nine-thousand dollars from the checking and savings accounts I shared with Kyle. Finally, I maxed out several credit cards to pay for a no-fault divorce." She turned the power off on the phone and stuck it back in her bag. "I was worried about the paper copies getting lost or ruined, so I bought a phone and took pictures, just to make sure that I had as many copies as possible of the evidence. I've been on the run ever since."

"Clare, I need to ask you an important question. What's the outcome you want?"

"Ah. That's the question I've been asking myself every hour of every day for the past two months. I know I can't ignore the buried chemicals." She ran down a long list of possible solutions, along with why they'd never work. "I knew right away that I couldn't go to the police. My former in-laws are in tight with the local law enforcement, and they have connections in government, too. The press is another possibility. But once I hand over the information, would the story become big enough to keep me safe? My former coworkers at EPA were definitely people I could reach out to, but my last boss retired a few years ago." Clare let her words trail off until she felt as if she were drowning in futility.

Isaac placed his hand on hers. "Clare—do you trust me? I can help you, but I need you to trust me."

She let him work his fingers between hers. The warmth of his touch was delicious, yet she had to stay focused, not get distracted by her attraction to him. Distraction could be dangerous—maybe deadly.

She moved her hand from beneath his. "So, what's your plan?"

Staying in Encantador was reckless, there was no doubt about it. But Decker was fascinated by the investigation. He'd watched the young girl discover the body and the chaos that followed.

The sheriff had been easy to spot. He'd spoken to a man and woman, taking them with him from the crime scene. But who were the people? Suspects? Cops in street clothes? Even for Decker, it was hard to tell.

But the couple—especially the woman—was intriguing.

Now he was a ghost—able to pass through town all but unseen. It gave him a sense of invincibility, yet he wanted more. He wanted people to fear him, to fear his name—to fear the very idea of him.

Just as they had his famous ancestor, Jack the Ripper.

Lifting the book that he'd stolen from the library, he scanned the table of contents.

Chapter 9: Defining a Serial Killer

He read: *By modern standards, a serial killer is a person who kills three or more people with a similar profile and/or commit the murders in a similar manner. Therefore, serial killing, as in a series of murders, are connected.*

Yet, in the late summer and early fall of 1888 that concept had yet to be defined or explored. All of that changed with Jack the Ripper. Even though death was everywhere in the crowded and impoverished neighborhood of Whitechapel, the gruesome nature of the first murder caught the attention of Metropolitan Police's Criminal Investigative Division straight away.

Decker set the book aside and started the engine. He pulled onto the street and turned left at the end of the block. A barbecue restaurant sat next to a motel. A large window allowed him a full view of the eatery's interior. He saw her and automatically Decker stepped on the brakes. The tires squealed as a cloud of burned rubber wafted over his vehicle.

Gripping the steering wheel, he cursed his reaction.

Slamming on the brakes in the middle of the road was sure to call attention to the car—and to Decker himself. He eased his foot onto the gas and drove away, thinking only of the woman. She was the one he'd seen with the sheriff. He turned right at the corner and then turned right again. He could circle the block a time or two— all the while deciding on his best move.

Then again, he already knew what he was going to do. He'd found his next victim.

Isaac's list of problems had just grown by one. Technically, he was still undercover, searching for a lead on Decker Newcombe. Now, though, he'd promised to help Clare. To protect her.

Well, it was a promise he intended to keep.

He sipped his tea. "There's really only one way to battle your ex and his family and that's to go after them—and hard. First thing I suggest is talking to the FBI. I'll introduce you to my contact in San Antonio."

"Is he the guy you called today?"

Isaac nodded. "Jason's a hard-ass, that's for sure. And that's what we want. Because from what you told me, there's enough evidence to start a criminal investigation. The FBI's office in Columbus will take over."

"How do I know that the Columbus FBI won't be influenced by my in-laws?" she asked. "They really are a big deal in Ohio. Friends with their congressperson. Both US senators attend their annual holiday party."

He understood why Clare had gone on the run. Nobody wanted enemies, but powerful enemies were hard to fight. Still, an influential family presented a different set of opportunities. "The press will be your best ally. The fact that the Chamberlains are well connected will make the story even more irresistible to the media. I have some regional contacts—San Antonio, Dallas, Denver. But my acquaintances will have friends at the networks. Cable news. National papers." His pulse was strong. His heartbeat was steady. He knew how to help Clare, and he was going to do whatever it took to keep her safe.

"How will this help me?"

"Once the world knows about the chemicals your father-in-law buried, Chamberlain Plastics Manufacturing will go on the defensive. They'll try and make plenty of counterarguments, defend themselves, and just to prepare you, they may go as low as an attempt at character assassination. I've seen it. But you have the evidence. Plus, you'll have set the narrative."

Clare sipped her tea. "They'll claim I had a breakdown."

"What if they do? You found out some pretty damning information about your husband's family. Then you overheard your husband and father-in-law discussing your murder. What you heard will go a long way in both the court of public opinion and the court of law."

Smiling, she wiped a bead of sweat from the side of her glass. "But you won't be with me for most of this, right? You'll be here working on the other case." She paused. "Decker Newcombe."

The thing was she was right. Isaac couldn't abandon the search for the hitman.

That was the moment when Isaac realized that somewhere in the back corner of his mind he'd allowed himself the luxury of asking the most dangerous question of all—what if?

He was saved from trying to put his thoughts and feelings into words by the opening of the kitchen door.

Phil, a tray of food balanced on his forearm, approached. Even from twenty paces, Isaac could see the steam rising from the plates. The salty, spicy scent of barbecue hung in the air and Isaac's stomach contracted painfully.

"Here you go." Phil set the plates on the table, along with sets of silverware and paper napkins. "How's that look?"

"Amazing," said Isaac.

"Enjoy," said the restaurant owner as he retreated to counter behind the cash register. The man was on the other side of the room and certainly far enough away that it'd be difficult to overhear any conversation.

Clare picked a fry off his plate and took a bite. As she chewed, Isaac couldn't help but feel… Well, he really couldn't categorize his emotion. But he definitely liked sharing his meal with her.

Finally, she spoke. "I'm not sure that I'll ever be safe." Sitting back, she folded her arms across her chest. "I've worked on cases like this before for the EPA. There's a battle on the horizon, but it'll be a legal one. There will be wrangling over fines and how much responsibility Chamberlain Plastics Manufacturing is forced to accept." She shook her head. "In the end, the only thing that Kyle and his family will lose is money. When it's all said and done, they won't be chastised—they'll be furious." Letting out a long sigh, Clare shook her head. "Then, they'll really want revenge."

It wasn't in Isaac's nature to give up or give in. "Eat." He pointed to her plate. "You need food for energy."

Reaching for her plate, she took a bite of the sandwich. She chewed and washed down her food with a swig of tea. "This is good."

They spent several minutes saying nothing and focusing only on their meals. When Isaac's brisket was gone, he cleared his throat. "I can start making calls for you tonight..."

His words trailed off as a car drove slowly past. The driver looked into the restaurant and ice shot down Isaac's spine.

He no longer had a beard or long hair. The face was thinner—gaunt, even—but the eyes were unmistakably the same.

Decker Newcombe.

Now what? Going to get his truck would waste time that he didn't have. Calling the sheriff was a must, but that'd take time, too. Decker was already in a car, so who knew where he would go? He had to know he'd been recognized. Isaac had to find and follow the car as best he could. Decision made, he stood abruptly.

"Isaac?" Clare spoke, alarm evident in her voice.

He moved to the window and watched the car as it drove slowly down the street. "I'd swear that was Decker Newcombe."

"Are you sure that was him?"

That was the exact question Isaac intended to answer. Sure, chasing the killer on foot was less than ideal, but he didn't have any other choices. Letting Decker get away was unacceptable. "Call the sheriff and tell him that Newcombe is in town."

"Where are you going?" Clare asked.

He squared his shoulders, ready for the fight of his life. "I'm going to catch that bastard."

Chapter 12

Decker drove, his hands already warm with the very thought of the woman's yet-to-be-spilled blood. He made several rapid turns, checking his tail after each one. After several minutes of driving, he slowly steered down an alleyway that ran behind the barbecue restaurant. He backed the car into a delivery bay at the rear of the eatery. After turning off the engine, he pulled two large trash cans next to the grille. It wasn't exactly camouflage, but maybe it was good enough for someone to overlook his car.

The restaurant's back door was propped open with a cinder block. Decker picked up the large brick while guiding the door to silently shut. The cook, his dark hair held back by a headband, stood at a stainless steel counter. He hummed along to music that played through wireless earbuds.

Moving silently, he came up from behind the man, who turned suddenly to grab a tub of onions from the storage rack behind him. Shock barely had the chance to register before Decker swung the cinder block as hard as he could. Concrete connected with the cook's chin, an arc of blood spewing from his mouth. Decker hit him with the cinder block again and again. There was the crunch of concrete on bone and the man slumped down, dead before he even hit the floor.

One of the earbuds came loose and a Huichol song came out of the small speaker. Decker stepped on the white plastic device, silencing the music forever. A block of kitchen utensils sat at the back of the counter. Decker selected a carving knife and stood next to the door, listening.

Clare stood next to the cash register, the acrid taste of panic in the back of her throat. Phil, the restaurant's owner, pressed the phone to his ear. "Yes, Undersheriff Glass, I need to speak to Sheriff Cafferty now."

As he spoke, Clare scanned the street. It was empty, save for a few cars parked at the curb. Where was Isaac? Had he found Decker? Where was the killer?

Speaking into the receiver, Phil said, "Yes, I know you said he's on a call with the highway patrol. But what do you think he'll do if you don't tell him that there's a dangerous criminal in town?" His voice was full of the same frustration that Clare felt. "Well then, why don't you pass him the message while I wait." Phone still at his ear, Phil let out a long sigh and shook his head.

"You think we should lock the front door?" Clare suggested.

"Good idea." Phil pulled a set of keys from his pocket and held them up. "The key to the front door is on the blue ring."

After finding the correct key, Clare locked the door. Just to be safe, she jiggled the handle to make sure it was secure.

When she returned, Phil was speaking into the phone. "Yes, we'll wait here. Glad to hear that he's on the way." He hung up and turned to Clare. "Well, you heard that."

"I did."

"You hungry?" Phil pointed to her half-eaten lunch. "You didn't finish your meal." He strode to the table, picked up her plate. "We can heat that barbecue right up for you."

Clare was too nervous to eat another bite. "You don't have to," she said, trying to be polite.

"Don't worry. It's no trouble whatsoever. Jorge!" he yelled. "Come here and get this plate. We got to get the food good and warm. Add French fries to the dish this time, too." For a moment, they stared at the kitchen door. It remained shut. "He loves loud music so he can't hear a darn thing I say."

Slowly the door opened. A man stood on the threshold. He was covered in blood. In one hand, he held a knife. In the other was a cinder block stained red. True, Clare had never seen a picture of the hitman. But she knew that the person before her had to be Decker Newcombe.

"What the..." Phil's voice trailed off, the plate falling from his hand, bread and meat tumbling to the floor.

"What do you want?" she asked, her body frozen with fear.

"You," he said, smiling. "I'm here for you."

* * *

Isaac scanned the street left and right. The sedan was gone.

He cursed in frustration as his phone began to ring. After fishing the cell from his pocket, he swiped the call open. "Yeah?"

"Is it true?" At once, Isaac recognized Sheriff Cafferty's voice. "Did you really see Decker Newcombe?"

Isaac mentally reviewed everything he'd seen. The guy in the car looked nothing like any of Decker's pictures, but there was something about the eyes. Something he just couldn't dismiss. Still, he had to at least ask himself if his mind was playing a trick. Just in case.

Deep down, though, he knew his instincts were on target. "Let's say that I'm ninety percent sure."

"I'd like it to be a certainty before we move on this," said the sheriff.

"Me and you both." Wherever Decker had gone, Isaac wasn't going to be able to find him on foot. He turned back toward the restaurant. "But ninety percent is a whole hell of a lot better than what we had before—which was nothing."

"I'm coming over to Phil's now. I'll have Glass send out an APB."

"Meet you in a minute."

Isaac jogged to the restaurant's rear entrance. Two trash cans were set at the end of a delivery bay. Behind them sat a sedan. Isaac's instincts jolted again. It was the car he'd noticed earlier. Quickly, he snapped a photo of the license plate.

Still, he stepped around the green plastic bins and

placed his hand on the hood. It was hot, but not from the sun. The engine was still warm.

That meant only one thing: Decker Newcombe had gone into the restaurant.

And looking toward door, Isaac realized Clare was facing the monster alone.

Decker watched the woman as her eyes filled with terror.

"Hey, you." A man in a bolo tie stepped forward. "You can't be here. Jorge!"

Decker cocked his head. "That your cook? Hmm. I don't think he'll be much help."

"What'd you do to Jorge?" panic tinged his voice.

Smiling, he held the cinder block higher. The corner was stained with blood. "I'll let you guess what happened to Jorge."

The man turned the color of used paste. He walked to the counter. There, he pushed a button on the cash register and a drawer opened. "It's all yours, just take it and leave."

"It's not money that I'm after." Energy coursed through Decker's system.

He looked at the woman. She stood near the door, a set of keys in hand. It was then that he understood— she'd locked the front door to keep herself safe from him. He wanted to laugh.

Instead, she'd created a trap.

"You need to get the hell out of here," said the man behind the counter. His voice held a defiant edge, but his hands shook. "Before I get rough."

Decker was on the man in a heartbeat, bringing the

cinder block down like a club on his skull. The impact sounded like a ripe melon hitting the pavement. The man's knees gave out and he crumpled to the ground. A pool of blood—so thick it looked black—seeped out of the head wound, slowly surrounding his prone form.

Keeping his gaze connected with the woman's, he moved from behind the counter. He pointed at her with a knife. She drew in a shaking breath and his chest warmed with satisfaction. "Bring those keys to me. Now."

In moments like this, when people were about to die, Decker had seen it all.

People soiled themselves. They cried. Pleaded. Made promises they'd never keep.

Some did all of that and more.

Yet, whatever it was that Decker had expected to see, it sure as hell wasn't a challenge from a woman radiating fear. "You want these keys? Come and take them."

Twin emotions—annoyance and amusement—fought for supremacy, with amusement winning out.

"You think you can take me on?"

She said nothing, only lifted her chin in defiance.

He dropped the brick at his feet and lifted the knife. He was a predator, ready to pounce. "Alright then, let's dance."

Sunlight glinted off the knife's edge and Clare's stomach dropped to her shoes. Her mind raced as fear gripped her body. What the hell did she know about dodging a murderer?

Newcombe blocked the door to the kitchen and the rear exit. The front door, just a few yards away, was now bolted. She'd never be able to unlock the door and escape in time.

That meant if Clare wanted to live, she was going to have to fight.

She scanned the room for a weapon.

"What do you want from me?" Even she could hear the fear in her voice. The last thing she wanted was to expose her raw nerves to a killer, but she was in uncharted territory. "How's Phil? Is he alive?"

Decker looked at the body behind the counter. "He's breathing, for now." Pause. "Why do you care?"

"Because nobody else needs to lose their life, Decker."

As if slapped, the killer's head snapped back. "How do you know my name?"

Well, there was no reason for her to lie. "I work at a bar where a lot of bikers hang out. Your name's been mentioned and put two and two together." She paused. "You've been missing for a year. You're on the run and wanted for the murder of some district attorney in Wyoming."

She glanced at the table and came up with a plan. Hesitating for only a moment, she took a step closer to the table.

"What're you doing?" The knife in Decker's hand twitched as he rolled his wrist. "Stop right there."

"I just want a drink of tea," she said, making her voice a hoarse whisper. She took walked slowly toward the table. Laying her hand on the back of a chair, she stopped. "Then I can tell you everything the police know."

"Just pick up the glass and nothing else." Decker was

clearly enjoying himself. Yet was his perverse happiness enough of a distraction?

She reached for the tea and brought it to her lips. After taking the last sip, she flung the glass at Decker's face. He lifted an arm to block the flying object. It bounced off his wrist and shattered on the floor. Next, she threw the plate at him, whirling it through the air. It connected with his hairline and a seam of blood opened on his forehead.

He growled. "You'll pay for that."

Clare ran for the kitchen. She pushed open the door and sprinted forward. Her feet slid out from beneath her. She landed hard on her back. The impact drove all the air from her lungs. Her head hit the floor. For a moment, everything went black.

A pinprick of light broke through the darkness and Clare touched the back of her skull. Her hand was wet. Sticky. Blinking hard, she looked at her palm. It was red with blood.

But it wasn't hers.

She looked around and swallowed a scream. A man lay in a pool of gore. His black hair was wet and matted. His eye socket was crushed. His nose, gone. His white t-shirt was scarlet. His black pants were wet with gore. She tried to scoot away. A spike of pain shot from the back of her head until she saw stars.

Then her vision returned. Standing above her was Decker Newcombe.

"You should've listened to me from the beginning. If you had, I would've been gentle and let you die easy-like. But not now," he said, grinning. "Now, I'm gonna kill you slow."

* * *

Isaac rushed to the restaurant's rear entrance and pushed on the handle. It didn't budge. He pushed again and once more. He had to get inside. But how?

He examined the door. The handle was a typical touch bar, and most likely the lock automatically engaged to the outside when closed. It meant that the mechanism was controlled by a roller strike. He could try to pick the lock, sure. But even with the right equipment, it could take hours—time he didn't have.

From inside the room, he heard metal crashing. A woman's scream. "Clare?"

He pounded on the door with the side of his fist. "Clare, can you hear me?" He waited, listening, for an answer.

There was nothing.

The silence fueled his worst fears. He slammed his fist against the door. "Clare, I'm coming. Just hold on."

Isaac ran back down the alley. Pulling the phone from his pocket, he placed the call.

The phone rang once. Twice. Three times.

"Come on. Come on. Answer your damn phone," he cursed as he ran.

On the fifth ring, the call was answered. "This is Cafferty."

"He's here. Decker Newcombe's at Phil's." His voice was a breathless wheeze.

Isaac had worried that Decker was responsible for Trinity's murder from the beginning, even though he had no proof. Now he was sure that the hitman was responsible for the first killing. And if he didn't get that door open, Clare would become the next victim.

"I'm on my way. You wait for me to get there before you try to go inside," said the sheriff. "You hear me?"

Isaac had heard, yet he had no intention of following the sheriff's orders.

He rounded the corner and sprinted for the front of the building. But would he get there in time to save Clare?

Somehow, Clare had kept the keys wedged between her fingers. Decker straddled her torso, keeping her pinned to the ground. He pressed one of her arms to the ground, but her hand with the keys was still free. She struck out with the sharp keys, focusing on his face. His arm. His hand. Any place she could do damage.

A long set of gashes on his forearm wept blood. Still, she wasn't going to be able to fight forever. Decker was stronger. Faster. Meaner. He'd killed more than once. And he was clearly determined to do it again.

Leaning forward, Decker pressed her chest down with his own. The stench of body odor surrounded her. She tried not to gag or worse, retch. Grabbing her wrists, Decker pinned her to the floor.

Clare's mind went blank with terror. If she wanted to live, she had to focus.

She was unable to move her arms to fight off his attack, but instinct took over.

She slammed the keys into his cheek. The ends punctured Decker's flesh. He roared with pain and pitched backward. Clare scrambled from beneath the killer. He grabbed her hair.

Decker drew back his fist and hit Clare in the temple. Pain erupted in her skull as her vision filled with a thousand tiny floating dots. She sprawled across the floor as the keys fell from her hand. They hit the tiles with a clatter and slid under a metal table. "Dammit."

Rolling to all fours, she scrambled to her feet. She was grabbed from behind again and spun around. She dug her heels into the floor, but Decker forced her toward the stove, where all six burners were lit. He grabbed the back of her hair. A sharp pain filled her scalp.

She reached back, slapping, hitting, clawing. Decker grabbed her wrists, pinning them to the back of her head. Her shoulders ached with the strain of being held at such an odd angle. Yet, that was the least of her worries. With his hand pressing the back of her head, Decker shoved her face toward a burner. The flame's heat danced along her skin. She closed her eyes. Yet, the fire still wavered behind her lids.

Clare refused to die. She tried to pull her hands free. His grip tightened, his fingers digging into her flesh. She screamed in pain, and he pushed her closer to the lit burner.

Clare refused to die. But what could she do to escape from the killer?

"Why are you doing this?" she asked, her voice trembling.

"Because." His breath washed over her ear as he spoke. "Being a killer is in my blood."

"You don't have to do this, you know. You can stop now." Clare was dangerously close to begging for her life. It was one thing she refused to do. "Let me go," she said, her tone flinty.

"Letting you go is one thing I won't do. It started generations ago with Old Jack. It's why I killed the red-head, too."

Clare couldn't believe how easily he'd just admitted he'd murdered Trinity. She knew he had no qualms about killing her, but what was she supposed to say to get more out of him—not to mention to hold him off at least until the sheriff arrived?

Without thought, she said, "She was a mom, you know. Now her daughter will grow up without a mother. And you took away her life. Why?"

Decker snarled, "Shut up."

He pushed her down harder, closer to the flame. Clare pushed her feet into the floor harder. It did her no good. The tile was too slick with grease and blood to gain any purchase.

Then again, maybe that was what she needed. She pressed her back into Decker's chest and brought back her skull, smashing his face with the back of her head. At the same moment, she lifted her feet, and pushed off the stove. The momentum sent them both tumbling to the ground. Clare was the first to regain her footing.

A knife lay on the prep table. Clare reached for the blade. Her hand found the hilt and she swung it toward Decker as he rose to his feet. The knife sliced open his shirt and the flesh beneath—but the cut wasn't deep enough to stop the killer. With a curse, he jumped to his feet and lunged at her. She brought the knife up and around, the blade catching his arm. With roar, Decker grabbed her wrist and wrenched her arm to the side. She screamed as her hand went numb. The knife slipped from her grip at the same moment she heard the sound of breaking glass.

Chapter 13

Isaac charged at the glass door, shoulder first. The pane shattered on impact, and he rushed into the restaurant, ignoring the shards of glass clinging to his flesh. The dining area was empty. Plates and glasses were strewn across the floor.

He'd heard Clare's scream and realized Decker had her in the kitchen. Pulling his gun from the waistband at his back, he ran toward the set of double doors.

A pool of blood was spread over the floor. A dead man, his face crushed, lay on the tile. Decker had Clare by the shoulders on the floor, where they struggled over a kitchen knife. Isaac lifted the firearm. "Let her go, Newcombe."

Decker held Clare to him and ducked down until she was a human shield. A knife was pressed to her throat. Isaac tried to get the killer in his sights, but it was impossible. There were no shots to take without the risk of killing Clare. But he didn't lower the gun. "Let her go," Isaac ordered.

"Why? So, you can shoot me?"

"You let her go and I won't shoot." Isaac hated to negotiate with the hitman. Yet, he'd do anything to save Clare's life.

"So, you can arrest me, then. No thanks."

Speaking to Clare, he said, "It'll be okay. I'll get you out of this."

Isaac remained by the doors to the dining area. But Decker was maneuvering toward the rear of the kitchen and the exit. Isaac couldn't let them escape. He aimed and pulled the trigger. The bullet punched a hole in the wall as the acrid scent of gunpowder mixed with the salty smell of grease and the coppery stench of blood.

"Don't move," Isaac warned. "I will shoot you."

The killer sneered. "I don't think so. If you had it in you to shoot your friend to get to me, you would have by now." He pressed the blade into Clare's shoulder. The wound wept blood.

Then, Decker kicked over a stainless steel table. It toppled to the ground, pinning Isaac next to the door.

With Clare still screaming, Decker pulled her by the arm and ran for the exit.

To follow, Isaac was forced to climb over the table, but Decker had already made it to his car and was speeding down the alleyway. Heart pounding and feet slapping the pavement, he gave chase.

The car turned the corner and the door opened. Clare tumbled from the driver's seat. Then, Decker punched the gas. Smoke rose from the tires and the smell of burning rubber filled the air.

Isaac ran to Clare's side. She lay on the ground, covered in blood.

Terror seized him, turning his hands icy.

Was she dead?

Dropping to her side, he smoothed her tangled hair from her face. She stared at him, her breath coming in short gasps. His eyes stung and he blinked hard. "You're alive. You got away."

"He didn't say anything. I don't know why he threw me from the car." She pushed herself up. Her palms were scraped and raw. Blood streamed down one arm from a cut to her elbow. There was a bruise on her cheek. He wanted to pull her into his arms and ease the fear and shock she must be feeling. Let the feel of her body pressed close to his ease his own disappointment at once again losing sight of his prey. Instead, he asked, "How bad are you hurt? I've got a med kit in the truck. We should get you to a doctor, Clare."

In leaving her at the scene, Isaac had been forced to decide—tend to Clare or continue to follow the killer. It was a brilliant decision on Decker's part, but Isaac hadn't even thought twice. He'd found Decker once, and he was sure that the killer would get careless now, making it easier to locate him again.

Because he was sure to come after Clare again, meaning she was in more danger than she'd been before. And while Isaac wanted to nail Decker, he was laser-focused on keeping Clare safe at all costs.

"I'm okay, I think." She reached for his arm. "Help me up."

"No, you just sit. I'll call an ambulance. You really should be seen by a doctor—you could be in shock, Clare."

"It's Phil." Clare used Isaac's shoulder as leverage to stand. He stood as well. "He's hurt bad."

Whatever Isaac wanted to say next was cut short by the shriek of a siren. Sheriff Cafferty slammed on the brakes, parking his cruiser in the middle of the alleyway. With the lights still flashing, he stepped from the car.

Holding on to Clare, Isaac called, "You need to call for backup. Newcombe was here, but got away." He gave a quick description of the car, along with the license plate number.

It took Mooky only a few seconds to send out another APB from the cruiser's radio. Stepping from the car, he asked, "What the hell happened?"

Isaac recalled the chaos in the restaurant. Sure, the restaurant was a crime scene, and anyone who entered would contaminate evidence. But Phil might be alive, and he'd be damned before he'd stand around and wait while a man needed savings. "Call an ambulance and follow me inside." He turned to Clare. "I know it's probably ridiculous to ask you to wait here."

Defiantly, she stared him down. "No way," she said. "I'm coming."

The sheriff made the call, then joined Isaac. The lawmen entered through the back door, Clare at Isaac's side. The dead cook lay on the floor. The room was still in shambles. Clare leaned heavily on his shoulder. "Phil's behind the counter."

The sheriff rushed into the dining area and Clare and

Isaac followed. Phil lay on the floor. An ugly purple bruise ran the length of his swollen jaw. Blood splatter covered the walls. A cinder block, the edge red with blood, sat on the ground.

Phil's breathing was shallow, although the bleeding seemed to have slowed. If he survived, it'd be nothing more than luck.

The sheriff applied a bandage to the head wound. He glanced at Clare. "How about you? Looks like you've been to hell and back."

She looked at her bloody elbow. "I think I'll be okay."

"And what about you?" The sheriff nodded to Isaac. "You've got glass all over your arms."

He picked a shard loose. "I'll survive."

Another siren could be heard in the distance. The sheriff looked up from Phil's side. "That's the EMTs now."

The ambulance parked in the back alley and the EMTs came in through the kitchen. Between them, they carried a medical kit and collapsible stretcher. Isaac pointed. "We have one victim behind the counter. He's alive but unconscious. There's another man in the kitchen. Deceased."

The sheriff and Clare moved into the dining area, giving the EMTs room to treat Phil's wounds. Isaac met them at a table. "Sit here," said Isaac to Clare. "This is a lot to take in, I know. You want a glass of water?"

She dropped into a chair, feeling the unsteadiness in her limbs, in her mind, as the adrenaline began to fade from her body. "Sure."

A stack of glasses and a water pitcher were stored on a table in the corner. Isaac retrieved three glasses, along with the pitcher and returned to the table. He poured water into a glass and handed it to Clare. "Here. It's not much, but maybe it'll help you feel better. For the moment, anyway."

She took a sip and gave him a wan smile. "Thanks."

He sat next to her and pulled another piece of glass from his arm. Sheriff Cafferty remained on his feet. Isaac spoke to the sheriff. "You have to go, I'm sure, and lead the search for Decker."

"I called the highway patrol. They got helicopters and airplanes looking for Newcombe's car. He might've gotten out of town, but he won't get far. For now, I need to know what happened here."

Clare spoke, her voice a whisper. "He told me that he killed Trinity."

"He said those words exactly?" asked the sheriff, his tone filled with incredulity.

"Not exactly, no. He said it's why he killed the redhead, too."

"That's a pretty compelling confession." The sheriff ran a hand down his face. "But why would he kill Ms. Jackson? You said he was a hitman and only killed for money."

Clare asked, "And why eviscerate her that way?"

"From what I can tell, nothing Decker Newcombe does makes sense." The sheriff folded his arms across his chest.

"It's wrong to think he's out of control. He's been nothing if not deliberate. Hiding for a year. Taking Trinity in Mercy and dumping her body in Encantador," Isaac said, just mentioning a few of Decker's recent crimes. "But his mode and motivation for killing has changed."

"Why?" asked the sheriff.

That was the most important question of all. He turned to Clare. "What else did he say? Even if it doesn't seem like a clue to you, it might be significant to the investigation."

Shaking her head, she said, "It's all such a blur. He came in through the kitchen. Then he attacked Phil. I'd locked the front door and knew I was trapped." Her voice broke on the last word. She picked up the glass. Her hand trembled and water sloshed over the rim. She took a sip and set the glass back on the table. "Like I said, it's all a damn blur. I wish I could remember but I don't."

She was frustrated. He could see that in the lines of worry between her brow and set of her jaw. He gave her arm a squeeze to show his support.

For now, he had no choice but to wait and see if Clare regained all her memories. Even if she did, Decker might not have shared anything germane to Trinity's murder or his plans. But Isaac had to get back to work. "Sheriff, I'd like to ask a favor of you."

"I'll help if I can."

Isaac was thankful for Cafferty's cooperation. "I need a private place to make a few phone calls. And a place for Clare to shower and a clean set of clothes for her."

"I can get you the clothes and a place to make calls." He paused. "Are you going to check in with SSA Jones? I could surely use the FBI's help."

Jason was the first person who Isaac planned to contact. "I imagine he'll be in touch with you soon."

He nodded his thanks. "I have just the place for you, then."

First, Isaac was forced to work with Ryan. Now the sheriff's office was involved in Newcombe's case as well. It was a hell of a way to be a singleton. But for the first time in a long while, he didn't mind having a team.

At Phil's, EMTs had examined Clare. Like she thought, all her injuries were minor. Her scrapes were cleaned, and her cuts were bandaged. They offered to take her to the emergency room, but she refused further treatment. With Phil so badly wounded, the doctor didn't need to worry about Clare.

Deputy Travers had scraped beneath her fingernails for evidence. He also gave her an Encantador Sheriff's Office T-shirt in exchange for her blood-soaked T-shirt, which was taken into evidence as well.

Likewise, the EMTs treated Isaac at the scene. The shards of glass were removed from his arm and all the cuts were treated and bandaged.

Then, Isaac and Clare were directed to the motel next to the restaurant. The Saddle Up Inn was a single-level motor inn that sat at the back of a parking lot. Half a dozen cars were parked in spots for a dozen rooms. The building was adobe, painted pink, with a roof of terracotta tiles. A sign on the street showed a lone saddle hanging on a peg, along with the words *Saddle Up*.

At the bottom of the sign, the word *VACANCY* was painted in red. There was a hook next to the vacancy sign and Clare guessed that in the motel office was the word *NO*, which was put out when all the rooms were filled.

Half a whiskey barrel had been converted into a fountain. It bubbled happily next to the front door.

"Looks like this is the place." Standing on the sidewalk, Isaac shaded his eyes. "I thought for sure that Cafferty would just put us back in the conference room at the sheriff's office."

"I just want to get out of these clothes and take a long hot shower," said Clare. She tried to ignore the image of holding Isaac's naked body next to hers beneath the spray of hot water. Yet, the fantasy left an indelible mark.

Without saying another word, they walked across the parking lot. Isaac pulled open the office door and a wave of air-conditioning crashed over Clare, leaving her instantly chilled. The desk clerk, a man with round glasses, looked up as they entered. Stockings of red and white hung in a line on the counter.

A radio played in the background. The announcer said, "You all know that last song was 'Jingle Bells'— and I hope that you sang along. Be sure to run all your holiday errands early today. A storm is moving into our area…" The clerk turned down the volume and smiled at Isaac and Clare. "You two must be the folks from the sheriff's office who need a room."

"We are."

"I've got your keys." He held up two worn plastic cards with a black magnetic strip. "Here you go."

Isaac took the cards and handed one to Clare.

The man continued, "That's for room ten. Turn right when you go back outside. Number ten is the third door from the end."

"And what about me?" Clare asked.

"That key will work on the lock, too."

"No," said Clare, clarifying her question. "What room am I supposed to be in?"

"Room ten."

"You don't understand," said Clare. "I need my own room."

Isaac removed his wallet from his back pocket. "I'll pay for another room," he said, a stack of bills in hand.

"Sorry, I can't help with that," said the desk clerk. "Three of our rooms are being renovated. The other ones are rented."

Clare glanced at Isaac, her face suddenly hot.

Then again, Decker Newcombe was still at large. If he showed back up, she didn't want to be alone. She nodded at the desk clerk. "Thanks."

They made their way down the walkway to number ten, and Clare waited as Isaac unlocked the hotel door. She crossed the threshold. The room was clean and comfortable. The Western motif that was popular around town was on full display. A barn door headboard sat at the top of a single full-size bed. Prints featuring riderless saddles hung on three of the four walls. The TV stand was an old wagon wheel with a glass top. A sign hung on the bathroom door as a joke: Outhouse.

"It's not the Ritz," said Isaac. "That's for sure."

A combo heat/air-conditioning unit clung to the wall beneath a window and blew a weak stream of almost-cool air. Clare adjusted the temperature and fan speed. The unit rattled the pane and icy cold wind gusted from the vents. She lifted her hair, letting the air-conditioner dry the sweat at the nape of her neck. "It's perfect," she said, dropping her bag on the TV table.

"Really?" Isaac sat on the end of one bed. "Look at these blankets. Cowboy-hat print? I haven't seen this since I was a kid."

The mention of his childhood left Clare wondering about Isaac. "Growing up, was your bedroom decorated with lots of cowboy stuff? After all, you did grow up in Texas."

"Me? Cowboys? No, I was more of a race-car kid." He laughed. "The more I look, the surer I am that this room is tacky."

"Cute," said Clare. Every part of her ached or hurt. "Enthusiastic," she added, rubbing the back of her neck.

"Which is a polite way to say tacky."

She laughed and her neck twinged. Clare didn't recall making a face, but she must've. Isaac's hand rested on her elbow. "Do you want me to call the hospital?"

She wanted to lean into him. To feel his hands on her, massaging the soreness, soothing the pain. Touching. Stroking. Stoking the heat in her veins.

She wanted him. It was that simple.

Then again, any kind of relationship with Isaac would create more issues than it fixed. "Phil's going to need a lot of care. I won't bother the doctor for a few bumps and bruises."

"I imagine that Phil has already been airlifted to a bigger hospital. Besides, I'm worried about you—and until you get examined, you won't know what's wrong."

She understood the wisdom of Isaac's words. But she ignored his comment altogether. "So, who gets the shower first? Me or you?"

"You go first. I'll call Jones." He took the phone from his pocket and sat on the edge of the bed.

"Alright, then."

She slipped into the bathroom and stripped out of her clothes. Turning on the cold tap in the tub, she plunged her pants into the stream. Clare waited as the runoff water turned from red to pink to clear.

Good enough. She twisted her jeans, wringing out the excess water, and then hung them on a towel hook to dry.

She adjusted the water temperature from cold to scalding and stepped under the spray. She closed her eyes and let the water sluice over her body. At the edge of her imagination, she sensed that memories of Decker Newcombe wanted to sneak into her mind.

She refused to think of him.

A complimentary bottle of body wash sat on the edge of the tub. Clare poured a dab into her palm and worked it into a lather. She ran her hand over her stomach, her chest, her breasts.

Isaac's face came to mind. What would it feel like to have his hands on her body? He would be a gentle but powerful lover, she decided, with her hands between her thighs.

Her own touch did nothing to excite her passions or ease the ache for Isaac's touch. Then she remembered the kiss. The power of his lips on hers. The sensual feel of his tongue in her mouth. Clare leaned against the tiles and explored her body. But it wasn't a fantasy that left her breathless and trembling. It was the memory of being touched by Isaac. Held by him, kissed by him.

She stood under the shower and turned her face to the spray. Isaac had come into her life at the exact wrong time. And that meant only one thing. There could be nothing between them beyond longing and unfulfilled desire.

Chapter 14

Isaac placed the call to Jason. The SSA answered after the first ring. "Have you got news for me?"

He filled his boss in quickly. "His intended victim is a woman named Clare Chamberlain." He hesitated. "One more thing. Decker's seen me. He knows that the police are looking for him. My cover's been blown."

To his credit, Jason remained calm. "I'm not pulling you off the case, yet. Tonight, I'll send in a team to Mercy and get more eyes at the bar."

Even though he was on the phone, Isaac nodded. "Solid plan." But there was more. "Decker admitted to Clare that he killed Trinity—the murder victim from this morning. A DNA swab was taken from the body. Soon, we'll know if it's a match with Decker, but I have no doubts."

"Interesting." Jason drew out the single word. "Why'd

a hitman who only killed for money start targeting women? And in such a brazen way that he's willing to attack others to gain access to his victim, no less?"

"I was hoping you had some insights."

After letting out a long breath, Jason said, "I'll run this by the behavioral sciences unit. They'll have a theory. For now, I want you to stay out of Mercy. The last thing we want is for you to be spotted by Decker."

A hard knot dropped into the middle of Isaac's chest. He hated to give up the case. But Jason was right. If Decker spotted him again, the hitman would know that Mercy was a trap and disappear. "What about Ryan?"

"He's still the bait," said Jason. "The undercover agents will be at the bar before it opens. If Decker shows up, we'll get him."

It didn't seem right to leave Ryan without protection. Then again, Jason had promised that backup was on the way. "I'll let him know. By the way, the local sheriff is looking for some federal help. Call me if you hear anything else."

"There is one other thing. I've finally gotten the authorization from DoD to task a satellite eight miles into Mexico. We're starting near where you found that phone. If all goes well, we'll have a location for the safe house by evening."

That would be good news. Then again… "Why would he go back to the place he's been holed up for a year? He told Ryan about it—I imagine Decker will find someplace else to hide."

"We have to follow every lead," said Jason, annoyance evident in his tone. "You know that."

"Yeah, I know. No stone, and all." He paused, wondering if now was the time to bring up Clare and the buried chemicals. "There's something else that needs you attention. I've seen some evidence that a company in Columbus, Ohio has buried some pretty toxic chemicals."

"You have a name for the company?"

"Chamberlain Enterprises," he said.

"I'm not making any promises, but my people will look into." Jason paused. "Anything else?"

"I'm keeping Decker's intended victim—the women he attacked—with me. We're staying in a motel in Encantador for now. If you need to talk to her, let me know."

"Eventually, I will. For now, my focus is on the DoD satellite. I'm hoping that we can get some images before the storm hits." Jason ended the call.

Isaac held his phone. Truly, he hated that he'd been told to stay away from Mercy for a variety of reasons. From the beginning, this had been his plan. He'd worked the case for months. It didn't seem fair that he'd given up a year of his life. Then, a team of undercover agents were going to show up and make the arrest.

He also loathed leaving Ryan on his own. It didn't take a gifted psychologist to help Isaac understand why he wanted to work as a singleton. For years, he'd carried Miguel's death around like a shield. It was meant to protect Isaac, but it also kept people away and it was exhausting.

He knew now that he'd never given Ryan enough credit. At great personal risk, he was trying to do the right thing. He wanted to bring Decker to justice and, at the same time, start over. True, Ryan would never replace Miguel, but he wouldn't have been a bad choice as a friend.

But if he had to lay low, as Jason said, there were worse places to be than a hotel room with Clare. He listened to the shower running in the bathroom. He imagined Clare's body, slick with soap, as water sluiced over her breasts.

He wanted to think that if he let himself into the bathroom, she'd welcome him with open arms and open thighs. But they'd only kissed once. And even he knew that hardly gave him the right to expect more. Still, it didn't stop him from wanting her.

He ignored his growing desire. Now wasn't the time to get drawn into adult fantasies. He had one more call to make. He pulled up his contacts and selected Ryan's number.

He answered the phone after the third ring. "I never thought I'd say this, but I'm glad to hear from you."

"Hey, man," said Isaac. "I have news. You alone?"

"I am. Go ahead."

"Decker's in the area." Isaac gave a simple recounting of the events after Trinity's body was discovered. He ended with, "The FBI will be sending several undercover agents to stake out your bar. I don't know who or how many, but enough that when Decker shows up, they'll be ready."

"Plus, I'll have you here."

Did Ryan already suspect that Isaac was being sidelined? "I'm staying in Encantador for now. Decker's seen me. If I show up in Mercy, he'll know there's a trap. Before he can be taken into custody, he'll take off. After that, we'll never find him."

On the other end of the line, Isaac could hear Ryan sigh. "There's not many people in the world I trust. Without you around…"

After a year of working together, he supposed they'd developed a respectful relationship of sorts. "The agents will keep you safe, man. They'll get Decker when he shows. Soon, all this will be over."

"I guess this is goodbye, then."

Isaac hadn't really thought about it that way, but Ryan was right. He was done with his time in Mercy. Despite the fact he'd hated the place, to know that he'd never go back was shocking, like ice water to the face. "I guess it is."

"I'll make good on that second chance, Isaac. I promise," said Ryan.

"I hope so," said Isaac. "You've earned it, man. And, Ryan—"

"Yeah?"

"Nothing. Just…be careful. And—good luck."

Then he ended the call.

Clare stayed in the bathroom to dry and redress. Thankfully, the sheriff's office T-shirt came to her thighs, and she need not put on her wet jeans. She and Isaac traded places, muttering polite nothings as they slipped past each other, Clare into the room and Isaac to the shower. Laying on the bed, she flipped through the TV channels, watching a local news station as it tracked a line of storms up from the Gulf of Mexico. The news anchor promised high winds, hail, rain and an unseasonable tornado watch.

Isaac exited the bathroom and Clare looked up from

the TV. His hair was still damp. He wore his jeans, no shirt.

After spending time with him, she knew that he was muscular and well-built. Yet, she was wholly unprepared for how he looked without his shirt. His arms were powerful, the lines of muscles were unmistakable. A dark sprinkling of hair covered his chest and abdomen.

Just seeing him left her breathless.

He ran a towel over his hair. "How're you holding up?"

She shrugged. "Sore. Tired. Worried."

"About Decker or your ex?"

"Both, I suppose." Using the remote, Clare turned off the TV. True, there hadn't been a lot of time to consider Isaac's suggestions for dealing with her in-laws, but she knew there were some flaws to his plan. She sat up, resting her back on the headboard. "As far as my ex, I have lots of concerns."

"Well, we'll be here for a while. Let's figure out how to ease them, if we can."

"Well, you mentioned bringing in the media and law enforcement. I agree that once the story becomes news, the Chamberlains will have to leave me alone. But how long will the world be fixated on some buried chemicals? Weeks? A month, maybe." She shrugged. "The investigation will eventually end, too. And then, who will be around to care what happens to me?"

"Me," said Isaac. "I'll care." He sat beside her, and their shoulders touched. Clare didn't bother to move away. "You could be my second client at Texas Law."

"I don't have money to pay you." She paused a beat before adding, "Except what I earned last night."

Smiling, he shook his head. "You can keep that cash. I won't charge you a dime."

"Really? Don't you need paying clients?"

"Sure, just not you." His thigh pressed against hers and she shivered with yearning. "For you, I just want to do the right thing."

Clare gave in to her longing to touch Isaac. Placing her hand on his cheek, she said, "Then I was right from the beginning."

"About what?"

"You really are kind."

"I don't know about that," he drawled. He leaned closer, so close that his mouth nearly touched hers. "Would a nice guy kiss you?" he asked.

"Only if I wanted a kiss," she said.

"Is that what you want, Clare?"

Without a word, she placed her lips on his. His mouth was strong. He reached around her waist, pulling her to him. Her breasts pressed against his chest. She sighed with the closeness, and he slipped his tongue into her mouth.

Winding her fingers through Isaac's hair, Clare pulled him closer. At first, the kiss was tentative—almost timid. As if he were reining in his passion. Or giving Clare a chance to retreat. Yet, she was done with running. She'd spent the past two months avoiding thoughts and feelings. Hell, she'd survived the hands of a killer.

Clare was ready to embrace her emotions again. She wanted to do more than simply survive. She wanted to claim this moment for her own and live.

She ran her palm over the muscles of his chest, a silent invitation. Holding her tighter, Isaac growled with pleasure.

His palm skimmed her side until Isaac found the hem of the T-shirt. He gently pulled it up, his fingertips branding her skin, traveling from her belly to her chest.

She began to burn, from the heat of his skin, from her own wanting. "Touch me," she whispered into the kiss. "Please, Isaac."

"Where?" he asked, slipping his finger inside her bra.

"Everywhere."

He rolled her nipple between finger and thumb, and she gasped with longing. Liquid heat settled low in her belly, and she ached for Isaac to explore every part of her. What's more, she wanted him inside her.

She couldn't recall ever feeling such intense desire—for any man. She'd never acted on her feelings so quickly before, ever. Sure, these were extenuating circumstances—to say the least!—but who knew what they faced in the coming days, or even hours? No matter which way she turned, she was being hunted.

So would it be such a crime to steal this moment for herself? Why should she deny herself the pleasure, the man, she'd been longing for?

Clare lay back on the bed. Isaac knelt on the mattress next her. She studied him—examining his shoulders, arms, chin, lips and eyes. How long had it been since she'd been so drawn to a man? For a moment, she couldn't remember. Then again, maybe she'd never been so attracted to anyone before now.

He ran his hand up her calf. Desire rushed through her veins.

"What're you looking at?" he asked, a small smile on his lips.

"You."

Isaac hovered over her. His fingers grazed the flesh of her stomach. "Tell me what you want."

Clare's blood buzzed and she gasped in anticipation as his fingers traced the silky fabric of her panties.

His voice low and husky, he asked, "Here?"

"Lower."

He gave her that smile she was starting to love. "I was hoping you'd say that."

Clare was already wet, swollen with want and desperate to have him inside her. Isaac slipped his hand into her underwear and ran a finger down the middle of her slit. She lifted her hips, and he slid a finger inside her. He began to move, and she drew in a short and shaking inhalation. He slipped another finger inside and she moaned with desire.

"Is this where you want to be touched?"

"Yes," she said, sighing. "Oh, yes."

He moved his fingers inside her as his thumb traced a circle over the top of her sex. She was still sensitive from her time in the shower. But having Isaac's touch was so different from her own. And really, it had been too long since she'd been properly stroked—or loved. The orgasm came on hard and fast. She cried out and clung to his shoulders. He smothered her cries with his kisses. Her heartbeat raced and every part of her body thrummed with ecstasy.

"Isaac," she whispered. "Oh, Isaac."

He kissed her again; deep and slow. Then, he moved his mouth to her neck, her shoulder, her chest. She stripped out of her T-shirt and dropped it to the floor. Next, she removed her bra.

He kissed her deeply. "You're perfect."

Clare wasn't sure that she believed him. Kyle had gone from being indifferent to planning her murder. And he certainly never called her perfect—or anything close. Yet, the look in his eyes told Clare that he saw her as beautiful and desirable.

"Better than perfect," he continued. "Clare, you're gorgeous."

Isaac lowered his mouth to her breast and took her nipple between his teeth. He bit gently. She hissed with the pleasure and the pain. He reached for her other breast and ran his thumb over her areola, until both of her nipples were hard.

Running her hands through Isaac's hair, she let the silky strands slip between her fingers. But she wanted— no, she needed—to feel more of him. She ran her hands down his chest, to his abs. To his hips. She traced his length through the fabric of his jeans.

"Oh, Clare," he moaned.

She worked the top button of his pants free.

"What're you doing?"

"Fair is fair," she said, pulling down on the zipper. Clare ran her hand inside his pants. He was hard and thick. She traced the head, moving her hand up and down his shaft.

Isaac kissed her hard. "Dammit, that feels good."

He got harder with her touch, but swiftly put a stop to her plans.

"Hold up." He held on to her wrist. "You gotta hold up."

"You don't like it?"

"Hell, I love it. It's just that I'll lose it unless you stop." He kissed her hard, gave her a wicked smile. "Take off those panties."

Clare did as she was told. While she disrobed, Isaac took off his jeans and underwear. She lay back on the bed and he stood, naked before her.

He bent down to kiss Clare and reached between her legs. He kissed her neck. Her shoulder. Her breasts. Lower still. Her stomach. Her hip. Then, his mouth was on her sex. He slid one finger inside her and then another.

The sensations were too much. Yet, she wanted more than to take her pleasure from Isaac—but to give him pleasure as well.

"Come here," she gasped, pulling him by the shoulders. "Lay on your back."

He rolled to the middle of the mattress and lay on his back. She was on his chest, with her rear toward his face. Clare studied Isaac's body. There was a scar on his chest and mole on his thigh. She wanted to investigate the map of his life and know everything she could about this man.

At the same time, she knew that any relationship between them—beyond the here and now—was impossible. So, Clare decided to drink in the moment until she was drunk with bliss. She ran her tongue around his tip and then, took him into her mouth. His tongue and fingers inside her. The pressure of ecstasy began to build, yet she'd never be able to climax again—not without Isaac inside her.

She swirled her tongue over him once more and nipped the inside of his thigh.

"Wait a second." Isaac rose from the bed and picked up his discarded jeans. From his back pocket, he took out his wallet. "Success." He held up a square foil packet.

Clare lay back as Isaac unrolled the translucent condom.

He knelt between her thighs. "So sexy," he murmured. He entered her slowly. "You are so freaking sexy."

She cried out as he drove hard at the very end. Isaac adopted the rhythm—a delicious torture—slow, slow, hard.

Clare's passion swelled. For her release, though, she needed more. Clare ran her tongue over Isaac's neck, savoring the salt on his skin. "Harder," she whispered into his ear. "I want you to take me harder. Faster. Now."

Isaac complied. His strokes carried the same urgency she felt. The wave of passion grew until it towered over Clare, threatening to drown her in her own pleasure. She cried out as she came. "Isaac. Isaac. Oh, Isaac."

The headboard slapped against the wall as he drove into her one final time. With a growl, he climaxed.

Heartbeat racing, he flopped down on Clare. He placed a kiss on her neck and gently bit the lob of her ear. "I like to hear you say my name like that."

"Like what?"

"Like when you come." He kissed her once more.

Her eyelids were heavy, yet Clare rolled to her side to watch Isaac. "That was really good."

He gave her a wide smile. "We are really good together."

Wrapping his arms around her middle, Isaac pulled Clare to him. They fit together perfectly, as if made for one another. Clare wanted to say or do something, but she was more than exhausted, and sleep came to claim her. As the last bit of consciousness faded, one word led her to her dreams. *Safe.*

Chapter 15

Filtered sunlight shone through the curtains, turning her hair that shade of gold that always made Isaac smile.

Was it wrong to want to hold on to the moment just a little bit longer? Was it horrible to create a place where it was just Clare and Isaac—and the rest of the world could keep spinning outside of their door? The condom began to leak, and Isaac supposed that he'd gotten his answer.

Slipping from the bed, he pulled the cowboy hat comforter over Clare. After placing a kiss on her head, he scooped up the pile of discarded clothes and doubled-timed it to the small bathroom. Isaac redressed in his boxers and jeans.

He wasn't sure what he noticed first. Was it that the air in the stuffy bathroom had grown softer? Or had he heard a breath? Seen a movement in the small mirror?

Lifting his eyes, he met her gaze through the mirror. Clare stood on the threshold, watching him. Her hair was tousled. Her lips were swollen from his kisses. She was clad only in the comforter and, honestly, Isaac had never seen anyone look more beautiful. He dropped his gaze.

Throughout the day, he'd come to realize one important truth. He was drawn to Clare. Yet, it was more than her looks or her mind or her sense of nobility. It was that being with Clare let Isaac be a decent man once again.

He wanted to tell her all that and more. He said, "You need to use the bathroom? I can get out of here, if you do."

Use the bathroom? Great way to woo a lady, Patton. Was there a less romantic phrase ever evented?

"I'm okay," she said.

They'd just had sex—no, that didn't do justice to the passion and pleasure that had passed between them. He really should say something. But what? Especially since his opening salvo for romance was all about using the loo.

He tried to find the right way to tell her how he felt. That after months of pretending to be someone who didn't care, Isaac had become apathetic. What's worse, he worried that his apathy had made him a lesser person. "The fact that you saw me as nice or kind gave me back a piece of myself that I thought was gone forever."

He let the fabric of his sentence unravel and hoped that she would pick up the thread.

Mutely, she watched him.

"Say something."

Clare stepped forward and placed her hand on the side of his face. "You are a good man. I know."

She let the blanket slip from her body. The fabric pooled around her feet. How had he gotten so lucky?

Isaac moved to Clare and placed his mouth on hers. They backed up into the wall. The kiss was hard and meant to claim. Hell, he was hard again as well. And what it wanted was Clare. He broke the embrace and found another condom—his last—in his wallet. With his mouth on hers again, he unbuttoned the fly of his jeans. He rolled on the condom and gripped Clare's rear.

She wrapped her legs around his hips, gloriously opening herself to him. He entered her in one deep stroke.

"Oh, Isaac," she moaned.

God, he loved hearing her say his name. Or to feel her breath on his shoulder. He remembered where and how she liked to be touched and reached between their bodies. He found the top of her sex and rubbed. Her muscles contracted around him as she neared another climax.

Isaac knew he wasn't far behind.

He pumped his hips, driving into Clare, as her moans of ecstasy echoed in the small room. She raked her nails over his back as she came.

He was close, so close. Pressing his lips on hers again, Isaac slipped his tongue into her mouth. They kissed and his world shrank until it contained only him and her.

As he came, Isaac realized that for months he'd been pretending to be something that he wasn't—until all that was left of Isaac was the shell of his former self. Yet, Clare had somehow filled him. Or maybe, she'd revived a part of him that had long been dormant. For the first time in months, Isaac found himself.

If Decker believed in anything beyond his own superiority, he'd have seen the past few hours as being fueled by sheer luck. Since leaving Encantador, he'd stolen and ditched three different vehicles. The last one was a pickup truck parked in the lot of a bar. He'd driven that truck to a secluded house at the end of a mile-long driveway. He now stood in the bathroom of that house with the shades drawn. Nearby, several flies droned in the late afternoon.

There were no neighbors, just an old dog that had been chained to the porch. The woman of the house must've been the vain sort. Her medicine cabinet was filled with dark brown hair dye and more cosmetics than a typical drugstore.

Not only had there been enough color for Decker's hair, but there was enough dye leftover to color the stubble on his cheeks and chin. True, he didn't have a full set of whiskers, but the skin beneath was stained and gave a passing appearance of a dark beard and mustache. A brown cosmetic pencil gave him a thick brow, and he decided to take it with him. Surely, he'd find a use for it along the way.

He donned a large flannel shirt and pants that were several sizes too big. He tucked a bed pillow into both. The added girth changed his body shape. He slipped on a set of reading glasses, before adding a baseball cap in blaze orange as the finishing touch. Standing in the bathroom, he examined himself in the mirror.

"Damn." Decker admired his disguise. He was a whole new man.

From the bathroom, he walked down a short hallway to the kitchen. With each step, he tried to adopt the stride of one who was heavier and older. A crockpot filled with chili sat on the counter. He found a box of crackers in the cabinet and a block of cheese in the refrigerator.

Whoever had made the chili was a good cook—and that was actually lucky. He finished one bowl of chili and then started on another. While eating, he planned and reflected.

Decker was surprised that the police knew all about him. And now, they knew he'd killed the woman in Mercy.

The blonde woman he'd attacked today was another problem. Certainly, she'd spoken to the police, and even now, every cop in southern Texas was looking for Decker—and likely had some half-assed ID for him, too. Although it didn't matter. He was done with this part of Texas—or he would be soon.

To stay one step ahead of the police, Decker needed funds—specifically the money Ryan owed to him. After one last stop in Mercy, he'd disappear.

Placing his empty bowl in the sink, Decker returned to the master bedroom. From the closet, he took two more pairs of pants and several button-up shirts. Certainly, the man—whoever he was—wouldn't mind lending his clothes to Decker.

He walked by the bathroom and pulled back the shower curtain. The couple lay in the tub, arms and legs tangled. Their life's blood now black. A spider crawled over the husband's face before disappearing into his hair.

Pulling the curtain shut, he thought of how the man had begged Decker not to do anything depraved to the woman he loved. As if Decker would ever find an old sow like that appealing. In the end, Decker was merciful. Two shots—both between the brows. The couple died within seconds of one another. He pulled the door closed.

In the kitchen once more, Decker slipped his newly acquired clothes into a plastic bag. Thank goodness the stove was gas. Then again, it's exactly what he expected this far from the main electrical grid. He turned on all the burners and the stink of rotten eggs filled the room. He also opened the gas valve for the oven. He picked up yesterday's newspaper and long-necked lighter. The last thing he did was grab a set of car keys from a pegboard on the wall.

With the fumes of natural gas filling the small house, Decker left through the front door. The old dog growled, showing a mouthful of discolored teeth. Decker crumpled up the newspaper, set it alight and let the bundle burn for a moment. Then, he threw the ball of flames into the house and pulled the door shut.

Keys in hand, he walked to the truck and started the engine. From the porch, the dog watched him with wide eyes—obviously aware that something was wrong.

For a moment, Decker was back at a similarly small house and a dog on a chain. To him, a young boy, the dog had been nothing but teeth and claws, and a dangerous beast on its best day. He hadn't understood that his fourth stepfather kept the dog hungry enough to be mean. Putting the car into Drive, he looked toward the road, but he couldn't take his foot off the brake.

A rawhide chew sat on the truck's floorboard. Decker slammed his fist in the steering wheel. "Dammit all to hell."

He shoved the gearshift into Park, grabbed the rawhide chew and opened the door. Striding up to the porch, he unwound the dog's chain and picked up a tin bowl filled with grimy water. "Come on." He gave the lead a tug.

The dog looked back at the house and dug his paws into the porch.

"They left you out here in the sun with only dirty water. That's no way to be treated. They didn't deserve you." Decker wasn't sorry that he'd killed the couple, but in hindsight a little bit of suffering might have been warranted. He tugged on the chain a second time and lifted the rawhide for the dog to see. "C'mon."

Head down, the dog ambled to the truck and jumped into the passenger seat. Decker slammed the door shut before rounding to the driver's side. He slid behind the steering wheel and pulled his own door closed. This time, when he put the gearshift into Drive, he let off the brake and drove down the road.

Tossing the chew into the passenger seat, he asked the dog, "What's your name, fella?" A round tag hung from a worn collar. "Old Blue," Decker read out loud. "It's an odd name for a brown dog."

Old Blue sighed in agreement.

There was a *whoosh* and Decker glanced into the rearview mirror. The house had caught fire and the windows exploded, black smoke billowing out into the gray light of the approaching storm. By the time the fire department arrived, Decker and Old Blue would be long gone.

Clare was in the thin space between sleep and wakefulness. In her dream, she was in London, encased in thick fog. Voices came to her. First was that of Dr. Garcia. *This woman has been disemboweled.*

And then, the tail end of the doctor's words were those of a killer. Decker said, *Being a killer is in my blood... It started generations ago with Old Jack. It's why I killed the redhead, too.*

She sat up, heartbeat racing. She knew why Trinity's wounds seemed so familiar—because they were. Clare looked around. She was still in the small hotel room with the saddle prints hanging on the wall. Outside, the wind howled—must be the storms promised by the TV news. She glanced at the bedside clock—5:17 p.m.

By her side, Isaac slept. With his head cradled in his arms, he snored softly. She knew that he'd been out the night before and imagined he was exhausted, but her revelation was too important to ignore.

She placed her hand on his arm. "Isaac. Wake up. I remembered something about Decker. I think it's important."

He opened his eyes with a sharp intake of breath. "What do you remember?"

"When we were in the kitchen." Clare could still feel the flames from the stove on her face. She inhaled and pushed the horror aside, focusing only on what was useful. With an exhale, she started over. "He said to me, *being a killer is in my blood… It started generations ago with Old Jack. It's why I killed the redhead, too."*

Isaac sat up and rubbed his face. *"Being a killer is in my blood,"* he repeated. "What's that supposed to mean?"

"I think I know."

"You know?" he asked, his tone incredulous.

Maybe knowing was too strong a term. "Let's say I have a hunch." Now what she needed was proof—and that meant getting her phone. Her tote bag sat on the table next to the TV. After the second round of lovemaking, Clare hadn't bothered to get dressed. She held the blanket under her arms, but her clothes were scattered across the floor.

Well, now wasn't the time for modesty. Naked, she rose from the bed and crossed the room to get her bag. Back at the bed, she slipped between the covers again. Inside her tote, she found her phone and pressed her thumb to the power button. The screen winked to life, and she accessed the motel's free Wi-Fi.

"Are you going to tell me about your hunch?" Isaac asked.

She entered several words into the search bar as she spoke. "It wasn't just what Decker said, but what he did to Trinity. The disemboweling, I mean." She pressed the spyglass icon. It took only minutes for over one-hundred thousand hits to appear. It was just as she'd suspected—and feared. Holding up the screen for Isaac to see, she said, "This is what he's doing."

He reached for the phone, his hand covering her own. He read the text, then met her gaze. "Everything you found is about Jack the Ripper. What does any of this have to do with Decker?"

"Trinity was killed and then disemboweled after her death." The more she spoke, the more certain she became of her hunch. "It's the same thing Jack the Ripper did to his victims."

"How do you know that?"

"A few years ago, Kyle and I went to England. When we were in London, we went on one of those Ripper tours. You know, you shlep all over Whitechapel, a guide shows people where crimes took place or bodies were found."

He considered her words, looking a little skeptical. "There are lots of other killings with postmortem mutilation. What makes you connect Jack the Ripper and Decker?"

"When we were…" The kitchen of the barbecue restaurant was the place that forever would be the source of Clare's nightmares. "Well, Decker told me he was like *Old Jack*. What other famous killer do you know of named Jack besides Jack the Ripper?"

Scrolling through her phone, he said nothing for a moment. "I'm not saying that the connection you've found is wrong. But I'm going to need more before I try to convince the FBI that Decker's started committing copycat killings based on murderer from Victorian England."

Was Isaac playing the devil's advocate in asking her for more facts? Or did he really not think her argument was compelling?

He continued, "Maybe a year of being alone was too much for Decker and he completely lost it. But it would explain why he's suddenly targeting women and not killing for a profit." Isaac paused. "I'll pass the information onto the Bureau. But I'll be honest, I hope that you're wrong."

Clare couldn't help it. She was offended by his remark. Sitting up taller, she gave him a side-eye. "Why's that?"

He held up her phone; the screen was filled with an article about the victims. "I'm no expert on Jack the Ripper but says here that his Autumn of Terror claimed the lives of five women. It means if Decker's copying the murders, then Trinity's death is just the beginning."

Isaac had to get in touch with Jason. Sure, the FBI would have to analyze Clare's theory. Even he agreed with her that Decker was copying Jack the Ripper's killing. After rising from the bed, he slipped into his boxer shorts. From there, he found his phone and sat back on the mattress.

He placed the call. His phone blared with three tones and a prerecorded message. *We're sorry but your call cannot go through.*

Looking over his shoulder, he glanced at Clare. She shrugged. "Weird. Try again."

He placed the call for the second time. It began to ring, the line filled with static.

Jason answered. "Isaac? Can you hear me?" In the background was a rushing noise. Immediately, Isaac pictured a locomotive rumbling past.

"I can hear you. Where are you?"

"I'm heading to the basement at my office building. Listen, San Antonio is under a state of emergency. Several tornados have touched down in the area. I'm not going to be able to send undercover agents to Mercy. Did you hear me? If you can get in touch with Ryan, you need to let him know."

"I can hear you," Isaac yelled into the phone. His chest tightened at the notion that Ryan would be left alone to deal with Decker.

"And one more thing," said Jason, his words breaking up as he spoke. "We found the safe house. It was just like he said, eight miles south of the border by where he dumped the phone. A team's ready to raid the place as soon as we can get there."

Isaac opened the drawer in the nightstand. There was a Bible, along with a pad of paper and a pen. "You got those coordinates for me?"

The phone beeped once. And the line went dead.

Isaac gripped the phone in his hand and cursed. "Dammit."

What was he supposed to do now? Did he stick with the original plan and stay in Encantador? Or did he go to Mercy and provide reinforcements for Ryan if—and when—Decker showed? Actually, Isaac didn't need to ask himself the question. He already knew what needed to be done.

"I'm going to Mercy." He stood and picked his pants up off the floor.

"Now?" Clare asked.

True, he wanted to be gone in the next few seconds— a minute at most. But Isaac had to think the scenario through. He needed to keep Clare safe and hidden. But where? He could leave her in Encantador and under the protection of the sheriff. Or did he take her with him to Mercy?

Or maybe it wasn't his decision to make.

"You heard what Jason said. I can't leave Ryan to deal with Decker alone. You still need protection. I can call Cafferty and request a deputy be placed on the street."

"Don't bother." Clare reached to the floor for her underwear. "I'm going with you."

Chapter 16

If Isaac's thinking about Decker's plans was right, the killer would still go to the House of Steele for his money. It meant that obviously Isaac couldn't work the bar, but would have to stay out of sight. If he waited in Ryan's office, he could arrest the killer when he arrived. As complicated as taking a hitman into custody would be, that was the easy part.

To Clare, he said, "In order to apprehend Decker, I'm going to hole up in Ryan's office. If you're in Mercy, I can't keep you with me. Newcombe has tried to kill you once. If he knows you're there, he'll try again."

"I can stay in your room," Clare suggested. "If the door's locked and the curtains are closed, he'd never even know that I was in town."

The situation was suboptimal, but her plan was decent. He nodded. "Let's get our stuff together and get out of here."

He redressed, putting on his jeans and shirt. Clare got her jeans from where they'd hung this whole time on a hook in the bathroom. She emerged a moment later, rubbing her hands on the front of her legs. "They're still damp, but they'll work."

"Don't forget your bag. Make sure you have the phone and the flash drive."

She picked up her tote bag and looked inside. "I've kept both of those safe for so long, it'd be a pity to lose them now." She looked at Isaac and met his gaze. "Now's not the time, I know. But I like your plan—law enforcement and media. It's better than what I have been doing. Which is basically hide and hope Kyle and his family never find me."

"We'll talk about this later." Maybe once the FBI agents arrived in Mercy, Isaac would take Clare back to San Antonio with him. Hell, he might bring her home for Christmas. He had no right to think about the holidays, or what sort of changes Clare might bring to his life—or he to hers. Not yet.

Not until the job was done.

Both keycards lay on the end table. He grabbed those along with the scant notes from his phone call with Jason. "Let's get out of here."

He pulled the door open. A gust of wind swirled through the room. The first thing Isaac noticed was the sky. It had gone from clear blue to roiling with clouds of gray-green. As every good Texan knew, a sky like that was a problem. "We might not have to worry about Decker showing up. Those are tornado clouds."

"I didn't think it was tornado season," said Clare, raising her voice to be heard over the wind.

"There's no season for anything anymore. Best to get back to Mercy and hunker down." He reached for Clare's hand. She slipped her palm into his and squeezed. Head down and shoulder into the gale, he moved down the walkway to the motel's office. He pulled the door open. The wind jerked it hard from his grasp and it slammed into the wall.

He waited for Clare to enter the building before following and pulling the door shut.

"Quite a night out there," said the desk clerk. "Although it's just wind now, but a storm's coming up from Mexico." A radio sat on a desk and blared the Emergency Broadcasting System's signal. A mechanized voice announced severe weather for the listening area. The clerk watched the radio as the warning played. He turned back to Isaac and Clare. "See?"

"We're getting out of here." He set the room keys on the counter. "Much obliged."

"You sure? It's much too risky to be out on the roads now." He gestured to the radio. "There's likely going to be shelter sirens going pretty soon."

Isaac couldn't leave Ryan to face Decker alone. If they left now and he drove fast, they'd be in Mercy before the worst of the weather hit. "I'm positive. What do I owe you?"

"Nothing. The room was covered by the sheriff's department." Isaac opened the door and the clerk called out, "Merry Christmas."

"Happy holidays," said Clare as they stepped back into the coming storm.

True, downtown Encantador wasn't big. But Isaac had left his truck parked in front of the diner. What had been an easy walk this morning was now treacherous. The street was empty, and all the businesses were closed. A plastic garbage can tumbled down the middle of the road. A streetlight hung above an intersection and swayed drunkenly in the brutal winds.

A fat raindrop hit the sidewalk as a fork of lightning illuminated the sky. A minute later, thunder sounded. Isaac gripped Clare's hand harder. "Can you run?"

She took off sprinting, pulling him along. The rain began to fall harder and faster. They came up next to the truck on the passenger side. He worked the key into the lock and pulled the door open for Clare. She slipped inside and slammed the door shut. Rainwater dripped from Isaac's hair. He wiped his face with a damp hand and moved to the driver's side. Once inside the car, he started the engine and backed out of the parking space.

He didn't know what waited for them in Mercy. And now he had to pray they'd make it there.

Kyle Chamberlain pulled into an empty parking spot at the Saddle Up Inn as the dark gray sky turned black. Pulling the phone from his pocket, he sent his father a one-word text. Here.

It had been a horrendous day of travel. Booking his flight from John Glenn International last minute, meant he had fly coach the whole way. From Ohio he made it to San Antonio in under five hours—even with a plane change in Atlanta. Once in Texas, he'd rented a car. While driving to Encantador, he'd fought deteriorating weather the whole way.

After turning off the engine, he stepped into the parking lot. His hands were sore. His knees ached. His head hurt and he could use a drink. The wind blew and a cold rain fell, a rivulet snaking down his back.

He ran for the office and pulled the door open.

A man with a round face and glasses to match stood behind the counter. "Good evening. You need a room?" he asked Kyle. "You're in luck. A couple just left."

What Kyle needed was information. He opened his phone and found a photo of Clare. He looked at her picture, his chest tightening with emotion. "I'm looking for my wife. Have you seen her?"

The man leaned forward to get a closer look at the phone. He sniffed. "I really can't talk about our guests."

I'll take that as a yes. "I'm sure you're very good at your job." He shoved the phone into his pocket and removed a wad of bills he kept secured with a money clip. Kyle peeled off $300. "It's important that I talk to my wife." He held up his hands like he was surrendering—it was just a happy coincidence that the man could see the money. "Her father had a heart attack," Kyle lied. Clare's dad had been gone for years. "I knew Clare would be here and it's important to me that I tell her myself."

"Well." The man put a book on the counter.

Was Kyle supposed to slip the money under the book? He shrugged and placed the cash under the novel.

"She's not here anymore, but you missed her by less than fifteen minutes."

Damn. "Where was she headed?"

"That I don't know."

But there was something else the man had said. *A couple just left.* Was Clare with another man? Kyle ground his back teeth together. Not only had his wife left him, but she was with a guy. Sure, he'd been upset before but now, he was furious.

He turned from the desk and walked across the small lobby. He jerked the door open.

"Merry Christmas," the clerk called after Kyle.

"Yeah, yeah. Merry freaking Christmas to you, too."

He ran through the deluge to his car and pulled open the door. He slid inside and cursed. What was he supposed to tell his father now? That not only had Clare stolen vital information about the company, but she had already had sex with some other guy?

He slammed his palm onto the steering wheel. Pain radiated from the heel of his hand and into his wrist. According to the desk clerk, he'd only missed her by minutes, but those minutes were valuable. By now, Clare could be in a hundred different places.

Or could she?

It wasn't like there were highways and roads all over the place. In truth, Clare could have gone anywhere but he doubted that she'd go far with the weather getting worse by the second.

He took out his phone. After opening a mapping app, he looked for towns within fifty miles. He counted seven, with the closest being a hamlet called Mercy— only thirty miles away.

It made sense to start his search in Mercy. Once he found his ex-wife, he'd convince her to come back to Columbus and let life be good—like it was before she found the damn memos. He'd talk nice to her and convince her of his love. He'd have to convince his father that Clare was loyal to the Chamberlain name—and it might mean cleaning up the contaminated soil without involving the government. But Kyle was sure that both his father and Clare would come around.

Unless Clare really was with another guy—and then, there'd be hell for her to pay.

Decker Newcombe found a secluded spot off the road that gave him a complete view of Mercy. The wind buffeted the truck, rocking it from side to side. Rain fell in sheets. Yet, from his vantage point, he could see everything. The plan was simple—find Ryan. Get the money. But one lesson he'd learned from the hit in Pleasant Pines was that even the simplest plans could get jacked up. Best to watch and wait. Settling back against the seat, Decker knew that it was going to be a long night.

Old Blue lifted a paw. A box of dog biscuits that Decker'd found behind the truck's bench seats sat between Decker's knees.

"You hungry, boy?" He held up a biscuit and the dog whined and nosed the treat but didn't take it. Decker set it on the seat and the dog gobbled up the food.

Another thing he had found stowed behind the seat was a set of binoculars. He held those as well and brought them to his eyes. Decker scanned the parking lot between the motel and the bar. Only a few cars were parked near the lot, which suited him just fine. The fewer people around meant fewer variables.

A set of headlights cut through the storm and Decker watched as a truck pulled into the lot. From the shadows in the truck, he could tell there was a driver and a passenger. They parked not by the bar but the motel. He lifted the binoculars to his eyes again. A man opened the driver's door and jumped from the truck.

Pulling the ocular from his eyes, Decker looked again.

He knew the guy. It was the man from Encantador with the gun—he was the one who stopped Decker from killing the woman. That must mean...

He turned his attention to the passenger side and watched as the blonde exited the truck. With a bag held tight to her chest, she ran to the motel's overhang. There, she smoothed her sodden hair from her face and spoke to the man. She pointed to a room but walked to another. The man produced a key and opened the door.

The woman stepped inside, and the man followed.

"Old Blue, looks like were in luck."

True, the man was most likely a cop—and if the cops were in Mercy, then Decker wouldn't get his cash. But in Encantador, he'd had no choice but to let the blonde woman go. She was unfinished business—and Decker hated unfinished business.

Now, though, he had a second chance. And this time, he'd take care of the blonde—for good.

The money could wait.

Isaac's room was the same exact size as the one where Clare had stayed the previous night. Yet, the dimensions were where the similarities ended. For starters, Isaac's room wasn't furnished like a hotel. And she was thankful that Isaac's living conditions were a little more, well, livable.

An unmade bed sat against the far wall. Next to it was a dresser. A recliner was tucked into the corner near the air-conditioning unit. Next to both was a metal footlocker that doubled as a table with a lamp. In the opposite corner sat a kitchen cart with a microwave and a coffee maker. A small refrigerator—the kind Clare had used in her college dorm room all those years ago—was beside the cart.

"It's cozy," she said, sitting in the chair. "I like it."

"I hate to just leave you here, but I need to let Ryan know that I'm back and that no reinforcements will show up tonight."

Lines of worry creased the corner of Isaac's eyes. She could guess what was bothering him. Without the FBI's help, the people of Mercy were on their own. "Don't worry, I know the plan. I stay put in the room. You'll go to the bar and watch from the office."

"Correct," said Isaac. "I want to do a little more research on Decker, too. See if there's something in his file linking him to Jack the Ripper that I might have overlooked before." He opened the footlocker and removed a sleek metallic laptop.

"You wouldn't happen to have another of those, would you?" she asked. "When I worked for the EPA, I wrote a few press releases. Since the media is where we'll start, I should…well, get started."

The lid to the footlocker was still open. "I don't have another laptop, but I have a tablet computer. It has a word-processing program." He rummaged through the trunk for a moment and then handed the device to Clare. "It should have a full charge."

Clare wasn't sure how to act in this situation. Part of her wanted to bawl and beg that Isaac stay with her. The other part—she supposed that independent streak that always wanted to do things on her own—wanted to remain calm. Yet, it would be stupid to be casual about a man as dangerous and deadly as Decker. "One more thing," she said, her mouth suddenly dry. "Do you have a gun I can keep with me?"

Isaac said nothing. Yet, from the trunk he removed a black metal safe with a fingerprint scanner. Isaac placed his thumb on the pad and the lock clicked open. "This isn't the same model we used earlier today, but the concept is the same."

"All guns are always loaded," she said, paraphrasing Isaac's first rule of firearm safety. "Put the sight over the target—which is the center mass. Pull the trigger. Shoot."

"And…" he encouraged.

"And never take a gun out unless you plan to use it."

"Correct." He set the gun on the nightstand. "You have your phone, right? There's no landline in this place, but if you need me, call. That is, if you can get a signal in this weather. I'll be at the bar and can get to you in seconds." He paused. "Are you sure that you're okay with this? I can stay here. Ryan can wait with us."

The offer of company was tempting.

She lifted the computer. "I've got a project. That'll help keep my mind off what happened. Besides, once the storm passes, it won't take long for the FBI to get here, right? I only need to wait a few hours." Then again, she knew that it took only seconds to change a life forever.

Isaac slipped the laptop into a backpack, also stored in the footlocker.

"What all do you keep in there?" she asked, half joking, half curious. "So far, there's been a laptop, a tablet, a gun and now a backpack."

"Let's just say this is my whole office in a box. I have lots of goodies. I'll show you—"

"Tomorrow. I will be fine, honestly."

"Honestly?"

After everything that had happened today, she suspected that she wouldn't actually be *fine* for a long while. Still, she said, "Now go."

"Do you need anything else?" He pointed to the kitchen area. "There's food. Water. Beer and juice in the fridge."

"I'll help myself if I get hungry." But did she need anything? Her suitcase was still in Trinity's room. Right now, Clare would love to get out of her clothes and change into something more comfortable. She was supposed to stay in the room and hidden, but surely she could walk down three doors and get her stuff.

"But…"

"But, what? I didn't say but?"

"I can see it on your face. You want to ask for something, so ask."

"My suitcase is in the other room," she began.

Isaac held out his palm. "Give me the key. I won't be gone for a minute."

She found the key and her cell phone in her tote. After handing the key to Isaac, she set the phone next to the handgun. As her fingertips grazed his palm, her hand filled with that same electric energy. It traveled up her arm and around to her chest until her heart skipped a beat. Yet, this time it was different. She now knew what his lips felt like on hers. She'd touch him and been touched by him in return. She knew that he fit inside her perfectly and that he gave a primal growl the moment he came. It was more than the raw sexuality of their coupling. Or even that Clare had come to Mercy lonely and alone. In Isaac, she'd found someone she could trust.

Clare had stood far too long while holding on to the key. She withdrew her hand. "Thanks."

"Lock the dead bolt and the chain when I leave. Don't open it for anyone but me."

"Got it." Clare stood by the door and held the handle as Isaac stepped out into the rain. She closed and locked the door. Her chest tightened and she could barely draw a breath. Pressing her forehead into the door, she forced an inhale. One, two, three. Exhale. One, two, three. On her tenth round of breathing, there was a rapping sound on the door.

"It's me. Let me in."

She recognized Isaac's voice. Her fingers trembled as she fought with the chain lock. "Just a second." Once that was free, she unlocked the dead bolt and pulled the door open.

He wheeled her suitcase into the room. "Here you go. Can you hand me my backpack?"

She maneuvered the suitcase into the room and moved onto the bed, where she picked up Isaac's computer bag. She held it out to him, and he took it from her hand.

Isaac stood at the door. Behind him, wind blew the rain sideways. Lightning flashed, illuminating an empty parking lot. He pulled her to him, placing his lips on hers. "Take care of yourself, Clare," he said, speaking into the kiss.

"You, too."

She locked the door behind him and then watched through a crack in the curtain as Isaac ran to his truck. There, he removed his gun from the glove box. He slipped it into the waistband at the back of his jeans and then sprinted into the rain. She stayed at the curtain and watched as his form blended with the darkness, realizing that she felt more for Isaac than simple lust. She liked his company. He was a good man who always did the right thing.

Had she come to care for him?

Then again, she shouldn't torture herself with wanting a relationship, especially since she had problems beyond Decker Newcombe. And he was a problem enough. If she took Isaac's advice, she was about to go to war with her former husband and his family. Even though the Chamberlains weren't as bloody as Decker, they were no less brutal and dangerous.

She had to get ready for the battle to come.

Chapter 17

Kyle stood at the gas pump and seethed. Across the road was a rattrap of a motel. Despite the storm, he'd seen it all so clearly. Clare stood at the door to a room and kissed another man. The guy had run to the bar, leaving her alone. After paying for his gas, he drove across the street and parked. Oblivious of the rain, he strode to the door and knocked.

"Clare? You in there? It's me. Kyle."

There was a window next to the door. He waited and watched. The curtains twitched. She'd peeked out and seen him.

He waited a minute. Then a minute more.

"Clare?"

Nothing. Not a sound. Kyle reached for the knob. It was stuck. He jiggled the handle. He tried to keep his temper in check, but he could feel the heat rising from his middle. Despite the cold rain, he started to perspire. Her new friend couldn't buy her all the things that Kyle could afford. So, what was she doing with some oaf who probably smelled like chewing tobacco and motor oil?

Slamming his palm on the door, he spit, "Open the damn door, right this freaking minute."

Nothing, still.

Well, Kyle refused to be ignored. He was going to get into that room one way or another—and then, he'd make Clare sorry.

There were no customers at the House of Steele. The weather kept everyone at home, even though the bar, tattoo parlor and motel were made of cinderblock and would withstand high winds and blowing debris. In truth, Isaac would have preferred a packed house to an empty room. With witnesses, Decker would have to be cautious. Without anyone around, Isaac would be forced to face the killer alone.

No, that wasn't necessarily true. He had Ryan and Clare.

Having people who he could rely on was a forgotten notion. For so long, he'd wanted to be a loner. But now? Well, he couldn't worry about now—not when the killer was still out there, somewhere.

At the moment, Isaac and Ryan were in Ryan's office at the back of the bar. And office was a generous term for the converted closet where the legitimate businesses were run. A filing cabinet sat in the back corner. In the middle of the room was a desk, along with a computer. The monitor was on. The screen was filled with four different pictures from security cameras. The bar's front door, exterior and interior. There was also a camera above the entrance to the tattoo parlor and one that gave a panoramic view of the parking lot. It was difficult to see anything other than rain, but if someone approached the building, they'd have time to react.

The light from a single lamp illuminated a pool in the middle of the desk. The rest of the room was shrouded in shadows. Isaac's gun was still tucked into the back of his jeans. Ryan held a shotgun, taken from behind the bar, across his lap.

Isaac's laptop was also on the desk and was connecting to the internet.

"You came back," said Ryan. From his mocking tone, he could tell that a joke was on the horizon. "You miss me?"

He'd already given the other man a rundown of the most recent events—including the hard truth that reinforcements couldn't get to Mercy. He also told him of the possible connection between Decker's most recent murders and Jack the Ripper. Instead of repeating the facts, he said, "Yeah, I missed you." And then, "You've known Decker for a long time. You ever notice a fascination with Jack the Ripper?"

"The only person who fascinates Decker is Decker."

The computer finally connected with the internet and Isaac was able to access his remote server for Texas Law. Isaac entered the secure site. "I get updates if anything's added to Decker's file. There hasn't been much recently, but let's start there. We might find something that was missed before."

Decker's mug shot was pinned to the top of an electronic document. It listed the crimes for which he'd been charged, and any time served. Isaac couldn't see anything in his criminal past that connected him to the Victorian era serial killer.

"You know Decker better than anyone," said Isaac. "When he attacked Clare in the restaurant, he said *being a killer is in my blood. First, there was the Old Jack. It's why I killed the redhead, too.* That mean anything to you?"

Ryan scratched the stubble on his chin. "When he called the other night, he asked if I knew anything about DNA testing. It made no sense to me then, but maybe there's a genetic predisposition to violence."

"You two grew up together. What were his parents like?"

"For a while, we lived near each other. We were kids and the same age, so we played together. As far as his parents…" Ryan shook his head. "His mom worked odd jobs to make ends meet. She had a tendency to get involved with guys who got violent with her and with Decker. I never met his real dad."

Isaac continued to scan through the file. He stopped. A new document had been attached. He only had a moment to wonder why there'd been no notification. Then again, it wasn't really an update to the case and therefore hadn't been flagged. *DNA Analysis, Newcombe, Decker.*

Ryan was reading the screen, too. "What the hell?"

Hell might be right. He clicked the link. It was a DNA profile, much like those done for a genealogy service. It listed places where genetic makeup originated, along with a list of ancestors. One name, Jeremiah Newcombe, was highlighted and an additional notation was attached. *Genetic link to sociopathy?*

Ryan already had out his phone. "This answers the question as to why Decker's become a copycat killer." He'd done his own internet search for the name Jeremiah Newcombe. The first hit came from an article published several years prior. *Identity of Jack the Ripper discovered through DNA.* "I wonder how he found out. Do you think he hacked into a computer system, or does he have a mole in Wyoming who's feeding him information?"

Both were interesting scenarios. But in reality, the *how* didn't matter nearly as much as the *why*. Decker was undoubtedly still out there. It was only a matter of time before he killed again—unless Isaac found him first and brought the murderer to justice.

Clare looked at the dark screen on her phone, not sure if she wanted to curse or cry. She'd left the device on with the internet connected for hours. Now there was no battery left and she couldn't call Isaac.

Outside, Kyle slammed his fist against the door. The frame rattled. "I saw you with him, you know. I saw you kiss that guy."

She found the charger in her bag and plugged in the phone. The screen winked to life. A message, gray words on a gray screen, appeared.

No service available.

"Come on," she urged the phone.

Kyle's voice came from the window. "Is that why you ran off, Clare. To be with that bastard? I loved you. I still do."

Clare might not know everything about love, but she did know that whatever possessiveness Kyle felt for her was the opposite of caring. She couldn't help but speak up after that baseless accusation. "You know why I left. I heard you on the phone with your father while talking about the little *accident* you two were planning for me."

"And to think, I came all this way to try and work things out with you." He gave a mirthless laugh. "My dad was right about you from the beginning. You are more trouble than you're worth."

"Why'd you track me down, then? You didn't need to come and find me."

Her words were followed by the crack of lightning and rumble of thunder. Was Kyle thinking about what she'd said? Had he left? She wanted to look outside— just to see where he'd gone. She moved slowly to the window and reached for the curtain. She pulled it away from the wall at the same moment the glass shattered. A brick skittered across the floor, bouncing off the footlocker.

Kyle shoved his hand through the broken pane, reaching for Clare. She dove toward the nightstand and snatched up the gun. She turned back to the window as Kyle pulled back the curtains. A long gash was open on the back of his hand, and it dripped blood onto the sill.

Clare remembered her brief shooting lessons. Isaac's words came back to her. If you take out a firearm, it's because you plan to *eliminate a threat. Aim for the center mass.* She lined up the sights with Kyle's chest.

"Get back in your car, Kyle, and go. I'm not leaving with you now or ever."

"That's where you're wrong," he began, lifting his foot to climb in through the broken window.

She fired once, striking the wall next to his head. "That's your warning. Come any closer and the next bullet will go through you."

His eyes went wide. "You wouldn't dare," he said, perching himself on the sill.

She fired again. A bullet struck Kyle in the shoulder. The impact shoved him back. With a curse, he tumbled out onto the sidewalk. Clare rushed for the window.

On the ground, her ex-husband held an arm across his abdomen and wheezed. "Christ! You shot me. You really shot me! Damn. I'm bleeding."

Her hand began to tremble. Yet, she pointed the barrel to the floor—just like Isaac had that morning. For a moment, Clare's ears buzzed and her eyesight went blurry. She blinked hard and forced herself to focus.

A large man in a hunter's cap lumbered across the parking lot. The rain fell and he seemed to materialize from the water. "I seen it all," he shouted to be heard above the wind. "I saw him break that window and you shoot." He had a phone in his hand. "I'll call 9-1-1."

Clare moved closer to the window. Without the pane, wind and rain blew into the room. "Go to the bar. Tell Isaac to come here." Lighting danced along the horizon.

The man placed a finger to his ear. "What'd you say? I'm hard of hearing. Speak up."

A rumble of thunder filled the night. She moved closer, leaning toward the man. "Go to the bar. Tell Isaac to come here."

It was then that he struck. Reaching for her arm, the

man pulled Clare through the window. A shard of glass caught her arm and she cried out in pain and anger.

Wrenching back, she held the gun by her free hand and lifted her arm. The man gripped the gun's barrel and flipped the firearm to face Clare.

"Who are you?" she asked, but she saw his eyes and knew.

"Miss me much?" he asked.

Before she could answer or even scream, he brought the butt end of the gun down on her head. For a minute, Clare saw nothing other than a blinding flash of white. The darkness encroached from all sides. She slipped down, down, down into oblivion.

Isaac looked up from his laptop and stared at Ryan. "Was that gunfire?"

Ryan was looking at the computer monitor and the stream coming from the safety cameras. "Three thunderclaps in a row? Unlikely. But I don't see anything." He tapped on the keyboard and brought up another set of cameras. There, on the feed from the front of the motel, was a big guy standing outside of Isaac's room. On the ground was a body. The guy lifted a gun. The picture was grainy, but there was enough detail for Isaac to know—the guy on the ground had been shot. His body went limp, and a pool of blood spread from behind his head.

Isaac was on his feet and sprinting from the office and across the empty bar before he even realized that he'd moved. He ran into the night in time to see a set of taillights swerving out of the parking lot and onto the road. It skidded on the wet pavement and disappeared, as if swallowed by the storm.

He kept running and slid to a stop on the sidewalk next to his room. The person who'd been shot was male. Isaac had never seen him before. There was a bullet wound to his shoulder and another through the center of his forehead. The curtains from Isaac's room billowed, blown by the wind. The glass pane was broken.

And Clare was missing.

The door was still closed and locked. At the window, he grabbed a handful of fabric and pulled the curtains and the rod out of the wall. The room was empty. He turned to the road. The car that had sped away was long gone.

Ryan, shotgun held tight to his chest, ran through the rain. "I saw it all on the camera." After placing the gun on the ground, muzzle pointed toward the parking lot, he knelt next to the body. In the dead guy's pocket, he found a wallet. "His name is Kyle Chamberlain from Columbus, Ohio." He looked up at Isaac. "He must be related to Clare."

How Kyle had found Clare was definitely a mystery. But the one he wanted to solve was where she'd gone. Ryan continued, "The big guy climbed in through the window and got Clare. She wasn't moving, but I don't know if she's dead or not."

Isaac threw a curtain panel over Clare's ex. Eventually, he'd call the sheriff and let him know about the homicide. "He's changed his look again, but we both know who took Clare." His throat was raw with terror and dread.

Ryan stood. "You think it's Decker?"

"You don't?" Isaac fished his keys from his pocket. "I'm going to get her back. You can come if you want. Or stay and call the cops. Tell them everything we know."

Reaching for his shotgun, Ryan stood. "You gotta be kidding me. I'm coming with."

Isaac held out the keys. "Start my truck. I need something from my room."

He hated wasting precious time in the search for Clare. But without his equipment, he'd never find her. Climbing through the broken window, he opened his footlocker. It really was what he'd told Clare—his workplace in a box. Instead of office equipment—printers, monitors and pens—Isaac had a sleek black drone that was controlled by an app on his phone. He also had a Smith and Wesson 500, along with an entire box of ammo.

He grabbed two bulletproof vests and a pair of dark jackets. Not bothering with the window, he unlatched each of the door's locks and walked to his truck. Ryan sat in the passenger seat, and he opened the door as he approached. "What's that?"

Isaac handed over the gear. Wiping the rain from his face, he jogged around the grille to the driver's side.

He backed out of the parking lot and followed the truck. His wipers moved back and forth across the windshield at top speed, but it did little to keep the rain off the glass. "That is a military-grade drone." He continued, "This can go twenty miles per hour and is whisper-silent. Two cameras—one in the front and one in the rear. It has a range of ten miles and a battery life of ninety minutes." He started the dual propellers and the drone lifted from the back of the truck. "It sends back pictures in real time to my phone." He held out the screen for Ryan to see.

"I changed my mind," said Ryan. "I don't want a gaming system for Christmas—I want that."

Isaac wasn't in the mood for jokes.

"How're we going to find Decker? For the drone to be effective, we have to be close to our target."

"We'll be close." He shared what Jason had said about Decker's possible safe house being eight miles from where they'd discovered the phone. He ignored the aching in his chest and the gritty burning in his eyes. "Well find Clare and bring Decker to justice in the process."

Yet, his words weren't entirely true. Isaac wasn't interested in cold and impartial justice anymore. What he was looking for was closer to vengeance. Decker had harmed the woman he loved more than once—now it was personal.

He tightened his grip on the steering wheel. Did he really love Clare?

Maybe he did. All he could do now is hope that he found her before it was too late to tell her.

Clare's eyes were still closed and yet her head throbbed with each beat of her heart. Her arms and legs were stiff and sore. Then, she recalled those harrowing seconds outside of Isaac's room and the terror came back. Her heart began to hammer against her chest and Clare struggled to sit up.

That's when she realized that she was bound—wrist and ankle—to something hard. A table?

"Oh, you're awake."

Clare looked to the left. Decker stood next to a shelf and smiled. His cheerful tone and friendly manner made her shiver.

"What do you want?" Her tongue was thick.

"You seem like a smart woman. I'm sure you've figured it out."

She had. "You're going to kill me. But why?" She bit back a sob. Clare refused to let this animal break her will.

Her arms and legs were tied to a table with worn rope. They were in a small room. A single electric bulb hung from a wire. Behind Decker was a counter. Upon the counter were several knives. Clare swallowed.

"There's more to your death than just murder." Decker picked up a knife. The razor-sharp edge glinted in the weak light. "Killing you will link my name with the most famous serial killer of all time. But I won't hide behind a pseudonym like he did."

Is that what motivated him? "So you're doing this for what? Fame? You want notoriety?"

Decker chuckled. "Fame is fleeting. I plan to be a legend. In a way, you're lucky. People will remember your name, too. So, I gotta ask you, Clare, are you ready for your death to make you immortal?"

Isaac drove through the storm to the exact place that he and Ryan had found Decker's phone. He parked on the side of the road.

"I'm going to call Jason once more." So far, his cell service had been disrupted by the storm. He placed the call. Immediately, three tones sounded. He didn't wait for the recorded voice to tell him that his call could not go through. He cursed and shoved his phone into his jacket pocket.

"Grab that drone," he said to Ryan. For the ride, it'd been stored on the passenger floorboard. "And come with me." He stepped out into the storm. Cold rain soaked his clothes and left his fingers stiff.

Carrying the drone, Ryan followed Isaac onto the empty road.

Black as a midnight sky, the drone was equipped with four rotors and two cameras. Isaac explained how the device worked. "It's controlled with an app on my phone." He continued, giving voice to his plan, "With the wind and the rain, these are crap conditions. But we'll send this bad boy up and see what we can. Best luck, we find the safe house. Worst luck, it gets blown to the ground and we find nothing." Which would mean that Isaac had no way to locate Clare.

After setting the unmanned craft on the asphalt, he opened the app. He tapped on the phone's screen and the propellers began to spin, their rotations a continual blur. Isaac entered the command and the device shot into the sky. After a few seconds, it blended with the endless sea of night.

The phone's screen was filled with an aerial picture taken in night-mode. Right now, there was nothing to see but rain and the ever-changing horizon as the drone fought against the wind to stay level. They went back to the truck and slid inside. Isaac adjusted the heat to the inferno setting and held out his phone so Ryan could watch the drone's progress.

Like many of his ideas, this one had been bold, brash, and there wasn't a guarantee of success. It's just that his resources were limited, and time was essential. Because if they didn't find Clare soon, she might not be alive for much longer.

"Wait," said Ryan, pointing at the screen. "Can you go back? I think I saw something."

"What?" Isaac reversed the drone's path midflight.

"It was a line. It looked like a fence."

From thirty feet above the ground, the fence did look like a black line had been drawn across the landscape. "Good catch," said Isaac. "Let's see where this leads. Left or right?"

"Right," said Ryan.

Isaac flew the drone along the fencing another quarter mile until they spotted a gate, and beyond that a road. He followed the road and found a small house sitting on a bluff. Next to the shack was a generator. A pickup truck was parked next to the door—it was the same one from the footage taken at the House of Steele.

Isaac exhaled a breath that he didn't know he'd been holding. Despite the odds, they'd found Decker's safe house. "Now," he said, "Let's go save Clare."

Chapter 18

Isaac was not a praying kind of guy. Still, he thanked whatever deity controlled the weather. Near the safe house, the storm was lessening. The rain still fell in a sheet, but the wind had calmed. From his truck, he was able to control the drone and survey the house.

There was a rickety front door with a cylinder lock. The rest of the wall was adobe. At the back of the house, there was a window with a cracked and dirty pane. The room beyond was dark, yet the camera captured the interior, along with a dirty mattress covered with blankets and lumpy pillows. At the edge of the house, the drone rounded another corner and passed the right wall. There were no windows. No doors.

On the final wall, there was a single window. Isaac maneuvered the camera to get a view inside and his hands began to shake with cold fury.

Clare was strapped to a table. Sure, he was thankful to see that she was alive. But that relief only lasted for a few seconds. Beside her, a small counter was cluttered with knives. Decker stood next to her, a blade in his hand.

"I've seen enough," said Isaac, his voice tight.

Ryan was right beside Isaac. "What's the plan?"

He hated that they couldn't drive right to the door. But if Decker heard an auto approaching, he'd kill Clare. "We get in close to the house. I take the front door. You cover the back of the house." Isaac put the truck into Drive. "And then, I finish this—even if it means finishing Decker Newcombe."

Sure, it was tough talk. But Isaac couldn't help but wonder if his plan would be enough to save Clare.

Clare stared at the knife in Decker's hand. Her limbs went rigid with fear. For the past two months, she'd had little to live for. But when she met Isaac, all of that changed. He'd offered her help and despite herself, she'd accepted. She'd finally found a potential way out of the danger that had sent her on the run from her life and everything, everyone in it.

Sure, she always wanted to be strong and independent. Yet with Isaac, she'd learned what it was to be a partner with another, rather than just dependent. She wanted to see him again and tell him that even though they hadn't known each other a long time, he'd brought her from the edges of existence and back to the possibility of living a real life.

So, she couldn't just lay on the table and die. Thrashing, she strained against her bindings and hoped the ropes would break. It was no use.

Or was it? She pulled her left arm, her muscles straining, her joints aching. Then she went limp. The rope had stretched but not enough. She needed time and that meant she had to keep Decker talking. What was she supposed to say, since she knew next to nothing about the man… Wait. That wasn't true.

Clare understood Decker's motivations.

She began. "The last time I was in London, I went on a Ripper Tour, you know."

The knife in his hand wobbled. "A what?"

"That's what they're called. Ripper Tours. A guide leads a group through London to visit all the places associated with Jack the Ripper." She developed a rhythm. Pull. Release. Pull. Release. The old rope gave a little with each motion. Clare twisted her wrist and tried to work out of the knot.

Decker regarded her for a moment, and she froze.

He asked, "What did you see?"

Her pulse raced and sweat snaked down her back. "What did I see where?"

He sighed. "On the tour. What places did you visit?"

She began to work her arm back and forth again, the movements smaller this time. "They go to all the places where the victims were found. I mean, the crimes took place more than a century ago, so every place is something different now. One of the crime scenes has been turned into a parking lot." Pull. Release. Pull. Release. "Kind of a letdown."

Decker stared at her. His blue eyes had turned black.

For the first time in her life, Clare knew what it felt like to look at pure evil. "Do you think," he began, "that one hundred years from now, people will visit this run-down old shack? Will they come to look at the place where you died?"

Isaac and Ryan made good time. Light from the house leaked out from beneath the door and made it visible from over a hundred yards away. Without a word, they donned the body armor and black jackets. Blending with the night, they approached the shack.

Then, Isaac heard a dog barking and froze.

Ryan heard it, too. Both men dropped into the mud.

"What the hell was that?" Ryan whispered. "He's got a dog now? Since when is he an animal lover?"

Isaac listened to the sound carefully. "Sounded like it came from the house."

Ryan turned to Isaac. "But that's impossible."

The barking started again, louder this time and more insistent.

Isaac didn't pretend to know anything about serial killers, but he knew a lot about Decker Newcombe. "He doesn't seem like the kind to keep a dog."

Ryan whispered, "He's not." Pause. "Is it a wild dog?"

Isaac shrugged. Maybe it was or maybe it wasn't. Then again, who cared? "All I know is that the dog has ruined the element of surprise and..."

"And what?"

"And we can't wait any longer. If we're going to get to Clare in time, we have to get in there right goddamn *now*."

* * *

To prevent Old Blue from being underfoot as he worked, Decker had put the dog in the bedroom and closed the door. If truth be told, he had wondered more than once if he'd been prudent to save the dog's life.

Yet, as Old Blue barked and scratched and howled, he knew he'd been right to take the canine in.

"Someone's outside." He stared at the door. *Who the hell could have found this place?*

Looking at Clare, he ran the knife down her lips, grinning as her eyes grew even wider in fear. "Not. One. Word." He couldn't imagine who'd hear her in the storm—or who was even out there in this weather—but he wasn't taking any chances.

Moving to the window, he peered into the darkness. It was hard to see anything through the constant rain. Yet, the dog continued to bellow.

For the first time in years, Decker felt exposed. His skin crawled as if a thousand ants covered his body. He'd learned to trust his instincts and his gut told him there was something wrong.

Could the feds have located him? After all this time? But how? He'd been so careful, even after killing that woman in Mercy. Still…something didn't feel right…

He slowly moved to the door. Turning the handle, he pulled it open. There was nothing to see—beyond the night and the continual rain. Then, a flash of light. A blaze of fire. And pain that stole his breath as the shape of a man bore down on him.

With Decker's back to the table, Clare struggled to break free, even as the dog's barking became more frenzied. *Where in the hell had a dog come from?* Finally, she pulled her wrist from the rope. Flipping to her side, she started working on the other knot, glancing back at the door, when the gunshot rang out.

It was like a thunderclap had exploded in the small room. Decker spun in a drunken circle, as a red blood-stain bloomed on his chest and shoulder. He fell to his back and stared at nothing.

Isaac rushed through the door, covered in mud as Clare struggled to pull her hand from the rope. Smoke wafted from the barrel of the gun in his hand. Her eyes watered in relief that they were both safe. She was overwhelmed with another feeling as well. It was a deeper emotion, more personal, and wholly connected to Isaac.

"You came! How did you even find me?"

"I did. Now, let's get you out of here." Grabbing one of the knives from the counter, Isaac cut through the ropes at Clare's ankles.

Ryan followed Isaac into the room. He was covered in mud as well. Decker lay on the floor, as a pool of blood spread across the floor.

She wondered if Decker was finally dead. The notion left her lightheaded with disbelief, after everything they'd been through. Ryan bent to Decker's prone form. He grabbed the killer's wrist—presumably to feel for a pulse.

Which was when everything went to hell.

For Isaac, the struggle erupted in slow motion. Decker must've been waiting for just the right moment to jump, and when Ryan reached for his wrist, the killer rolled to his side, knife in hand. Yanking Ryan to the floor, the two men struggled as blood and mud flew everywhere.

Isaac rushed forward as the dog began to howl, the sound taking on a hollow quality as if they were all lost in a cave. Ryan screamed in agony as Decker swung the blade into his side up and under the body armor. The handle protruded haphazardly.

Then, Decker rose to his feet and staggered into the night.

Isaac fell to the floor beside Ryan, who was clearly in agonizing pain. But Ryan gritted his teeth and held onto the wall for support, trying not to pass out. "I'll be fine. Just catch Decker, dammit. Don't let him get away after all this!"

Clare was at Ryan's side. "I'll stay with him."

Ryan grimaced, "We'll keep trying to get a hold of Jason."

He gave a terse nod and ran into the storm. Earlier, he'd set the drone down next to the house. Thankfully, it was still there. Pulling his phone from his pocket, he turned on the rotors. Rain still fell, but the wind no longer blew. The device lifted straight into the air. With the cameras on, he watched and searched for signs of Decker.

He found him within minutes.

The hitman staggered across the uneven ground, less than a quarter mile from the house. Water dripped from his hair, but the rain wasn't enough to wash away the blood that was coming from his chest. Isaac watched as Decker stumbled to the ground. He never got up. He wasn't sure if his truck would make it over the uneven terrain. The last thing he wanted was to break down.

Isaac had no choice but to go after the hitman on foot. He sprinted into the desert. Within minutes, Isaac was soaked with rain and sweat both. He found the spot where Decker had fallen. Yet, the hitman was gone.

Clare found little in the small shack that was helpful. As she'd guessed, a dog was locked in the bedroom. It shied away from Clare when she opened the door, but eventually came to stand at her side as she rifled through Decker's room.

There was a dirty blanket, which she used to stanch the bleeding, and a pillow, which she placed behind Ryan's back.

"Is that better?" she asked as he settled against the pillow. She knew enough to leave the knife alone. Once it was removed, he'd start to bleed again.

"A little," he grimaced. "Thanks." The dog stood in the doorway that separated the main room from the bedroom. "How'd Decker end up with a dog, do you think?"

She had no idea and simply shook her head. "We should call someone. Sheriff Cafferty, maybe? Or the feds that Isaac's been working with."

"The feds are stuck in San Antonio with the storm." He held out his phone. "Encantador isn't too far away. Call the sheriff."

Clare found the contact information and placed the call. "This is Clare Chamberlain," she began as Mooky answered the phone. "There's been an incident…"

As she spoke, Ryan patted the floor. "Come here, boy." Head down, the dog ambled to Ryan's side and lay down.

Having given the sheriff all the pertinent information, she ended the call. Turning to Ryan, she said, "I think the dog likes you."

He scratched the dog's ears. "I've always wanted a dog."

Ryan's shotgun stood against the wall. She picked it up and cradled it against her chest.

"You know how to use one of those things?" he asked.

Not really, but she said, "Isaac taught me how to shoot a handgun."

"Well, careful with that thing. It has a nasty kick when it's fired."

She took note of his warning. "If Decker comes back, I'll be ready."

It wasn't Decker who returned to the shack, but after some time, the sheriff arrived, leading a long line of county vehicles with sirens and lights.

Clare met them outside. The rain still fell, and the wind still blew. But the worst of the storm was over.

Cafferty's cruiser was the first to stop near the door. "Christ almighty," he said getting out of his car. "You either have the best or worst luck in the world to tangle with that son of a bitch twice."

A pair of EMTs rushed past Clare and into the shack. The rain from before had lessened and now the sky only spit drizzle. She watched for a moment as Ryan began to get treatment for the knife that was still stuck in his side.

"Decker kidnapped me from Mercy and brought me here. He was shot and I thought he was dead."

"But he wasn't."

"He stabbed Ryan and ran into the storm. Isaac is trying to find him." A hard kernel of worry clogged her throat. She had no idea if he'd found Decker, where he'd gone or even if he was okay.

As the storm lessened, Isaac deployed the drone for a second time. After searching, he had to admit that the killer had disappeared once again. What's more, he'd used the unmanned aircraft to view the safe house. On the app, he'd seen over a dozen different emergency vehicles at the shack. There were cars from both the sheriff's office, the highway patrol and the Mexican police—the Federales. With all those reinforcements, Decker was as sure as found—or so he had to believe.

He jogged back to the shack with the drone under his arm. He arrived as Ryan was being taken from the small house. Strapped to a gurney, an oxygen mask covered his face. As Isaac approached, he lowered the mask. "You find him?"

Isaac hated to admit the truth. "No."

"He won't get far—not this time." And then, "I need a favor. The dog needs someone to get it home. Old Blue's address is on his collar's tag."

"Sure, I'll take care of him."

"Thanks, man. I don't want to see him left on his own." He let out a pained, shuddering breath. "I appreciate everything, man. Thanks."

For the first time, he liked hearing Ryan saying those words.

An EMT placed the oxygen mask over Ryan's nose and mouth. "You have to keep the mask on, sir."

Ryan gave a thumbs-up as he was lifted into the back of the waiting ambulance. Once the doors were closed, they drove away. Isaac set the drone on the ground, near the sheriff's cruiser, and looked at all the gathered vehicles. Without the storm to interfere with the cellular service, he'd be able to call Jason soon.

The sky was lightening from ebony to soft gray. True, they didn't have Decker in custody or his corpse in a body bag. But they'd survived the night and that had to count for something.

It left Isaac with a single need. He wanted to see Clare.

He turned to see her standing on the threshold, speaking to Sheriff Cafferty.

"Clare." He whispered her name.

She turned and looked over her shoulder. Their eyes met and Isaac's pulse jumped. He moved across the ground, oblivious to anything but her. She held out her hand to him. He slipped his palm into hers and pulled her to him. He inhaled, breathing in her scent. She wrapped her arms around him, holding him to her.

There were so many things that he wanted to tell her—like that her embrace was the one place he wanted to claim for his own.

"Good to see you, buddy," said the sheriff, interrupting the moment. "What'd you find?"

"A lot of sand and rocks and rain," he said. "But no Decker."

The horizon was filled with a cloud of dust. "That must be the feds," said Cafferty. The look on Isaac's face must've asked what was on his mind because the sheriff continued, "He was already on his way when I called."

It took Jason only a few minutes to arrive. He introduced his team, which consisted of four special agents and a forensic pathologist, Michael O'Brien. Dr. O'Brien was with the team when they left San Antonio and tasked with the forensic examination of Trinity's body. But with Decker wounded and missing, the physician was asked to help with the search and to give his analysis of any trace evidence they managed to find. Jason mentioned that dogs and their handlers were on the way.

The first thing on the agenda was a video taken from the drone. Using the app, he found the moments when Decker was spotted, stumbling through the night. On the screen, the killer fell.

"Stop the video," said Michael. "Can I see your phone?"

Isaac liked the other guy's combination of command and courtesy. He handed him the cell. "Sure thing."

"Until we have a body, I won't proclaim anyone to be deceased," the doctor said.

"Patient. Surgery. I thought you were a forensic pathologist," said Jason. "Doesn't that mean you conduct tests on tissues or examine blood and urine for toxins? Besides, all your patients are already dead."

"True enough," said Michael. "But I did go to medical school. I can sew up a bullet wound if needed."

Yep, Isaac definitely liked Dr. Michael O'Brien.

If Jason were offended by the slight rebuff, he made no comment. Instead, he said, "We need to walk from here to where Decker was last seen. Everyone needs to be shoulder to shoulder. If you find something, stop and let us know. It'll get tagged and bagged for evidence. Understood?"

There were plenty of law enforcement officers for the job and Isaac need not volunteer. Yet, Decker was still his responsibility. "I'll go, too," he said as the line was forming.

"I'm coming, too," said Clare.

Jason shook his head. "No way."

"He attacked me twice," she said. "I'm done running away and hiding. Besides, I've spent time with him. I know how he thinks."

Jason glanced at Isaac. He shrugged. "She has a point."

The fed sighed. "I don't have time to argue. You can come along."

Clare stood next to Isaac as they walked into the desert. He took reassurance from her presence and longed for the moment when he could talk to her about everything that had gone down between them. About everything he'd started thinking and feeling about her, about them.

Still, this was hardly the place or time.

The line of people moved forward as one. With last night's storm, the typical hard-packed earth was silty. The wind continued to blow, sending dust devils skittering across the ground.

Using the coordinates taken from the drone's video, they returned to the place Decker was last seen. A detective from the Federales stopped. *"Tengo algo." I have something.*

Everyone broke ranks and formed a loose circle around the man. Partially buried in the sand was a bloody and torn shoe. The detective said what everyone had to be thinking. "He was attacked by an animal."

Jason marked the shoe with an evidence card #1. Another FBI agent began to take pictures.

Clare turned to the doctor. "I'm curious what you think. You saw Decker's wounds. You've seen this shoe. Is he even alive?"

Michael took a knee. "I need to get this to my lab. The teeth marks look canine, but I'd have to analyze the saliva for DNA. Likewise with the shoe. Sure, there's blood on the fabric but it might not have come from a human. And furthermore, we can't assume that shoe belongs to Decker."

"If it's not his, whose would it be?" Clare asked. Isaac thought it was a good question and he was curious for an answer.

The doctor said, "I can only deal with medically proven facts. If the blood on the shoe is Decker's, then I can tell you. And as far as his condition, until we have a body, medically speaking, we have to consider that he's possibly alive. And if he was attacked by an animal, then chances are that we'll find proof of that attack."

The search continued for several more hours. Mile after mile of desert was covered, one at a time. The sun climbed in the sky, and the heat along with it. By 11:00 a.m., nothing else had been found. The team reversed their search. It was midafternoon by the time they made it back to the shack and took a break.

It was Clare who broached the subject of procedures again. "The desert is a big place. How much longer will we search for Decker?"

Jason was handing out water bottles. "The simple answer is until he's found and in custody or the morgue. The more complicated answer is an active investigation can only continue for so long. Like the cop said, he might've encountered a wild animal who saw him as he was—wounded prey. The weather last night could have washed away any evidence there was to find, and now, the dust is covering anything left for us to find today. Basically, unless Mother Nature spits up his body, Decker may never be found."

"But you *do* think he's dead," Clare pressed.

"I didn't say that, either. Like the doctor said, until we have him in custody—or evidence of his death—the FBI will consider Decker Newcombe a fugitive."

"Fugitive?" Clare scoffed. She twisted the cap off her water bottle and took a drink. "That sounds like you'll quit looking." Isaac felt her frustration himself. It was born of the futility of finding a body in the desert, along with having survived a harrowing twenty-four hours. And in Clare's case, also being on the run for over two months.

"We'll never quit looking. But you're talking about an active search, and I can't tell you anything other than it's not over today." Jason finished the last swallow of water in the bottle. "Let's get this shack processed as a crime scene, and while we're at it, I'll bring in fixed wing air support."

Search aircraft had positives and drawbacks. On the plus side, they could cover a much larger area than individuals on foot. A huge minus—there were plenty of small clues on the ground that they'd never see. But either way, Isaac knew it was time to go.

"Hey, Jason. I need a minute of your time."

Isaac stepped away from the group. Both Clare and Jason followed. "If you need something more from us, we'll stay…"

"Go," said Jason. "It sounds like the past twenty-four hours have been traumatic."

"It was," said Isaac.

Clare just nodded.

"And about our agreement—you did a good job. Make sure you have your phone handy. The FBI will be reaching out for your services again—and soon."

"What about the other case I mentioned to you?" Isaac asked. "You remember, Chamberlain Enterprises."

Jason shook his head and chuckled. "Most people would be happy to have their plan to catch a killer work—even if the subject isn't in custody. But not you—you're ready to move on to the next case. You're a tenacious bastard, I'll give you that."

Tenacious bastard? He'd take it. "So have you heard anything?"

"Actually, I did. The CDC has a pocket of renal cancers in Columbus. The testing is just starting." Jason turned to Clare, "If you can get me all your information, we can see if there's a connection."

Clare gave him a quick nod. "I can get you those documents to you as soon as I get back to Mercy."

Jason nodded to them both. "I'll be in touch."

For Isaac, it was a good start. "You ready?" he asked Clare. They still had to walk back to his truck, and he was looking forward to a few minutes alone with her. There was so much he wanted to say… "Clare. Wait a minute."

He jogged back to the small house.

"Where are you going?" Clare shaded her eyes with a hand.

"I made a promise to a friend, and I have to keep it." He collected Old Blue and his water dish. In the truck Decker stole, he found a leash and the dog happily trotted at his side. "You walk him," said Isaac, holding out the lead to Clare. "I'll carry the drone."

With so many emergency vehicles having driven to the safe house, the road back to Isaac's truck was easy to follow.

"Why the dog?"

"Well, Ryan was worried about him. Besides, I couldn't just leave him there. I think he's been through a lot."

"See?" She gestured to the dog. "You might try to fight your nature, but you really are kind."

"Not always," he amended.

"Always with me," she said.

He gave her a small smile. "That's because you're special."

She glanced at him as they walked. "Oh?"

Only moments before, he'd struggled with what to say. Now he couldn't restrain himself from speaking. He stopped walking and reached for Clare's shoulders, turning her to face him. "Since Miguel died, I haven't cared about anyone or anything. Then, you walked into the bar and all that changed. I changed." He swallowed. "When we were driving—hoping to find Decker's safe house—and you, I realized. Well, I realized that I care deeply for you." Did he love Clare? He thought he might. Still, it was too early for him to be able to put those feelings into words. "I know we've only had a little more than a day together. But I want to see what a week would be like with you. A month."

He didn't add *a year or a lifetime*, though the words came to him.

She sighed. "When Decker had me in that room, I didn't want to die. But I wasn't sure what there was to live for, or to fight for, either. I'd been so alone for so long, fighting everything on my own, betrayed so badly by Kyle. But you, Isaac. You came to mind." She scratched Old Blue on the head and the dog leaned into her leg. "Just thinking about you gave me the strength to fight and survive." Clare shook her head and scanned the horizon. "I'm sorry about what happened to Kyle—although I'm thankful that he's not after me anymore. But I didn't want Decker to kill him, that's for sure."

"I'm sure Decker will be charged with his murder," said Isaac. With the crime being recorded by the cameras at the bar, a conviction would come easy—once they found the killer, that is. "Eventually, there will be justice for Kyle."

She didn't reply and he let the silence settle over them.

She spoke again. "He was my husband and I hate that everything turned out the way it did. One thing I don't regret, Isaac, is you. I'm not sure what comes next. But whatever it is, I'm glad that we're together."

Reaching for Clare, he pulled her to him and placed his lips on hers. He held her tight, pressing her body against his. God, it felt good just to hold her. As he kissed her deeply, he wasn't sure where the road would take them, but he would unquestionably enjoy the ride.

Epilogue

Clare wore a bikini and linen cover-up. She dug her toes into the sand and let the waves wash over her ankles. She looked out over the Pacific Ocean and sighed, not sure if she should really believe that her New Year was starting in paradise. This close to the equator, the sun was just starting to slip toward the horizon.

Before leaving to visit her mother in Hawaii, she and Isaac had paid a visit to Trinity's daughter and ex-husband. The little girl was eight years old and looked exactly like her mother in miniature. She assured the girl that she was very much loved by her mother—and as proof she gave her the locket that Trinity always wore.

The girl's father seemed to appreciate the visit, so Clare and Isaac hadn't felt unwelcome.

A phone pinged with an incoming message. She turned around to look at Isaac, who stood at her back in the surf. Since arriving in Kauai days earlier, he'd been getting messages and calls nonstop. Many were from well-wishers who'd seen the media coverage about Decker Newcombe, the modern era's Jack the Ripper. In fact, Clare had even been interviewed by various cable news networks more than once. Many others who reached out to Isaac were looking for his firm, Texas Law, to take on their cases.

It looked like his professional success was guaranteed.

He wore a set of swim trunks and a short-sleeved shirt, open at the chest. He pulled the phone from his pocket and glanced at the screen.

"Admirer or client?" she asked.

"Neither. It's Ryan." The day after Christmas, Ryan had been released from the San Antonio Area Medical Center. After getting out of the hospital, he'd met with the local US attorney and had his criminal record cleared, per his agreement with Isaac and the FBI. Then, he'd returned to Mercy, collected his clothes and personal belongings—along with Old Blue, whose family had been killed by Decker—and left. "He sent a link to a podcast. Same old stuff, theories about what happened to Newcombe." Using his thumbs, Isaac typed a reply. "I asked him if he heard anything useful in the episode."

Within seconds, Ryan sent a reply. "He says no. Unless space aliens are real."

Clare laughed. Everyone had their own conspiracy as

to what had happened to Decker. Some were absurd—like a Martian abduction. Others thought they could prove that he'd perished in the desert somewhere, while others knew just how he'd survived. But until the killer was actually found, Clare wouldn't rest easy.

No, that wasn't entirely true. Since surviving the day where the lines had blurred between hunter and the hunted, Clare found solace from her fears in Isaac's arms. The first few nights had been plagued by nightmares, but eventually, slowly, she began to recover from the trauma. Now, though her sleep was still far from peaceful, the bad dreams were finally starting to fade. Some of that was due to the therapist the FBI had referred her to, and some was because of Isaac. Leaning into his chest, she breathed in the salt air and his male scent. She wanted to stay here forever, but Clare knew that Isaac had a business to run in Texas.

He wrapped his arm around her and held her tighter. His phone pinged again.

"Give that thing to me. I'm going to throw it in the ocean," she said, joking. Or mostly joking, at least. Still, she grabbed it from his hand and noticed that the message came from Jason Jones. It began RE: Columbus Case. She handed back the device to Isaac. "It's about the Chamberlains."

He opened the message and held the screen so she could read as well.

DOJ opened a case into Chamberlain Plastics Manufacturing for both environmental crimes and conspiracy to commit murder. Target letters have been sent. Expect indictments soon.

"That's good news." Clare had worked at the EPA long enough to know that a DOJ case meant criminal charges. Chamberlain Plastics Manufacturing would have to pay a fine. But she didn't know if it was enough to put them out of business. Then again, it might not matter. The people who buried and hid the chemicals were certain to spend time in jail. "Now, turn off your phone already! I want to just enjoy the moment."

"Just a moment?" Isaac asked, powering down the device and slipping it into his pocket.

Clare pulled her to him and brushed her lips on his. "We can start with now and see how the rest of our story unfolds."

"Fine with me." Isaac enveloped her in his arms and together, they watched the sun set over the water.

* * * * *

Look for Michael's story,
the next installment of Texas Law,
Jennifer D. Bokal's new miniseries for
Harlequin Romantic Suspense.

Coming soon!

#2211 COLTON'S ULTIMATE TEST
The Coltons of Colorado • by Beth Cornelison

Despite an awkward history with bar owner Roman DiMera, Morgan Colton enlists his help in tracking down a dangerous fugitive. As they work together, the straightlaced lawyer and the ex-con discover that opposites attract, but Morgan's past could be a bigger threat to their future than the fugitive they're tracking.

#2212 SECRET ALASKAN HIDEAWAY
Karen Whiddon

Dr. McKenzie Taylor travels to her new Alaskan home and witnesses a terrible accident. She feels compelled to take in a mysterious man with no memory. As she protects her patient from oncoming threats, she has to shield her heart against her growing attraction to the man with no name.

#2213 DANGER IN BIG SKY COUNTRY
Big Sky Justice • by Kimberly Van Meter

When a beloved family is murdered in the middle of the night, police detective Luna Griffin must work side by side with the victim's brother, Ben, to bring the killer to justice. With each turn, more questions than answers are revealed. The killer could end up costing them their lives, but there's no turning back for Luna or Ben, not even when their feelings for each other threaten to turn their worlds upside down...

#2214 BOOKED TO KILL
Danielle M. Haas

Widow Olivia Hickman's emotional attachment to a loft she can longer afford forces her to rent the NYC home to tourists. But when a killer stops at nothing to claim the loft—as well as Olivia—as his own, she must do whatever it takes to survive, including letting a handsome detective help her stay out of danger.

Get 4 FREE REWARDS!

We'll send you 2 FREE Books plus 2 FREE Mystery Gifts.

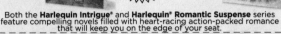

FREE
Value Over
$20

Both the **Harlequin Intrigue®** and **Harlequin® Romantic Suspense** series
feature compelling novels filled with heart-racing action-packed romance
that will keep you on the edge of your seat.

HARLEQUIN
PLUS

Announcing a **BRAND-NEW**
multimedia subscription service
for romance fans like you!

Read, Watch and Play.

Experience the easiest way to get
the romance content you crave.

Start your **FREE 7 DAY TRIAL** at
<u>www.harlequinplus.com/freetrial</u>.